The Price of an Orphan

The Price of an Orphan

Patricia Carlon

First published in Great Britain by Hodder and Stoughton

Copyright © 1964 by Patricia Carlon;
first published in the United States of America in 1999.

Published by
Soho Press Inc.
853 Broadway
New York, NY 10003

Library of Congress Cataloging-in-Publication Data

Carlon, Patrica, 1927-
The price of an orphan / Patricia Carlon.
        p.   cm.
    ISBN 1-56947-173-8 (alk. paper)
              I. Title
        PR9619.3.C37P75   1999
823–dc21   99-30787
                  CIP

10 9 8 7 6 5 4 3 2 1

CHAPTER ONE

MEGAN GALE was singing. Once, more years ago than she would have willingly admitted to, she had been told her voice was tuneless. She had just thrown back her head—mouse-brown her hair had been then, and not skilfully bleached as now—and snapped out the jerky, rough laughter that was as unattractive as her singing voice and square, stubby-fingered hands.

"Who's to worry?" had been her retort. "I'm tone deaf. It doesn't worry me and when I'm pleased it's got to come out some way or I'd come apart at the seams."

She was pleased now as the little car bucketed through the swirl of reddish dust on the country road. The car was hers. Second-hand, but paid for down to the last cent. That was one item of deep pleasure. The second was her hair. She had stopped off the previous day in a bigger town than any she had passed through on her trip and had her hair redone. She hadn't expected it would look much. The salon had been a two-chair, dim little place with faded adverts in the window. But it had been good. Better even than she had been used to back home. She gave a quick upward flick of glance at the mirror, wanting to admire it again, then remembered the scarf that covered it.

It was gaudy yellow that clashed with the bright-red sundress, but the clash failed to mar her pleasure. The red dress was the third item in her delight. She had paid more for it than she had ever paid before for a dress. There was a jacket to go over the bare top and when she reached her destination she meant to put it on, and the scarf could come off. For the moment it had to stay put. It was the only scarf she possessed and it kept the dust out of her hair and that was all that mattered for the present moment.

The dust cloud was getting thicker ahead and for a fraction of time her pencilled-in brows drew together. The she laughed, drowning out the sound of the engine. What the dickens did dust matter? She wasn't going to let it spoil her day or the thought of what lay ahead.

She flung back her head so that the tied ends of the yellow scarf stuck out in aggressive absurdity under her pink chin, waggling like floppety rabbit ears as she sang, "I gotta a date with a real swell guy . . ."

A mile further on she and the car engine became abruptly silent. For a moment, as she reached for cigarette and lighter and lit up, the world about seemed completely still, then gradually, as she sat there, drawing in smoke jerkily and expelling it with great ugly, but to her, enjoyable gusts, noise drifted into the world again, to swell in her consciousness and become part of her satisfied pleasure.

The cicadas were a shrill, monotonous background that seemed to soak into the blazing warmth of the day and become part of it. Just what heat ought to sound like if it could ever sound off, she told herself and then giggled. When she was silent again she could pick out, over the background noise, a piercing, bell-like note of some bird somewhere on her left. Apart from that there was silence and for a moment she felt oddly disappointed, with the feeling that something expected was missing. Then she realised what it was. There was no sound of traffic. She had lived for so long with the constant hum of traffic as a near neighbour the world seemed wrong without it, but now apparently her little green car had the whole wide, red-earthed road to itself.

"And I got all that blue sky to myself," she laughed, tilting her head still further back. "And all that blazing old sun. And the cicadas and their bumble, hum, hum, hum."

She laughed again, arching her arm to throw the cigarette aside. Then she remembered the warning notices she had passed along the whole of her route. Carefully she pinched out the glowing end before tossing the cigarette to the side of the road where parched trees and grey-green of undergrowth screened everything further than a few yards in her sight.

Even the signpost had a parched look about it and one arm was pointing dejectedly to the ground. She laughed again as she noticed that, tilting her head sideways to read the black letters—"Quidong. Private road. No through road."

With a little nod, and ignoring the other arm that pointed straight ahead to somewhere called Caragnoo, she turned the car to the

6

right. Private the road might be, but she had business along it. And the sign wasn't fooling her any, she told herself with the continued bubbling self-satisfaction, by pointing downwards, as though her destination lay in the nether regions.

It was going to be just the opposite, she thought contentedly, then winced as the car bounced in and out of a gaping pothole. For a minute the way ahead was completely obscured by dust, then she came out into comparatively clear air again, squinting ahead.

The trees here pressed much closer towards the car. Some of the branches stuck out like pointing fingers, as though an army of draggled drabs was jeering at her. She was annoyed at the thought, then forgot it as she saw the figure ahead.

She pulled the car up with such violence the world became one vast red dust cloud. She sat still, appalled at it, not game to open the windows or get out. In the swirling mass of it she could make out the dim figure, throwing up an arm to shield a stricken face and bending forward as though lungs were being tortured.

She flung open the left side door and called. When the door was closed again Megan looked into the flushed features and said humbly, "I'm real sorry about that. I'm not used to this sort of road and I didn't expect it to kick up like that. There's been a real dry spell around here, hasn't there?"

The answer came huskily as though her companion was still unwillingly savouring dust throat deep. "It's always like this in the summer. And use your brakes that way and you'll have the car on the scrap heap before you know it."

Megan's voice held an injured note as she gave back, "That was your fault, popping out like a grub out of an apple at me. I got a shock and of course I trod on the brakes. But not to worry. I got here, didn't I?"

"Yes."

The one word was so unenthusiastic that even Megan's self-satisfaction was punctured. She said with a flatness to equal the other's tone, "You said I could come. That you'd meet me along here and that we'd . . ."

"Yes. Don't worry. I'm just full of dust." A handkerchief was scrubbed vigorously over dust-smeared features. "How was the trip?"

"I wouldn't say it was downright enjoyable, but it didn't skin my nose either. And," she repeated, this time with complete satisfaction, "I got here."

"Yes. If you'll start up—slowly, *slowly*, woman!—how long do you expect this car to last? Oh, well, never mind. I'll direct you. Take it slowly. You'll see a track on the right a bit ahead. We turn off there. It'll be bad going for a short distance I'm afraid."

"Not to worry." Megan threw her head back and promptly, remembering the scarf she had intended to remove, stepped on the brakes again. "Oh, lordy, I'm sorry, I'm sorry. Honey, you're positively scowling and it doesn't suit, honest."

She untied the scarf, took a glance in the mirror to make sure the golden waves weren't crushed, then smiled expectantly at her companion. "You wouldn't think it was done at some little hole of Calcutta in a two by four township, now would you?"

"Am I supposed to be an expert on hairdressing?"

Megan giggled. "Well I guess not, darling, but not to worry." There was a hint of wistfulness in her voice as she added, "I like to look good. Like the dress?" She leaned back so it could be seen properly. Then she added, with a sudden lick at her lips, "It skinned me right out. The dress and . . . there's a jacket goes with it. I'll show you later. And my hair, and the car and everything new." She flicked a glance sideways, "I spent more than I planned on."

Her companion gave her one swift, thrusting glance that caused a slide of uneasiness under the red dress.

"I agreed, because I had no choice," the voice came with monotonous flatness, "to give you what you asked. You're here to collect and you'll get it. Don't imagine, though, that now I can agree to more demands. I may," the flatness gave way to a weary mocking, "have been a goose, but don't expect me to start laying golden eggs."

Megan sniggered. The sound was ugly. As though realising it herself she said swiftly, as she started the car again, "Not to worry. I wasn't . . . oh well, I was to be honest, hinting that . . . but . . . oh just forget it, honey."

Because her former feeling of ballooning satisfaction seemed to be running out of the necessary air to keep it rounded and firm,

8

Megan threw back her head again and tortured the air with a rowdy, "I gotta date with a real swell guy . . ."

The first notes brought back all the satisfaction that had been with her on the main road; a satisfaction that was not even dinted by her companion clapping hands to ears.

Megan giggled, explaining, "I'm happy. You know what I'm like—I've just got to let the whole world know. That the lane there?" The car was again jammed to a halt. "Not much, is it? Just as well, maybe I couldn't run to a bigger car, humm?"

Her companion didn't answer. With a faint shrug of her bare white shoulders Megan launched into the open bars of the song again.

Her companion said wearily, "I've told you often, Megan, you sing as well as my mother's dead canary."

Megan gave a shout of laughter, and was answered by a faint smile.

"I'm damned if I know why you've always thought that the craziest joke you've ever heard."

"It tickles my funny bone, that's all I know. Don't ask me why it makes me roar, but it does. But like I said, I'm pleased with life." She gave her companion a quick, beaming smile, "but anything to oblige, that's my motto. If you can't stand me carrolling, how about me letting off steam with a recitation instead?" She gave a quick, flickering glance sideways, "Remember that piece about living for the day that . . . what's her name? . . . used to recite? I always . . ."

"Why not just talk?" her companion broke in. "Meet anyone interesting on the way down, for instance?"

"No." Megan suddenly scowled. "You wouldn't believe some of the snooty types you meet around. Give them the time of day and they act like you're handing them a case of bubonic plague. Not that a bar of it fretted me," she gave a defiant toss of her head, "I wasn't stopping over anywhere longer than a few hours, but I feel a bit out of it." Her tone was suddenly wistful. "There were those bus tours all round and everyone on them so friendly with each other. You know, sometime," again she gave that quick, calculating glance sideways, "I'd like to go off on one of those. It'd be a nice way to see everything."

9

"There's a lot to see right here."

"All I've seen is trees . . ." then she straightened, slowing down till they stopped. She looked round in bewilderment. Her voice was several notes higher when she asked, "Hey, where've we landed?"

"The caves. Drive on over there," the way was pointed out. "Under the trees. They'll keep the sun off the car."

There was such a note of authority that Megan obeyed; then, realising she had just been given an order, her mouth set angrily. The car came to an abrupt, shuddering halt just short of the trees.

"Just what do you think . . .?" she began.

"I want to talk to you and this spot is private."

Megan half turned in her seat. The bush was thicker here. It seemed to close in, grey-green, all around except where the thin line of track disappeared behind them and where in front there was a fairly clear area, that finished in a scrub-covered rocky barrier twenty feet high.

"I thought we were going to your place. Where is it?"

"Over there."

"All I can see over there," was the tart rejoinder, "is trees, and I don't like them. You wouldn't know what sort of bugs were hiding in there. Where's the houses?"

"Nearest one is Quidong homestead. Four miles away, as the crow flies."

"Well I'm no crow, but we're not flying either. How far've I got to drive till we reach home? And where's the road?"

"I'll show you in a minute. When we've talked."

"I talk best with my fanny on a cushion, my feet on another and a cold glass in my hand. Come off it, honey," her voice dropped to a wheedling note. "These sort of spots give me the creeps. If it was a nice bit of scenery now."

"It is. We're at the caves. Didn't I tell you about them? They honeycomb quite an area. I'm not sure for exactly how far. No one's ever tried exploring very far, but you can get an odd echo in some spots just by standing still and throwing your voice towards the ground. Quidong means place of an echo for that matter. The crystallised limestone in some of the caves is unbelievable. Unfortunately you can't reach the lower ones, but you can peek down from the front cave. The front cave's quite a sight, too. Unfortunately they're all dangerous. Otherwise I suppose there'd be a tourist resort out here."

"You don't say."

"We can get into the main cave. I'll show you. It's a fairyland when you look down with a torch."

"I ceased believing in fairies when I was in short socks." Megan snapped the words out. She felt uneasy, but didn't know why. Maybe it was because she had had the whole day planned out and now her timetable was being thrown off balance. She'd always been like that, ever since a bit of a kid, she reminded herself.

"I thought you'd enjoy it," her companion sounded disappointed, "but of course . . ."

Megan was suddenly contrite. Here she was being offered a treat and she was grumbling and whining. It wasn't the way to start their new life off. She said briskly, "Why sure I would. It's just that driving all day I was thinking of a good long drink . . ."

"You drink too much."

Megan's cheeks flamed beneath their spots of rouge. She said with what dignity she could dredge up, "It'll be different now. You'll see." She opened the car door on her side and put one foot out. "Come on and show me this fairyland. Where is it?"

"Over to your right."

She wished, after a few steps, that she had worn flat-heeled shoes. The ground was hard, studded with little and big stones and there were dry twigs everywhere. She stopped, half turning, to call back as her companion stepped out, "Hey, lend us an arm, honey. These shoes . . .

The impact broke off her words. She didn't even have breath left to cry out. It was if the world had exploded in her spine. She was thrust downwards, forwards, sprawling with limbs and body all flat to the stone-studded ground.

She tried to scrabble upwards, tried to feel round towards the burning pain in her back, but she couldn't move. She finally gained breath from somewhere. She managed to whisper upwards, "You shot me."

"No. I don't mean you to be found but if you are, bullets can be traced. I threw a spanner at you. You drink too much and you can't be trusted and my life would be hell."

Megan tried to slew her head sideways, to look up. There was only the two stalks of trousered legs in her sight. They reminded her of the parched rows of trees along her route and her thinking they were pointing jeering fingers at her happiness.

She whispered, "You've broken my spine. You must've," but her mind wasn't on the blazing pain. It seemed to have receded and her mind had turned inwards and backwards while her hands scrabbled feebly at the reddish-brown, powder dry earth. Then stopped when the spanner descended again on the nape of her neck.

.   .   .

Whoever had screwed on the number plates had done a job for permanency. It was unexpectedly hard to get them off, but at last they were placed on the ground. That had been the first thing, after dragging the woman's body into the shelter of the scrub. Now if anyone ventured along the track, by some remote possibility, all they would see was a small green car, and there was no number plate to catch the eye and be remembered and brought forward at some future embarrassing date.

Although planning had made it almost certain that Megan would never be found for years, if at all, the number plates of the little green Mini would be causes of possible trouble until they were destroyed. No one was likely to ask where Megan was. There were plenty of women like her—floating from one address to the other; never making true friends because her best friend was the bottle. No one cared where they went. But if the number plates were ever found the question would arise what they were doing off the car they belonged to. Questions would be asked as to who owned them. They would be traced back to Megan's name, and from that would rise the question of where Megan herself happened to be, and it might be possible, even a long time ahead, for her journey to be traced.

For the time being the plates were put in a position selected days previous—the hole in the split trunk of a tree to one side of the car. They were too dangerous to be taken home where chance might cause someone else to discover them. It was unlikely anyone at all would visit the caves. Beyond probability that if so visiting, coincidence would take them straight to that hollow tree to delve inside it. And later, as soon as possible, they could be removed out of the district to a final resting place.

With the plates disposed of there was the body to strip. Shreds of clothes on a skeleton might possibly be traced some day. And there were her rings. None of them valuable. They could be hidden away and in the future sold over some city jewellery store counter.

As the number plates had proved unexpectedly hard to remove, so was Megan's body unexpectedly hard to strip. At moments it was a sluggish, leaden weight. At others the still warm flesh seemed palpably alive under sweating, groping hands. The job of stripping her seemed endless and by the time it was done exhaustion was beginning to set in.

Although the urgency of the final job of hiding her and the car pressed relentlessly, five minutes were expended on the luxury of one reviving cigarette. It was a luxury that paid unexpected dividends, because it brought to light one thing completely overlooked in the long days of planning for this particular afternoon.

Megan's hair suddenly became another source of betrayal. Hair was supposed to last long after flesh and blood had become nothing but bone. If by some unfortunate stroke of fate Megan was found within a year, or even two, that freshly waved and bleached hair might be the means of Megan coming to life again in the description of some country hairdresser who had found satisfaction in Megan's harsh, strident voice of praise, and who had been told of Megan's journey.

So the hair would have to come off. The thought was unpleasant, but the unpleasantness was given no time to grow into a monstrous revulsion that could flay nerves into overlooking one single strand of golden hair. It was necessary first to search through Megan's one case for a pair of scissors. The only ones were a tiny pair in a cheap manicure case and the task of cutting through the bleached and now earth-dulled hair was one maddening frustration of sweat and aching thumb where the handle of the scissors gripped uncomfortably tight, wealing the flesh on either side.

13

The hair was bundled into the cheap pink nylon slip for later disposal, together with the clothes and suitcase and Megan's false teeth.

The body, which had taken on a look of complete horror with its sunken cheeks, puckered mouth and hairless head, was left well hidden while the next part of the job was carried out.

The entrance to the front cave had long ago been striped across with boards that were bolted through into holes drilled in the rock round the entrance. It had taken several days of furtive visits before the bolts had finally been loosened so that one quick tug at each would remove them, the boards, and the warning notice with its "Keep Out—Extreme Danger."

The entrance was right at the base of the rock barrier. With the boards gone it gaped darkly with no hint that beyond it a flashing torchlight could bring to life pendants curled and twisted like vast sea shells hanging from the roof with one gaping crack crossing it, and columns arching up from the floor in several places, while far inside there was a small cavity leading down into depths unknown, where torchlight could pick out fluted columns, vast shells and other forms wrought through countless dark, silent, undisturbed years.

Sunshine pricked delicately across the entrance, stopping a bare few inches inside, revealing nothing, and there was no time or wish to bring the place to life with the fluttering of a torch. There was too much still to be done, with that pressing reminder of flying time always nagging.

If the body had been hard to strip, it was harder still to drag back and replace in the front of the car. It seemed to suddenly possess again a fleeting, horrible life that caused a limb to thrust out, the head to loll, the puckered mouth to gape, the trunk to twist, but finally the ghastly job was done and Megan was huddled down against the left hand doorway.

It had been a mistake to put her in the front though. It meant that she was in sight and that her dead feet sprawled indecently close to living ones as the car was driven carefully towards the entrance. That had been carefully measured and it was a certainty that the car would go in, but only just. It had been Winifred buying the little Mini that had actually decided her fate. A fact that it was a pity Megan, with her sometimes ironic turn of humour, could not appreciate.

With the car pointing directly into darkness, and the engine still running, but the brake on, the car was left driverless. Then the brake was released. The car shot forward even before the door had been slammed shut. It swung wildly free, scraping the sides of the cave mouth, jamming for one heart-wrenching moment before it scraped free. The car went rushing straight on and hell seemed to break loose.

There was a crash, a dull rumble, and echoes of disaster that rose in crescendo as dust swelled out with a moaning gust into the sunshine. The whole silent bush came alive with wild upward sweeps of wings and the cave's anguished voice was echoed in a hundred bird cries from the blue sky.

But surprisingly the whole thing was over in a bare few minutes. It seemed unbelievable. Planning had allowed for a much greater length of time before the world was still again; had allowed indeed for someone possibly to hear the noise and come to investigate.

But everything became still with no one arriving and the final steps were hastily put into action. One glance at the blocked cave entrance revealed that things were fully as hoped for. It had been expected that the car would smash across the sloping floor till it tumbled past the deeper entrance and crashed over into the chasm right at the back where water from some underground river could be darkly picked up by torchlight. That the fragile pendant shells of the roof might crash as well had been hoped for; that the cracked rock above that should tumble as well had been hoped for but not really expected.

But it had happened. The cave mouth was completely blocked and a cave-in had been expected for so long that no one was going to query the fact that it had finally happened.

But equally, no one would be likely to believe that a cave-in had neatly removed the protecting boards and stacked them aside. If they were found removed it would be thought some fool had gone inside and been trapped and the long job of removing the fallen rock and limestone would be undertaken, and Megan might be found.

So the boards were carefully replaced. The bolts, loosened,

were now still loose, but that could be accounted for, if discovered, by the action of time, and the probability that the cave-in had jerked them partly free, and at leisure they could be securely cemented back.

Surprisingly, there was little rubble outside the entrance. What there was was tidied in minutes and with the boards fixed there was no sign at casual glance that anything had happened at all. A tree branch, vigorously wielded, swept out the tyre tracks leading to the cave mouth and when it was tossed aside the suitcase was collected and carried to the other car, parked well out of sight, to the far east of the caves, and the car itself was driven away.

Megan's false teeth were buried in the bush and later, where bush gave way to cleared paddocks a tiny fire disposed of the golden bleached waves of hair. Each separate strand seemed to come alive for one brief second, to curl and blacken and vanish in a vestige of time that seemed indecent. A few kicks and nothing was left of Megan's last vanity. It took longer to burn the few papers from the case—a passport, two hotel receipts, her driver's licence, and wedding certificate folded round a photograph. They were thrown on to the flames after one quick glance brought memories, clustering, whispering, fighting for their rightful place in thought that wanted none of them.

CHAPTER TWO

"BIG fat bottoms."

Johnnie said the words aloud and then repeated them, but nobody paid him a scrap of attention. The few people passing were intent on getting somewhere else. They weren't interested in Johnnie Bradford or his words. Neither were the backs.

There was a long row of them in front of him. Ten of them, he counted disgustedly. Ten big fat backs turned to him while their owners leaned forward, resting sunburned arms on the upper rail of the fence. There were ten feet resting on the bottom rail and ten feet on the ground. Johnnie had wriggled between them to find out what was happening, only to discover to his disgust that it was bullocks—a long line of them with their heavy rears turned to the rail while they waited judging.

"Big fat bottoms," he told them disgustedly and wriggled away again, to stand idly kicking at the ground till he remembered Stuart's strictures about taking care.

Remembering, his mouth set mutinously. The Welfare had told him to call them mum and dad, but he hadn't been able to, any more than he had been able to agree with her that life in the country was one big whopping excitement. He was honest enough to admit that in the beginning, when he had first been told of his new foster home was with Stuart and Kay Heath, he had thought the idea great. But that, he reminded himself furiously, had been because he had been stuffed up with yarns about how nice it was going to be with him riding a pony and helping with the animals.

He had never in his life met a horse or a bullock. The bullocks could have been elephants as far as he was concerned. He was scared of the size of them. And horse riding made him sick.

That had made Stuart mad. His brilliant blue eyes had blazed down from his darkly tanned face as he'd said, "You're the damndest nine-year-old I've ever struck. Most boys would give their eye teeth to have a pony of their own, but *you* throw up."

It had been Kay who had suggested, "Maybe a doctor could give him something," so next clinic day Stuart had taken him to Caragnoo. Johnnie had objected strongly to the resultant prodding, with all the vigour of one who had learned more bad language before his ninth birthday than most men learned in a lifetime. He had stopped only when he noticed that Stuart's six feet was tensing in a manner he had learned by then meant trouble—for Johnnie himself.

But the doctor had just looked at him thoughtfully before saying impatiently, "Substitution of aggressiveness for fright. Quite common. He's healthy enough. You'll get nowhere forcing him to ride. Just give him time."

Outside Stuart and Johnnie had eyed one another with the wary summing-up that had quickly become usual between them. Then Stuart had put out a hand, ruffled Johnnie's shock of brown hair and asked, "If you won't ride, how the devil are you going to get to school? It's five miles. Five miles back. Every day except Saturday and Sunday."

Johnnie had gazed down at his boots, about to demand didn't he have feet for cripes' sake, but at the thought of his feet—his own two feet that were used to city pavements and short city blocks—doing a dance through ten miles of bush road, he had remained silent.

Stuart had suggested, "I reckon Kay might take you in and out. Or Miss Webber."

Johnnie had pulled a face at the latter suggestion but had been rather taken with the idea of Kay chauffering him. Ever since the morning, soon after his arrival, when he had come across her in the first flush of dawn, swimming in the dam with her long fair hair floating on top of the water behind her, she had held a fascination for him.

But she hadn't agreed to take him in and out. She had said nothing about it and neither had Miss Webber, but suddenly, overnight, there had been an old bike in the toolshed and Stuart had told him he was to use that for getting about.

He had been wary of Kay after that, because it seemed she wasn't too keen on his company and he was wary of Stuart because he obviously considered his foster son a disappointment. There was

Miss Webber, too. He soon got wary of her darting at him all through the long dusty days of school.

"Where's your handkerchief, Johnnie? Where're your pencils? Where's your composition book? Where's your speller?"

She never gave him a chance to show he had the articles in question right there at hand. Almost before she had mentioned composition or drawing or arithmetic she was dancing forward on the little feet that looked so absurd with her bulk, and demanding to know, even as he fetched the necessary things from his desk, where they were.

Johnnie had quickly become wary of lots of people. Jackie Light, the Quidong stockman, who belied his name by being the chocolate colour of his aboriginal ancestors, for instance. Johnnie would be a long time forgetting the way the man had stood him up and shied stones at him—quite gently, but enough to hit and sting—to show him what the stock felt when Johnnie shied stones at them.

And there was Mr. Waters with his everlasting talk about the good times ahead, when you were dead. Johnnie had asked him flatly on their fourth meeting, "If it's that good up there," he had jerked a brown thumb skywards, "Why'd you make off when we met that snake? If you'd let it bite you you'd be up there now, spoonin' up the gravy."

Mrs. Waters had laughed, Johnnie remembered. She had what he described as a chuckly laugh that made you want to join in. He had liked her at first, but now he kept out of her way, too, because lately every time she cornered him it was to tell him how Mr. Waters, who had been whisked off to hospital in Sydney, was worrying about Johnnie's behaviour. Johnnie had suggested she only tell her husband the good bits and he had thought she was going to laugh, but then she had frowned instead and retorted, "Mr. Waters would call that a sin by omission, I'm afraid," which had merely left him bewildered, but he couldn't stand her reproachful looks every time he fell into another lot of disgrace.

There was Miss Mings, too. Johnnie didn't dislike her. To him she was a god-like being, owning Quidong station and all the cattle and horses and dogs—everything right down to Stuart's hours of work, but he kept out of her way, because, god-like again, she would look down on him and boom out the same thing every time, "Well, Johnnie?" and he had never discovered what she meant him to say to it.

There were only two things he wasn't wary about—his bike and the caves. He loved the first passionately and his devotion to the second was half because of the solitude, where he could make-believe he was important and no one could tell him differently, and half because it was a forbidden delight that he had to savour secretly.

He had collected Stuart's hand on his seat when the man had discovered him trying to prise off the boards that covered the caves entrance. Everyone had later impressed on him the caves were dangerous and Stuart had later taken him up and prised off one of the boards, flashing powerful lamplight inside and holding Johnnie up to see the curling shells hanging from the roof. Then he had the board back and said, "You know what it's like now, but you can't go in. It's dangerous."

But the one amazing glimpse had fevered Johnnie's imagination until he had discovered another way in.

To Johnnie the caves were a paradise and today, when the show they had all been raving about for weeks had proved such a fraud to him, he decided to sneak away.

"Big fat bottoms," he said again to the ten backs leaning against the rail. Nobody paid any attention. The women, he knew, were skiting over their cooking and the men were looking at bullocks and machinery and horses and the kids were having pony races, the thought of which made him sick to the stomach.

"Goodbye," Johnnie said to the unresponsive backs. "You keep your rotten old show and races."

He trotted off, a thin brown figure with a shock of brown hair and huge grey eyes above a pointed nose and chin. His legs, in brief brown boxer shorts, went faster and faster as he neared the place where he had left the precious bike.

His hand touched it gently, running over it in gentle caress in the way he had seen Stuart touch the big black stallion he rode. He made the same little sizzling sound he had heard the man do as he stroked.

Peace welled over him. He went on stroking, eyes half closed, then abruptly opened them wide and gazed round him quickly. He didn't want anyone catching him stroking the bike. They wouldn't understand how he felt about it. As he mounted and rode away he thought of Stuart saying disgustedly, "fancy a boy preferring a bit of steel and a few nuts and bolts to a flesh and blood horse."

He put the thought aside, concentrating on the fact that ahead of him lay a whole golden afternoon to himself. No one was going to miss him. If anyone looked for him in one corner and didn't find him, there were three other corners he could be in and they wouldn't fret.

He put on speed, took his hands off the handlebars and crossed them on his narrow chest, grinning as he sped down the slight incline. He was whistling when he turned on to the caves track, going more slowly because it was rough ground and he was afraid the bike would be hurt.

He left it where he had often cached it, on the west of the caves. "I'll be back soon," he told it as he opened the leather pouch that swung from the back of the saddle. He gave a couple of flicks to the torch to make sure the battery was working, then started to scramble through the scrub. The hole that he finally wriggled through would have been overlooked by most people.

Johnnie grinned to himself as he eased himself carefully upright. He knew it didn't pay to play tricks in the caves that were a trap for unwary feet and actions. He went carefully across the tiny cave, wriggling through into a second larger one, and then went through another hole into the front cave. He had found it, on first exploration, a disappointment because there hadn't seemed so many pendant shells as there had been in that brief glimpse from outside, and the great crack in the rock frightened him. But he was fascinated by the water that flickered blue-black in torchlight, and more than fascinated by the glories torchlight revealed when it was thrust through the small cavity leading into the cave below.

There was another fascination to the place, too, the way a spoken word, whispered, would be taunted back at him to merge in a humming vibration all through the caves.

He took them all in turn, playing torchlight down on to the water, then down into the cave below, then throwing his voice down into the cave, on to the still water, up to the crack in the roof till the whole place was humming and whispering back at him. But long after he stopped talking the humming went on. It took him a minute to realise that there was a car coming down the track. The sound carried to him clearly through the spaces between the slats of board across the cave mouth.

Johnnie cursed, fluently, disgustedly. It wouldn't be a local person he knew. Everyone for miles round was set like a jelly among the bullocks at the show. This'd be a picnic party—one of the groups who ignored the private road sign and came up in the hope of a quiet picnic spot.

They might stumble on his bike, he realised, in an agony of apprehension. They might damage it. He scrambled up from the floor, then gave a jump of fright. There was a noise like the cracking of stockwhips over the brown backs of cattle. Something went past him in the darkness. He didn't know where it went but the noise had disturbed the whispering world about him. The vibrating was growing and swelling. He knew one of the pendant shells above him must have snapped off a small piece and the vibration of it had caused other vibrations.

He swung the torchlight upwards in sharp apprehension. He didn't know whether to start moving or stay still. He was still trying to make up his mind when the sound and vibrating began to die. Gently he started to move, then remembered the car. He went towards the cave mouth, pressing his face up against the boards so he could peer through the space between the two bottom ones. It wasn't much of a viewpoint and he couldn't see any car at all for a minute. Then he got a glimpse of brighter green near the trees.

It was a good distance off, but he saw the door open and a woman in a bright red dress getting out.

"Ah, fall down and skin y'nose," he threw at her, then gulped in sheer astonishment as she threw out her arms and crashed. He felt a knot of sympathy tighten his stomach muscles. He knew just how she felt. He'd gone like that himself off the bike once. Then he saw someone coming to pick her up—someone in gaberdine pants and an old felt hat.

But Felt Hat didn't seem in a hurry. Probably, Johnnie reflected in sharp disgust, he was another like Stuart. The sort who just said, "Up you get, Johnnie. If you wait around for the world to pick you up you won't get far. That's a lesson for you to remember."

In sudden primness, he threw towards Felt Hat, "That's no way to treat a lady, see."

But afterwards he was heartily thankful that Felt Hat hadn't heard him. It took him several minutes to get his wits working and his stomach back in its proper place but finally he knew, in sick bewilderment, that he had really seen all that—seen an upraised arm and something shiny that crashed down on the red lady's body twice; seen Felt Hat grip her and drag her, all twisted feet and flopping arms, into the scrub.

He pressed against the boards and felt them wobble. For a minute he thought they were going to burst out and himself with them. With a gurgle of fright he wriggled back. When he had recovered from the second shock he looked out again. Felt Hat was round the back of the little green car doing something. Then he got up and went over to the trees. He stood there for a bit then came back and vanished into the scrub behind the car.

"Jeez!" whispered Johnnie and suddenly one of his dad's warnings popped into his head.

"If you get your nose rubbed into somethin' dirty, wipe it clean and clear out, at the double."

"Jeez!" he whispered again.

As quickly as he dared he crossed the cave, wriggled through into the middle one and on into the third one. He took a good look out of the entrance hole before daring to venture out. The car was right out of sight now, and Felt Hat, too. Johnnie didn't dare think about the red lady. He wriggled across to the bike, but then stopped. He wasn't game to go back to the track. Felt Hat would see him for a certainty. But he wasn't game to hang around either.

In the end he headed west. He had learned enough from Stuart to know how to take direction from the sun. He went quickly, disregarding resulting scratches and discomfort, but long before he was anywhere in sight of the main road, he gave up, exhausted, and frightened again because there was a terrific noise somewhere and the ground seemed to rumble under his feet for a couple of minutes.

He crouched down, drawing the bike down with him. It was then he saw the scratches on the blue paint. He had instinctively, without real thought, tried to protect the precious possession throughout his journey, and there were only two scratches. But they *were* scratches. He looked at them, touching them with one grubby-nailed hand, gently, and then suddenly he was crying.

"Jeez!" he muttered through the tears. "I'm sorry," he told the bike aloud and told himself fiercely that it was all right to blub a bit over the bike being hurt. He wasn't crying about the red lady or Felt Hat. There were plenty of things he had seen in city alleys that would raise anyone's hair and the red lady was no skin off his nose.

"Just the same," he whispered to the bike, "I wish she'd get to hell out of m'think-box."

CHAPTER THREE

KAY pulled herself out of the dam to kneel on the outspread towel, thrusting her wet hands up to string the long blonde hair back against the bones of her head.

She raised her face, her grey eyes looking into the palely washed blue of the dawn sky and found herself immediately wishing, with an intensity that was sheer pain, that the blue was the sea—curling in, white-capped, along miles of golden-sanded coastline.

She knew only too well why she was thinking of the sea. She and Stuart had spent their honeymoon there two years before. They had walked barefooted on the tide line where the waves had spent themselves in washing over their feet in cold caress. Occasionally they had bent to pick up a shell, to hold it in cupped hands and exclaim over it before Stuart would ask, "Think the kid would like that one?"

The kid . . . not a child of their own, though they had planned for three. But a foster child. A lot of people would have called it absurd, ridiculous, to discuss the taking of a foster child when they had been married a bare few days. Now, looking back over two years, Kay knew it *had* been ridiculous—a ridiculous gallantry that had paid off with untold heartbreak.

But she had married Stuart after two years of long letters during their separation while he was in the country and she in the city; of deliriously gay meetings when they talked themselves into a wonderful silence; or her journeys to the country to him and his to her in the city.

The first time he had ever mentioned a foster child it had seemed supremely right to her that it should come true. She had known by then of his upbringing in an orphanage. She had felt pain for him in his solemn, "So I feel I ought to do something for some other kid without a real home. I always promised myself that when I was married I'd ask my wife to take a homeless youngster into the house . . ."

She had agreed with him even more through the letters that had

25

followed when he had spoken of the bitterness of no privacy; no possessions; no love of his very own.

"We'll have a foster child," she had written back.

Stuart had been working as manager of a small station in the south when they married. He had come east for their delirious two weeks of honeymoon by the sea and together they had gone to the appropriate authorities at the end of that time and stated their wish to take a foster child into their home.

Kay could remember the astonishment on the face of the middle-aged woman who had interviewed them. She had pointed out gently that they only sent children to settled households. "They come from broken homes mostly you know," she had pointed out, "so they need a feeling of security."

She had gone on to speak of the difficulties of adjusting during the first year of marriage; of the possibility of a baby of Kay's own leaving her with little free time. She had agreed quite eagerly that at twenty-eight and thirty-four respectively Kay and Stuart were quite old enough to deal with the problems of a child from a broken home; and that Stuart, himself the product of such a home, would understand and cope probably far better than most men.

"Wait a year, and then come back to see me and we'll talk again," she had promised at last.

Kay moved restlessly on the towel, fingering her still soaked hair. If only she and Stuart had left things at that, but they hadn't. If only she had started a baby, perhaps they would have given up the idea. But she hadn't, and at the end of the year when Stuart had gained the job with Miss Mings, and the wonderful modern cottage below the main homestead at Quidong, they had decided to delay no longer in asking for a foster child to share their happiness.

"And we got Johnnie," Kay muttered through set teeth.

But even then, with anger welling over her, she knew the anger was mostly for herself and Stuart because they had failed so dismally to live up to the ideas of their own worth.

But a lot of the anger was for Johnnie himself. Cheeky and lazy, and cowardly and stubborn, were all adjectives that fitted him like a glove. And he was the worst little liar in creation.

She thought again of the previous evening and Johnnie's absurd tale of a woman being bashed to death near the caves. She and Stuart had arrived home, hot, tired and frantic, because a search of the showground and all round it had revealed no trace of Johnnie at all. It had been wild relief to see lights in the cottage as they had driven up, and then . . . Kay's lips compressed . . . the little pig had rushed out with that story.

She had simply gone on inside without a word and turned on the bath, meaning to wash the dust of the day off herself and slip into a housecoat before getting something to eat. But Stuart had bent down to the boy's level. He had said slowly, "I reckon you're lying, Johnnie. You're always lying. There was that snake at the school-house. Remember? And the wild Alsatian? And the car that was bogged down by the river. And you getting lost. Remember them?" Then he had stood up again, clamping his felt hat back on his dark hair. "But all right, we're going to the caves, and then . . ."

He had started for the door and impatiently she had called, "Stuart, for heaven's sake, you know it's not true."

He had turned back, smiling at her mirthlessly, his face a shadowed mask of sunburned skin and white teeth and brilliant blue eyes as he had retorted, "Remember the boy who cried wolf? I have nightmares sometimes thinking one day he'll tell us the truth and we won't recognise it. I won't be long."

Kay sighed again, raising her face to the now deepening blue of the morning sky.

Of course Johnnie had finally admitted the story was a lie, but not until he had added gallons of spilt blood, two hooded men and wild shrieks to his story.

The two of them had long ago agreed that the best way of dealing with Johnnie's lies was to have them out, and then ignore them and him as being totally beneath a sensible person's interest or notice.

They had played the evening out in that fashion. Johnnie had admitted his lie, had his bath and eaten cold chicken and salad in his pyjamas, while she and Stuart had talked determinedly of the show and the fat stock prices.

But whan Johnnie had been put to bed Stuart had said bleakly, "He'll have to go back."

"So you've finally realised it," she had responded quietly, and had loathed her very quietness. She and Stuart no longer quarrelled

27

over Johnnie. Or anything else. When they talked it was about Johnnie or the fat stock prices. Little else. That, she knew, was the whole tragedy of the last year.

At first they had argued, planned and debated Johnnie, Stuart's new job and a thousand things with their usual spirited give and take that had been to her Omar's book of verse and flask of wine. Then slowly they had drifted into silences and polite discussions that nothing seemed to bridge. They eyed one another warily, over Johnnie's brown head, each silently blaming the other for their failure to come to grips with the boy and turn him into something worthwhile. They had, in that year found weaknesses in their own character brought ruthlessly to light and both had resented it.

Stuart had stood revealed to her as a man who was not the easy-going, even-tempered person she had thought. He had stood revealed as a conformist of rigid views. She imagined that in the orphanage he was always the boy who got the biggest slice of cake, simply because he shined his shoes, ate his meals, slept and played, in conformance with rules laid down by the authorities, and now he conformed to the accepted standards of a station manager. He drank the exact number of beers in the Caragnoo local that conformity suggested was right for a man with responsibilities; he shouted drinks as, when and to whom his predecessor had done; he gave to the same charities in the same ratio.

And he expected his foster son to conform to the image of a manager's son. That Johnnie had different ideas and was as stubborn as a mule about putting them into action meant that Stuart was left at a loss.

Kay could have drawn a perfect portrait of the foster son Stuart had dreamed about. He was tall and sturdy, with a good-natured grin. His clothes were usually clean and his schoolwork average to good. He was popular with people and excellent with animals and could make at least the first three in local horse races. He was average to good at sports and he loved the wide, open, red-earthed, cruel countryside as Stuart did.

In only one way did Johnnie conform to that portrait. He was good at lessons. Even though Miss Webber claimed he lacked concentration she had to admit he was quick-witted and usually made out far better than the country children his age.

Stuart had groped hopefully at that small piece of conformity and had tried too hard to coach the boy to take an intelligent interest in the country—thrusting it into Johnnie's consciousness under the guise of history, geography, and the arithmetic of station management.

But Johnnie had quickly seen through the ruse and turned stubborn. She remembered that only the previous week Stuart had admitted defeat there and had said, "It makes me sick to see four stone and a bit of humanity going to waste like that. It's . . . indecent, somehow." And when she had looked at him with a little quirk of question upraising eyebrows, he had gone on, "He weighed himself in Caragnoo when I took him in last Saturday. Do you know the little tyke's proud of the fact country living's put no flesh on him."

Then in a sudden attempt at humour he had mimicked Johnnie's gruff tones, "Just shows y'the blatherskite they feed you about country air. The Welfare said I'd fatten up till I didn't know m'self."

The previous evening, with Johnnie in bed, when they had decided he had to go back and they had to admit to authority that they had failed, she had said, "The Welfare is Johnnie's natural enemy. The Welfare and the Cops. How he loathes them!"

"I don't blame him for that," he had pointed out. "The Cops put his father away for two years and the Welfare must seem like chocolate packers—one little chocolate in this space, and another in that and the little chocolates have no say where they go, even if they're cramped."

She had said lightly, "I don't think Johnnie would be flattered at being compared with a chocolate," and then had been surprised at the bitterness in his answering:

"He's like one. The sort that are full of nuts. You think you've just finished with them when crack, you've snapped your teeth on another. One mistake we made," he hadn't looked at her, "was giving him that bike. You said driving him in and out would make him different from the other kids and that they'd jeer at him. That was right. But the bike was wrong. I reckon he should have been made to walk until he took to horseback. This way he's had locomotion and he won't look at horses."

She had taken the blame without protest or comment, and they had gone silently to bed. To lie, she remembered bitterly, as far apart as the bed permitted.

She put her hands against her hair. It was still soaking wet and for the thousandth time she debated having it cut short. But Stuart liked the crown of fairness that she looped it into during the day.

Stuart, she thought, pain in her heart, and was suddenly conscious of being watched.

She turned and saw he was standing there pressed against the bole of a nearby gum tree, his gun under one arm and his felt hat tilted to the back of his dark hair. The pale blue shirt was open at the throat, and his bright blue eyes were squinting towards her through a thin trail of cigarette smoke.

"You sneaked out before I was awake," he said in a voice that gave no hint of the fact he had been watching her for some time and admiring the modelling of her face. Usually the heavy crown of fair hair distracted the viewer's eyes away from her high cheekbones and the perfect modelling of generous mouth and stubborn chin. Now, with the water-drenched hair scraping the bones of her head and flowing down her back she had a clean-lined beauty that was absurdly disturbing. Absurd, because no woman should be more attractive when drenched and pale of face than she was when made-up to face the world, unless she was ugly as sin, and Kay was far from that.

"I thought you might as well sleep in," she said, and thought with renewed anger how trivial were the things they discussed now. And he hadn't kissed her. Not even blown one to her with a quick gesture of wide mobile mouth.

"After last night I needed it. You're still sure . . ." he began in the soft voice that went so oddly with his tall, solid, vigorous looking body.

"I thought we'd thrashed the whole thing out," she said unemotionally, "Though I do wonder, you know, why Johnnie told that particular lie." She went on quickly, not wanting him to break her train of thought, "I mean, his lies are usually plausible. That wild Alsatian for instance. He'd heard some calves had been savaged and the stockmen thought an Alsatian-dingo cross was prowling the neighbourhood. So he dreamed up a wild, slavering Alsatian chasing him. And we wouldn't have found out it was a lie if Dr. Pope hadn't tricked the truth out of him. And there's the snake in the schoolhouse . . ."

"A wholloping bastard of a stinkin' snake," he mimicked.

"Yes. One of the other boys at school had found a deadly snake in his bedroom. Johnnie thought he'd share the limelight and see one in the schoolhouse and he wouldn't have been found out there either, only he had to boast to a younger child who let it out unwittingly. And there was the episode of him being lost."

Her mouth tightened at the memory of the day six weeks before when Miss Webber had rung the cottage and reported Johnnie's non-appearance at school. Kay had done nothing about it except prepare a lecture on truancy for the boy's homecoming, but night came and Stuart, but no Johnnie.

Even then she and Stuart hadn't quarrelled. He had just flung at her, dull voice, "If you'd done something this morning he might have been found quickly. Now . . . it might be too late."

The search party had found him, grubby and babbling of walking in circles and being scared to death, in the morning. If only white men had been involved Johnnie would have been cossetted and believed, but Jackie Light's grandfather, grizzled of hair and voice, had pointed out signs telling him the boy had walked straight as an arrow through the bush and then stayed there waiting for the district to be roused to find him.

She still flinched at the memory of the apologies she and Stuart had faltered to the search parties.

"You must admit," she said slowly, "that his lies are usually appallingly good, and based on something he's heard or read. Oh, I know, too," she broke across his voice, "that this episode was almost certainly based on those ghastly blood-and-thunders he gets off the other boys, but . . . it was such an *implausible* lie this time!"

He asked, "Doesn't it occur to you he might have wanted to be sent away? That he reckoned a few lies like this would be the final straw?"

The colour rushed up under her cheeks. "I . . . well of course I know he's not happy."

Then suddenly she rose to her feet. She went towards him,

31

barefooted, the white swimsuit dry now against her slim body, but the long fair hair still floating damply down her back. "Stuart, do you blame me for . . . this failure?"

He said, abruptly crushing out the cigarette with deliberate grinding of one boot, "You never tried to help him. Or change him. You let him run wild," and then he turned and walked rapidly away.

She felt like laughing. Instead she felt the hot humiliation of tears on her cheeks. So her delicate treading—her watchful reminders to herself not to nag, not to complain, were now thrown back at her. In Stuart's eyes she was condemned because she hadn't lost her temper; had failed to nag; hadn't forced Johnnie to change into the little boy Stuart had dreamed of having as a foster son.

. . .

The main homestead at Quidong was the usual country house— a square of rooms surrounded by a wide veranda. Iron-roofed, with the veranda screened in completely with fly-wire, it should have been a hideous eyesore. Instead it blended, like others of its kind, into the crude, often primitively ugly landscape around it.

When Kay went in through the veranda's screen door, she heard Miss Mings call, "We're round here."

She went round the corner of the square and found the two women eating breakfast at a table laid outside the open kitchen doorway.

"Have some toast," Miss Mings urged. "And marmalade. Bad for the figure, but good for the taste buds."

Her ugly, lined face creased in a smile that showed her big even white teeth, and Kay, as always, felt a wicked desire to pluck off the round, dark-rimmed glasses. She had sometimes wondered if Miss Mings had groped down a lucky dip when making the selection, because they were so completely wrong. There was a certain measure of attractiveness about the sundarkened face that was lined in a myriad little creases round eyes and mouth and with two deep creases either side of the long nose. And there was attractiveness, in the round dark eyes, too, and the short-cut, but naturally wavy grey hair. But with the round glasses Miss Mings looked remarkably like a wise old ugly owl.

In contrast, Miss Webber knew what suited her. Her hair was always carefully rinsed to a darkness that refused to give way to passing years. Her complexion was babied to paleness with cosmetics, and her pale eyes were framed by upswept blue-framed spectacles. She was proud of her small feet and in spite of the fact she must have known her high heels were a source of amusement in the district, she continued to teeter along on them.

When Kay shook her head to toast and marmalade and Miss Mings' version of a nice cup of tea, which she claimed wasn't drinkable unless stewed at least twenty minutes, Miss Mings said briskly, "Have a chair then. Or something."

"Like a nice headache powder," Miss Webber suggested smilingly. "That Johnnie!"

Kay frowned. She felt a sudden furious dislike of Stuart because he had told others of the boy's story, and now everyone was going to laugh at Johnnie . . . again.

She asked, "How did you know?"

Miss Mings' big teeth bit into golden toast. She said indistinctly, "Your husband took Jackie with him last night. Jackie told Jess this morning," she jerked her grey head towards the kitchen where Kay could see the half-caste girl at work. "Jess told us. Told her," she added more clearly, the mouthful disposed of, "to keep quiet. Not fair to make the little beggar a laughing stock."

"Are you going to send him back?" Miss Webber leaned forward, pale eyes glittering.

"We haven't decided anything," Kay retorted evasively. She had no intention of discussing the decision with anyone until the welfare people had been told and some plans made that would satisfy Johnnie himself. She only hoped that they could get through the interval without Johnnie seeing gangsters in the the kitchen or even . . . she stifled a sudden desire to burst out laughing . . . Miss Webber kissing the school inspector behind the blackboard. He was quite capable of it and Miss Webber's sense of humour was so lacking she might possibly be overwhelmed with humiliation. Then she remembered that for all Johnnie's sins, really hurting people wasn't something he did. Not that is, if he realised it would hurt and sting.

She said slowly, "We mightn't have him much longer though,

because his father is . . ." she stopped, then finished, "because his father might be able to have him soon."

Miss Webber asked, "Did you know he's kept to the fiction all this time that his father's in the Antarctic. Pitiful, isn't it? None of the children believe him of course, because unfortunately he confided in one of the other boys soon after he came and the boy told."

Kay said violently, "No wonder he didn't make friends here. It's a wonder he's not a lot worse than he is."

Miss Webber stood up. "I'll get along, Miss Mings. Plenty to help with at the church fête with poor Mr. Waters still in Sydney, and I must do my little bit. It doesn't seem right to have no clergyman of our own, does it, and it's not the same thing just having someone visiting from another district every third Sunday."

She went trotting away on her absurd high heels and Miss Mings said gruffly, "Ellen Waters is worth two of her husband anyway. He's another who doesn't fit into country life." She savoured the last crumb left on her plate and gave a little sigh of satisfaction, "Ah, that was good." Then she blinked owlishly at the younger woman. "Think I like my food too much?"

Kay blushed because she had often thought exactly that. She had several times been to the main homestead with Stuart to eat up there. Each time Miss Mings had savoured and lingered in rich satisfaction over her food, finishing long after the rest of them.

Miss Mings chuckled. "Don't be embarrassed. I get my main satisfaction these days out of food. I can't bear seeing it wasted either. It's a hangover from Malaya. You'd understand if it happened to you." Her face was no longer ugly and alive. It was faded and tired and bleak. She said slowly, "Never thought I'd get out of that particular hell."

Kay sat silent. She had known, ever since coming to Quidong, that Hilary Mings had once lived in Malaya, had been a victim of the Japanese advance and been rescued only when the tide of war had flown out again, but never before had the elder woman mentioned it to her.

But now she went on, "We never thought the Nips would come. Didn't seem possible. My parents sold out you know, when my brother died. We had a plantation there. They moved to Australia and settled. I wouldn't go. I was engaged." She flashed the girl the brief smile that lifted some of the ugly lines from her face. "Hard to believe? I wasn't bad looking in those days. He was a doctor. Mission work. I moved into the mission too. We all talked about the war and the Nips, but we never thought they'd arrive."

"I was shopping that day. Down in the market. I was there when everything stopped. I can still see it. The little Malayan stallholder holding up a bunch of vegetables and staying like that, frozen. And a little boy howling, and suddenly silent, his mouth still open. Everything stopped. Then the first of the Nips walked down the road. I never went back home."

Her mouth twisted. "I had the shopping with me. That was a mercy. None of us—there were dozens—were given a thing to eat for four days. We lived on my vegetables. Afterwards . . ." she shook her head, "that's better forgotten. They weren't cruel—just ignored us. Penned us up like chickens and expected us to scratch for food. Funny thing was, you never got used to it. Think you would, wouldn't you? But no, every day you felt the same old pinpricks and hunger all over again.

"Then it was over. They never even told us. Just vanished. And when we knew . . . I've never understood it, but they started dying like flies. People who'd seemed tough as oak all through it just lay down . . . oh, well," she gave a long sigh.

"There was no help either. The Nips had gone and most of the Malayans had fled. I wandered around for a while, then finally some sort of order came back. I went to hospital and learned there was a trustee here. My people were dead. They hadn't known whether I was dead or alive. I came on over. There was nothing else to do. I had no friends anywhere. The place was in a terrible state. In debt, too. My father had brought some abos here and tried to work them like Malayans. They kept going walkabout and probably thought him a great joke. Must have been funny, you know. Oh well, that was a long time back. It's a good place now, and I haven't grudged an inch of the work I've put into it."

She gave her tall, thin body a brisk shake. "I've got the mollycobbles this morning. Don't know why I pushed all that nonsense on to you. Especially considering you've enough on your shoulders. I suppose you came to collect Jess and the food for the fête? I'll be down later on."

She pulled herself upright, sun-browned hands clutching the table edge. She said briskly, "Give Johnnie something to do with his hands. He's good with a hammer and saw. Keep him busy and he'll be all right."

Kay nodded, going in search of Jess. Poor Johnnie, she thought, with a sudden conviction that they all, from herself and Stuart, down to his schoolmates, had failed him.

CHAPTER FOUR

"Poor Johnnie!"

Johnnie yelled out the words to the trees as he whizzed by them on the bike.

"Poor Johnnie!" he yelled to the blue sky and repeated it to the red-winged parrot that flew upwards with an angry screech at being disturbed.

He knew now that he was going to be sent back to The Welfare. A good listen at the kitchen door the previous night had told him that. He wasn't surprised, and there was one thing to hold on to . . . he might see his dad soon.

The mere thought of his dad made his mouth fill up. Maybe because he wouldn't let the fill-up happen to his eyes instead. He knew quite well what The Cops and The Welfare thought of his dad, but they didn't know what his dad could be like. Johnnie was quite aware that his dad wasn't to be trusted with other people's property, but he considered that a mild failing when compared to others he had known in his short life. There had been old Hogg, for instance who had boarded with them when Johnnie's mother had been alive. Hogg had kept so many full bottles hidden round the premises it had hardly been safe to sit down. And there had been the newsagent on the corner who had regularly blacked his wife's eyes, and Mr. Davies who had collected his pay Friday nights and lost the lot at Saturday's races, so that his wife and kids scrounged off the neighbours for the rest of the week.

And above everything Johnnie knew his dad was kind. When you were sick, Johnnie remembered, the old man was right there, with hot water bottles and rubbing your legs. Just like, he told himself, the way he himself rubbed his bike and Stuart rubbed the big black stallion.

He had tried not to think of his dad for a long time, but now he felt it was fairly safe to start thinking again because it looked like they'd come together again. The letter that had brought that news had been kept from Stuart and Kay. That was one thing he liked

37

about them—they never pried in things they thought concerned him alone.

Parts of the letter Johnnie had learned by heart. One such part ran: "When I get things settled I can apply to The Welfare to have you back. I asked Rose to find out and she did. Her name's Rose, Johnnie, and it suits her too. You've never met her, but I've known her for plenty of time—before your mum passed away. We'd got together again for the first time in ages just before I was sent up, and Rose has been visiting me all through my spell inside. She says she thinks we can make a good go of marriage, but I've got to latch myself on to a job first. That may take a bit of time. Soon as I'm set though, Rose and me will tie up and I'll have you stand up as my best man if the clergyman agrees, and then we'll tackle The Welfare."

It had a nice ring about it, that bit—tackling The Welfare was a phrase after Johnnie's own heart. He could clearly picture The Welfare falling over like nine-pins under his father's onslaught. But he hoped desperately that Stuart didn't let on to them about the previous evening. If he did they might decide Johnnie needed a special school or something.

Every time he thought about the wretched mess he had flopped into he felt like asking someone to kick him.

If only he had remembered his dad saying, "If you're in trouble keep your flaming mouth shut and no one can pin you down to anything, see!"

Well he hadn't. He had finally reached home and then developed the horrors. The house had been empty and he had kept picturing Felt Hat riding up and whisking him away to finish up with the lady in red. By the time Stuart had walked in Johnnie had been in such a sweat he had just rushed forward, gripped one trousered leg and spilled out the lot. The only thing he hadn't mentioned was about being in the caves, and by the time Stuart demanded, "And where were you when you saw all this?" he had scrounged enough self-control back to say:

"Up a tree. Honest. I looked down and there was this lady and she went whack! . . . on the ground and got her brains beat out'n then . . ."

Stuart had said very slowly and deliberately, bending down so

38

their faces were on a level, "I reckon you're lying. As usual. When I prove it I'll brain you. See?"

Just for a moment Johnnie had toyed with the idea of throwing off a laugh and saying, "Jeez, I didn't think you'd believe me, but it was a good yarn wasn't it?" and making out it was a lot of baloney, because by then he had realised what he had done.

Instead of wiping his nose clean and clearing out he had spilled the beans and dropped himself up to the neck in the dirt. Felt Hat was going to hear the tale and he'd be scared. It was certain, Johnnie reasoned that Felt Hat would have ants in his pants wondering what else Johnnie had seen—his face for instance, or whether Johnnie would be able some time in the future to trot out some means of identifying him. In fact he couldn't be sure Felt Hat was a man or not, he was too far away. But he guessed a man.

Felt Hat, he had quickly decided, wouldn't be half so scared as Johnnie was at the idea. Johnnie's diet of blood-and-thunder had left him with no illusions as to what happened when a murderer thought someone could identify him.

But it had been too late by then to recall what he had spilled. Stuart had started off and been joined up by Jackie Light. Johnnie had reluctantly pointed out the spot and been uneasy when there was no sign of blood.

The two men had poked around in the scrub, at first impatiently, and then in silent weariness. Then Stuart had sketched a mirthless smile and said, "Well, Johnnie, your dead lady's upped and beat it."

Johnnie hadn't known what to make out of it for a minute. No body, no blood, no anything, was a bit much. For a moment he had toyed hopefully with the idea that he had had a nightmare, but he had known it wouldn't wash. He had just stayed silent, pondering. He had known that even if Stuart kept quiet, Jackie would tell Jess and she had a tongue like a river in flood, so sooner or later Felt Hat was going to hear.

Then he had had the brilliant idea, and had begun to pile one lie on top of another, calling vividly on imagination. Tales of hooded men had poured from his lips. One with limp. One without. One with one hand and one with two. He had nearly doubled up with laughter at the way Jackie Light had rolled his eyes, but sheer fright had helped keep him solemn, for he had known that the best he could hope for was that Felt Hat would get the idea he knew nothing worthwhile and would leave him alone.

He was still uneasy though as he rode that morning back to the caves, after dodging Kay. He intended to search the scrub and see if he couldn't find the lady in red. Then they would have to believe him and make sure Felt Hat didn't come through the window one dark night.

He wished, though, that he could see his dad. His dad had always been able to sift fact from fiction with uncanny ease and would have done something at the double.

He parked the bike where he thought the green car had been parked the previous afternoon. Then he went fearfully into the scrub. But when the bush closed round him he was scared. It looked so big and silent and Felt Hat, he realised, could have taken the woman a couple of miles in any direction.

He poked around for a while, while his enthusiasm slowly chilled, and finally he went back to the bike. He tried to make out where the lady in red had fallen but there were no traces to guide him. Finally he hunched down beside the bike again, going over everything from the time he had wriggled through the entrance to when he had gone for his life.

That was it, he thought suddenly. He'd go back through the caves and press his nose to the boards and look out as he had done before. Maybe he had made a mistake as to where the green car had been. If he looked out again the same way he'd see his mistake.

He went quickly, before he could get scared about it, but a few minutes later he stared blankly at the piled ruins that confronted him. He couldn't get into the front cave, though he could reach a hand through to shine the torch a little way. He backed away again, muttering, "Jeez!" as he remembered the way the caves had vibrated and hummed and the way something had swished past him.

His legs developed the wobbles when he realised that probably the roof had crashed in just after he had left. For a moment the wobbles wiped out his horror of Felt Hat. It was only when he had wriggled back into sunshine that he remembered what he had come for, and remembered that he couldnt tell anyone of his narrow escape, or he would be smacked for being in the caves at all.

He walked back towards the bike, then remembered how Felt Hat had done something to the back of the car, then gone off into the trees. He walked slowly along the way he thought Felt Hat had gone, then the sight of a rent tree trunk brought further inspiration. He plunged in a hand, reckless of possible snakes, then cursed when his clutch brought out only dead leaves. The next hole he tried yielded no better and the third presented him with a dead lizard.

He cast the find aside with one hand while holding his nose with the other. It was simply because he had nothing better to do to fill in time and because he had no desire to go to the church fête and have everyone ragging him, that he continued through the bush, plunging his hand into likely holes.

When he found the number plates he dropped them like hot coals.

.　　.　　.

Jess Dickens wasn't a gossip for spite's sake but she did love the pleasant sensation of being able to tell something new, especially when it was funny. She had thought Jackie's story, recounted over a cup of tea at the first faint flush of piccaninny dawn, the funniest she had heard for a long time and when the exchange opened she passed it on to the aboriginal girl at the Prescott's, who passed it on to a friend further on.

By ten o'clock, when a red dust cloud marked the hurrying passage of a traveller towards the caves, the district was echoing to the sound of, "That Johnnie!"

.　　.　　.

Johnnie went like a streak into the surrounding bush when he heard the sound of someone coming. In the hot, still air, over the iron hard ground, the noise of the new visitor to the caves sounded alarmingly loud to his ears.

He went, clutching the number plates to his chest to throw himself flat when he was sure he was out of sight.

For a minute the newcomer stood silent, looking at the bike that betrayed the boy's presence. The lovingly cared for chromework winked in the sunlight, but there was no sign of its owner. Sure there was no sound, the newcomer went swiftly through the bush till he was sure the boy was nowhere close by, then even more swiftly went to the tree.

The soft stream of curses that were spoken were so lowly voiced they barely stroked the hot air. After a moment's silent listening a cigarette was lit as an aid to thought and stilling wild panic, then the bay mare was unloosed from its sliprein over the branch of a tree and ridden away.

With panic stilled it had been easy to remember that Johnnie had never come to grips with the bush. He wouldn't dare penetrate very far into it for fear he got lost and it was obvious from the deserted bike that the boy had heard the horse coming and dashed off in fright.

A search was the obvious thing and might just as obviously fail as a search in one direction might let him back to the bike from another. The easiest way to catch him was simply to wait for him to sneak out when he thought he was alone again.

The cigarette was drawn on in short angry drags as the problem was debated of what to do with Johnnie. That the boy had seen Megan's death and the hiding of something was obvious. It was as certain he had then fled before the final disposal of the body and car or else he would have told that as well. But how much had he seen of the person disposing of Megan? There was the possibility he had not the faintest inkling of the truth; there was the other possibility that he knew, but was sure of being disbelieved, and had dreamed up the tale of hooded men, on finding the body gone, in an effort to make the killer believe he could never make identification and so was no danger.

He had obviously forgotten the matter of something being hidden until that morning, and whether of not he was believed when he told of finding the plates, there was going to remain the fact that there were two number plates, and no car. But just taking the plates off him wasn't going to be enough. His memory was excellent and if he made enough fuss some enquiry might be found as to who possessed that particular number, and then, if he could describe

Megan and the description fitted her well enough, the question would arise—where is Megan Dale now?

·　　·　　·

Johnnie had unfortunately gone to earth in a spot where leaves and decaying vegetation had formed a soft, damp area. He came up for breath with the knowledge his face was damp and filthy. Putting the plates beside him he reached for an already grubby handkerchief and rubbed vigorously over cheeks and nose. That reminded him of his dad's strictures about keeping his nose clean and out of trouble.

"Jeez!" he muttered faintly and spread the two plates out, gazing at them in wonderment. He didn't have a clue as to why they had been in the tree, but it was pretty certain they belonged to Felt Hat. Ears alert for sounds of danger he pondered, memory groping through stories from borrowed comics. It wasn't till he heard the horse's hooves receding down the trail that he settled for the idea of false number plates.

That was it, he told himself. The murderer had put false number plates on the green car while he drove the lady in red to the caves. That was so if he was seen the Cops would go looking for the wrong number and dig themselves into a hole deeper than a wombat's burrow. When the murder was done Felt Hat had dropped the false ones and put on the real ones, so he could . . . well what? After more thought Johnnie settled for him driving off to the show.

The thought was decidedly unpleasant, because it turned Felt Hat into someone who belonged in the district—someone who had put away the plates for just a bit till they could destroy them. Johnnie spared no thought as to how Felt Hat had managed to get the false plates. In the realms of literature false plates were as common as a pound of tea at the grocer's.

"Jeez!" he whispered, listening till the horse's hooves vanished into silence. He slipped the plates down inside his striped T-shirt and started wriggling through the scrub when he realised he was in a mess again.

If that had been Felt Hat on the horse, he realised, he had obviously come in search of the plates and instead had found the bike. So he would simply pretend to go away and then when Johnnie

43

sauntered out of the bush he was going to be grabbed like a kooka sighting a snake. Johnnie felt a shudder go straight down his spine and tickle his toes as he remembered what the kooka then did with the unfortunate snake.

He sat there, feeling his mouth fill up. That made him think of his dad, which was quite unprofitable. He tried to think of Stuart instead. Stuart, he thought hopefully, might come in search of him. Or Kay. Then he rejected Kay. If she found he had lit out without waiting for her to drive him to the fête in Caragnoo she would simply go off without him. She had a policy of non-interference in his affairs that at first had pleased him and then irked him unbearably because he had come to the decision it meant sheer indifference about him.

Then he had such an amazing thought that, on the point of rising, he sat down again with a thud. What if Felt Hat was Stuart. Or Kay. A woman. Maybe it had been a woman. He hadn't thought of that. He tried to tell himself that idea was good for a laugh, but it persisted. He hadn't had a good look at Felt Hat. He couldn't even be sure if the figure had been short or tall or anything else. All he could remember was a Felt Hat and gaberdine pants.

Felt Hat, he realised in dismay, could be anybody from Miss Mings to Sergeant Coombs, the Caragnoo policeman. Most of the men wore gaberdine pants and felt hats and so did the women when they went out helping with the cattle.

He hugged himself so tightly the edges of the number plates pressed cruelly into his skin, but he hardly noticed it. He was realising there wasn't anyone in the district he dared to go to with the plates for fear of being bashed himself. His mouth started to fill up and he thought of his dad again. That was it, of course, he realised. Someway he had to get his dad to Caragnoo, or himself to Sydney.

He tried to work out how long it would take his dad to get a letter telling him about things. It would get to Sydney by Monday probably, he decided, then realised there had been no address on the letter. One of the bits he had memorised was that his dad was looking for a bit of a room. He had said something about it being difficult to find something cheap and it had to be cheap because

44

he didn't have a penny due to his stay inside and he had to save up so he could tie up with Rose.

That meant Johnnie writing to The Welfare and asking them to post on a letter. But it might take them a week, he fretted, and besides they'd be sure to snoop inside it.

He went on sitting there trying to plan out how to get to Sydney. It was no more productive of ideas than trying to decide whether to stay there in the scrub until it was dark and someone came to find him, or whether to take the risk of rushing back to the bike and being grabbed and having his head bashed against the nearest tree like a kookaburra's dinner.

.   .   .

Kay almost decided to go without bothering to find Johnnie. She knew quite well that he spent most of his spare time hanging round the caves, but as she was under the delusion he knew no way in, she had never told Stuart. She had told herself Johnnie was en-titled to what privacy he needed and true to her policy of non-interference unless unavoidable, she had remained silent.

It was remembrance of Stuart's flat, "You've let him run wild," that compressed her mouth and decided her to go to the caves, rout Johnnie out and take him to the fête whether he liked it or not. Until he was finally out of her care he would get so much super-vision, she decided that not even Stuart could cast blame on her.

She drove rapidly towards the caves track. Even after a year at Quidong she still felt a faint revulsion of the way cleared land would suddenly give way to undisturbed, silent bush, so that she gained the impression a mysterious, primitive world was for ever on her doorstep.

And she hated the caves. She couldn't understand the fascination they held for Stuart. He had come rushing to her some three months after their arrival to tell her he had discovered another way in. He had obviously expected her to be thrilled at the idea of exploring, and just to please him she had followed him through an entrance that was barely more than a dark hole. They had gone through into the boarded-up front cave and Stuart had flickered powerful light down into the cave below over the limestone moulded by quiet centuries. She had known he had expected her to give way to rapture. Instead she had cried out, "It frightens me! Nature working away, making all that to last for centuries and she blows us away in sixty or seventy years. We should be worth more effort than she's given us. It's as though . . . it makes me feel so horribly unimportant . . ." she had let the confused explanation trail into silence. "I don't want to see any more," she had said finally.

He hadn't tried to persuade her to stay, but as they had reached sunlight again he had pressed, "Don't let on to Miss Mings about the entrance or she'll have it closed and some time I'd like to let myself down into the bottom cave and poke around."

She had told him curtly he was being a fool; warned him of possible dangers; and then given up. She hadn't returned to the caves and had no way of knowing that Johnnie's eyes had seen her and Stuart, had marked the spot and claimed the entrance as his own from then on.

As soon as she reached the end of the track and cut the engine she saw the bike, but there was no sign of Johnnie. She got out of the car, calling his name, her voice rising impatiently when she wasn't answered.

Johnnie had heard her the first time. He had heard the car coming too and had been debating whether or not he should go out. On the one hand was rescue from trouble; on the other was the possibility that while the person on the horse had been all right, the person in the car was Felt Hat.

But as the voice came closer he realised it was Kay. He decided to go on out. For one thing he was being investigated by a convoy of bull-dog ants. For another he knew he could outrun Kay if it came to the point, because he had asked her to pace him a couple of times and he had out-distanced her easily.

Thirdly he couldn't really imagine Kay as Felt Hat, though he had to admit to himself that she had been funny lately. Jumpy and starting sentences and then stopping, and looking through him as though she hardly saw him.

He wished he could confide in her, but there was Stuart. If Stuart was Felt Hat, Kay might be in it, too. And Stuart had been decidedly odd recently, Johnnie remembered unhappily. As jumpy as Kay and hardly being in the cottage at all except to eat and sleep.

46

All Kay said when he came sneaking out was, "There you are, at last. What on earth were you doing? You're filthy. And what are you clutching down your shirt?"

He wasn't used to her questioning him like that, with her voice sharp and her mouth settling into tight lines. He said uneasily, "Just some bits of wood. I thought I could make somethin', maybe."

"Why don't you ask Stuart for wood? We're going into Caragnoo. You had no right to go off like this."

Johnnie hesitated. She sounded altogether different and he was suddenly uneasy and frightened. He opened his mouth to protest that he didn't want to go, then he saw that Jess was in the car, too. So it was all right. He'd go to Caragnoo, he decided, and stay among crowds. Felt Hat couldn't get him then.

Jess was smiling and as he fixed the bike in the back of the car, he wondered if it might be safe to confide in her, but then he knew it wouldn't be. Felt Hat had had his sleeves rolled down, and his back turned. And Johnnie, for the life of him, couldn't have said whether the hands with the shiny weapon had been white, sunbrowned or chocolate-brown aboriginal. So he couldn't rule out Jess. Or Jackie Light or the other stockmen.

He decided there was nothing for it than to get to his dad. If Mr. Waters had been around Johnnie could have gone to him he reasoned because even his vivid imagination boggled at the idea of a clergyman bashing people over the head. But Mr. Waters was in hospital and the other clergyman wasn't due for another fortnight. Which just left his dad.

And he would have to hide the plates somewhere, too, he remembered. It wasn't going to be any good putting them back where he had found them, in case Felt Hat hadn't yet returned, and then just telling his dad about them. By then they'd be gone and Johnnie knew what The Cops were like. His dad had been in prison and he could talk till the cows turned blue before they believed him or Johnnie without something to back them up. Whatever the risk the plates had to be hidden until his dad could hear the story and say what to do.

He said suddenly, as the car turned on to the road for Caragnoo. "I listened to y'last night. You're sending me back."

He saw, without real interest, that her cheeks went red and her teeth clamped down into her bottom lip.

Then she said, "I'm sorry you heard that."

He said gruffly. "Don't mind. Honest I don't. See, m'dad's out. He wrote me. And I want t'get back to him, see."

Kay said, a little bleakly, "Have you been terribly unhappy here, Johnnie?"

"I guess . . . I wasn't what you expected, umm?"

"And I guess we and the country weren't what you expected. I'm sorry, Johnnie."

"Well, see," he brushed that aside, "M'dad's out and he's tying up with Rose. I don't know her other name, but they're going to see The Welfare about me'n . . ."

Relief broke over Kay in clean, healing waves. "He's getting married? I'm so glad, Johnnie. Once they set up a home for you I'm sure the welfare people will let you go back to him."

"When?" he asked explosively.

"I . . . well frankly I don't know. Perhaps in a couple of months."

Johnnie was crushed into a dismayed silence in which he hardly heard her going on, "Just remember that Stuart and I wanted you and that none of us are really to blame because . . . you didn't fit in. You see, Johnnie, there are some people who belong in big cities and some who need . . ."

"When can I see m'dad? Couldn't I go this week?"

Kay said, bemused by his anxiety, "That's rushing things, Johnnie. It will all have to be discussed and . . ."

"Jeez!" was Johnnie's sole, disgusted comment. He wanted to rant at her that if he wasn't allowed back in Sydney double-quick he'd light out. But probably she'd only laugh, he reflected. And if Felt Hat was anyone with a say in his disposal he was going to see an unpleasant reason for Johnnie wanting his dad in a hurry and he was going to make certain the idea came to nothing.

He slumped down in his seat, clutching tightly to his chest. He had the plates, and the proof he wasn't altogether lying, and his dad would go to The Cops and then they'd have to search all the scrub and while they were searching they would keep him safe.

But first, he thought gloomily, he had to get to his dad.

48

CHAPTER FIVE

THAT Johnnie was determined to remain among crowds was obvious, but he still had to be watched, ready for the moment when caution failed him and he was alone, or for another when he finally made up his mind to confide in somebody.

It was easy to sit, slumped down, in the shade outside the Caragnoo hall, face in profile to the window, felt hat slid forward on forehead, hands lazily on stomach, eyes apparently closed, and yet see inside the hall where Johnnie sat cross-legged, on the floor, apparently engrossed in discarded items of jumble, but obviously, to someone with intent interest in him, more interested in what the women were saying.

It was easy not to answer a soft, enquiring "Asleep?" and hear footsteps tip-toe away so softly that it was still easy to hear Ellen Waters asking, "Why don't people realise we can't possibly sell dirty clothes?"

Kay Heath's head, with its crown of fair hair, lifted, her gaze going from the price tickets she was stapling, going upwards in fleeting interest in the grey and white spotted silk being shaken out for her appraisal.

She asked, "Who sent it?"

"I haven't the faintest clue. You know what it's like, but of course you don't," she promptly amended, easing one foot out of a sensible low-heeled shoe, then slowly pressing it back into its leather prison again. "This is your first time here. But it's held the day after the show and races, not only because people can stay overnight and enjoy both things, but because it gives everyone for miles around a chance to bring their jumble in on Friday. And their junk. You know, I sometimes think total strangers drive for miles just to dump things on us that even the garbage collectors in the towns wouldn't take." She added, at Kay's laughter, "I shouldn't talk like this. It's blessed to give, of course . . ."

"But hell to receive, sometimes?" Kay suggested.

Ellen gave a stifled gurgle of laughter. "I'm afraid you're so horribly right, but here's something . . . it's a bit startling of course. The native girls would like it, though."

And Megan had liked it, had preened and postured in it, with her pale plumpness rising out of the too-tight top of it. It was too easy to remember that with Johnnie sliding to his feet, wide gaze fixed on the splash of colour as the dress was spread out, grubby hands reaching for it and then sliding hastily away as the women turned in surprise and amusement.

Ellen held it up against her body, the red clashing with her greying red hair, as she asked, "Do you like it, Johnnie?"

It was easy to come yawningly awake, eyes open to the world, body tensed and waiting, but finally Johnnie backed away with only a soft, unhappy, "Jeez!" that brought instant wrath down on his small head.

"You mustn't say that Johnnie," Ellen Waters protested, "Mr. Waters explained that to you."

It was easy to move inside; to suggest, coming up to them, "You'd like an ice cream, eh, Johnnie?' and know, with cold relief, by the look in his wide grey eyes, that he was going with you and that you could take him and the ice cream right away with you.

But Kay interfered. She stood up and said she would come, too; that the tea tent should by now be geared for a cup of tea and that she needed it. It was hard not to show how you felt, but you managed it with a smile and a pleasant, "I'll shout you that and Johnnie the ice cream and myself a cold glass of beer."

Afterwards it was necessary to remain affably at Kays side and talk to her of the fat stock prices and the best of yesterday's cattle, while still all the time keeping one eye on Johnnie as he huddled down on himself in one corner, licking away at the ice cream till the sweetness was all gone and the cone was left, a sodden ragged thing, clutched in one grubby hand. His other hand clutched his thin body across his chest, in desperate affection.

When Kay said she must go back it was easy to stand up with her and say, "I'll keep an eye on the boy till he's finished the ice-cream and send him back afterwards," and then to move slowly towards him while planning how to get him alone. It was obvious he was going to be wary of being alone with anyone until he had worked things out. The best thing would be to say that Kay wanted him outside at the car to help her carry a box into the hall, and once he was among the deserted parked cars he could be easily dealt with and driven away. Later there would be a search for him, of course, but when he was finally found, floating in some water-hole, it would be put down to one of the simple tragedies so often heard or read about—a small boy unable to swim because he refused to learn, wandering away and slipping into deep water and drowning. If anyone remembered his story of the lady in red they were unlikely to think, let alone say aloud, "How odd he should have died right after that impossible story he told," because his lies and his antics were a district joke.

It was annoying, the plan made, to find him surrounded by other children, laughing and jeering, while he huddled down sullenly, still clutching the sodden cone and the front of his striped T-shirt.

It was obvious that he knew he was in for a bad time, for his latest lie had confounded the rules of childhood. Lies were considered one of the few advantages of being different from adults, and the bigger and more impressive they were the more credit the liar attained among his peers. The greatest lie in the world, if it dazzled and confounded an adult, put the liar on top of a pedestal of glee, while the lowliest, if it was discovered a lie, placed the liar beneath a pedestal of gloom and scorn.

It was easy, in fact, to know Johnnie's heart and mind as he said huskily, his face blank of expression, "Go get lost. The whole flamin' mob of you, see."

. . .

Watching Johnnie was like watching a silent film unfold reel by jerky reel. First the huddled-down silence, the muteness, the stolid acceptance of jeers and laughter; then the pensive pursing of lips; the sharp upward thrusting of glance into youthful faces; the dawning of surprise and delight that broke out into a husky, "She was *real*, see. 'N the chap had false number plates."

It was necessary to stand silent and mute, pretending an interest in words poured into ears that were straining for Johnnie's words instead, while the boy tugged a hand down the neck of his T-shirt, then threw away the sodden cone and used both hands while he babbled, "He hid 'em down a tree trunk in the scrub, see'n he's gonna go back and find 'em gone'n he's comin' after me'n then . . ."

It was necessary to stand quite still and smile pleasantly into a mouthing face whose words made no sense, while concentrating on Johnnie and the bigger boy who had reached out to grab at the striped T-shirt, with an impatient, "Pull your shirt out of your pants, silly, and get them out that way."

You could hear Johnnie's odd little snort of laughter and see the yellow background of one plate slide into view, while you said a pleasant good-bye to the person whose conversation you had never heard at all.

It was easy then, to concentrate on the sharp, horrified, "Stone the crows, Johnnie's gone and pinched someone's number plates. You'll be skinned, Johnnie!"

It was still necessary to stand quite still, apparently absorbed in the meaningless scribbles your hand and pencil made in a large notebook, while watching Johnnie press his hands to his middle to stop the plates sliding any further into the light.

His small, pointed face belonged again to the flickering silent screen of an old-time film. There was the fading of brief relief; the dulling of bright eyes; the sharp awareness of laughter and horrified whispers; the blankness of expression that changed to stubborn firming of small mouth, then to a flashing, furious, "They're false ones!"

His expression changed again to thrusting-chinned, pouting-lipped sullenness as he was told, "Quit it. You pinched 'em. You'd better hand them to Mrs. Waters and she'll call the number out and hand 'em back."

It would have been easy then to have walked forward, with a sharp, "What have you been up to, Johnnie?" and a demand for the plates and a stern, "I'll deal with this," with the knowledge Johnnie himself would later be dealt with into the bargain, if a hand hadn't clutched and held, and another face mouthed happily and smiled at you.

It was necessary to stand still and smile and nod, and wave to someone passing who waved back, while from the play of emotion across Johnnie's face, from worry to horror, it was only too easy to guess his thoughts and to know, in despair, that he was not going

52

to agree to the suggestion, because he had been bright enough to work out that having the number called out over the loudspeaker was going to give Megan's killer a chance to come calmly forward and say, "they were taken off *my* car". No one would question that, because few people had even the vaguest idea of the numbers on the cars of neighbours and acquaintances and even friends, while if Johnnie insisted on linking the plates with his story about Megan —insisted on saying he had found the plates in the bush—it would be easy to turn his story aside into mocking laughter with a swift, "I suppose you hid them in the bush, did you, Johnnie, meaning to make your foster-dad be talked into having another search around for your dead lady? And then you'd lead him to the hidden plates, wouldn't you, and have a fine old time while he made a fool of himself tracing them? Wouldn't your foster-dad play, Johnnie? So that you were left with the plates and the other kids made you hand them in."

It would be easy, but dangerous, because if Megan was ever found the episode of the plates might be remembered, and also the name of the person who had come forward, but the comforting fact remained that it was unlikely Megan ever would be found at all. Almost certainly at that moment her body and car lay under the blue-black sheen of water below the earth.

It would be dangerous in another way, too—in the fact that coming forward would tell Johnnie beyond all doubt the name of Megan's killer, but the fact remained there that no one would believe him, or listen to him, if he dared to speak out, and a fortunate "accident" could still take care of him.

His look of frantic dismay, as he bundled the number plates back into hiding and notched his belt tighter round his thin body, might have been caused by working it out for himself, and knowing real fear. Fear, it was obvious, was hidden deep in his red-faced rage as he rounded on the children, with a desperate, "No, I won't. I won't be skinned neither unless you pimp. You do and I'll paste y'till your eyes pop out'n then . . ."

With mouthing acquaintance passing on it was simple to go forward, frown lines on forehead, prepared to say shortly, "Johnnie, your language! You watch your step, you little terror or else . . ."

But it was necessary to stand still as someone else came laughing and mouthing about how lovely the day was, and wasn't the fête *fun?* When they had passed on, Miss Mings, in a printed silk dress of an indeterminate brown and white pattern with an odd appearance of feathers about it, that made her look more owl-like than ever, was beside him, saying grimly, "Use that sort of language and you'll go to hell."

It was easy to see, by the look in Johnnie's wary grey eyes, that at that moment he considered hell a far cooler proposition than his present whereabouts, then he said uneasily, "They takin' a mickey out of me."

She countered, "You asked for it."

He gave a faint grin, then abruptly, still keeping one arm firmly pressed round his body, he gripped her brown and white sleeve with the other hand and whispered up to her, so ears had to strain to hear, "Miss Mings, I don't want to stay around no more because see . . ."

"Kids unkind to you, eh?" she bent her grey head down to his brown one.

He gave her arm a little shake, "Would y'lend me the fare to Sydney? M'dad's out and he'd pay y'back. Honest. And m'dad's gettin' tied up, see . . .

"What? Good heavens, boy, no! Your father wouldn't welcome you either."

It was obvious that that had flicked him on the raw, by the redness, the rage, in his small face. Then she added hastily, still bending down towards him, "Don't mean he doesn't want you. Far from it. But he's only just out of . . ." she suddenly burst into a crescendo of short barking coughs. "Pardon. Mean, he has to make a living. Find a place to live. He couldn't have you with him till he's settled."

Johnnie's hand slipped away from her arm. He managed, "How far's it to Sydney anyway?" and looked down at his sandalled feet appraisingly, as though debating their fitness for the journey ahead.

But his head jerked up again and just missed her nose as she answered, still bending, "About three-fifty as the crows fly and by road . . ."

"Jeez!" he jerked faintly, his grey eyes dimming with panic. He stood, open-mouthed, his face again a silent play of emotion.

He might have been seeing the journey in terms of red earth

roads and towering anthills; in grey green bush and scrub and yellow-brown dried-up river beds; in lonely drab railway sidings and homesteads and purple mountain ranges; in the grey corrugations of iron water tanks and the brown, slowly moving backs of cattle; in the wild howls of dingoes and in the brilliance of star-studded nights and the harshness of cloudless brazen-sunned days.

Then he was promptly, quietly and thoroughly sick.

.   .   .

It was Kay, coming in search of him with her new policy of constant supervision in mind, who rendered first aid. She was quick, deft and quite kind, but she wasn't his dad. But he finally grinned cheekily, if shakily, up at her, and said, "Jeez, but you oughta've seen old Mings and some of the others around jump when I let fly."

"Little pig," Kay said dispassionately. She had indeed seen several people jump away hastily before she had hurried forward and taken Johnnie outside. "I suppose you've spent the morning stuffing yourself."

Johnnie wriggled under her hand, uneasy again, because her voice and her face both seemed tight and hard.

He said gruffly, "I'm O.K. I'll be off."

"Oh no, you won't," she said tightly. "You're going to pack jumble for Mrs. Waters." When he didn't move she said, and was instantly appalled at the shrillness in her voice, "You heard me. Go on. Hurry up."

Johnnie was suddenly frightened. Her eyes had taken on a glittery look that scared him. He fled in search of Mrs. Waters, still clutching his middle and reflecting that it had been a good thing that the neck of his T-shirt was so tight or else the plates would have shot into view when Kay had bent him over.

And what was Kay odd about anyway, he wondered unhappily. She was acting as though she had sat on an anthill and was still feeling the results. He didn't care for dwelling on the thought that she might know he had the plates and was itching to get them off him, because that meant she was either Felt Hat or knew who he was and that meant . . .

Then he suddenly realised that Stuart and Kay had both

55

known the previous night that he had seen the lady in red and old Felt Hat. So if either of them were Felt Hat why hadn't they gone and collected the plates and hidden them somewhere else?

He drew a long relieved breath. He clutched at her arm and began, "Kay, you know that woman? Well, see, she's real'n and she's buried out there and . . ."

"Johnnie!" He drew sharply backwards, so sharply that he banged into Miss Mings, who had arrived with water, powders, a light rug and a cushion. He just skirted her, and went on backing away, his wary gaze fixed on Kay's glittering eyes.

She said furiously, "If you ever dare mention that woman again I'll . . . I'll kill you. Do you understand?" Her voice went wavering up on a note of real hysteria and appalled, she clapped her hands together, then arched them up, over her mouth. She said in another minute, her voice quieter, "If you try to lie to me again I'll thrash you. Is that plain? Very well then. Go straight back into the hall to Mrs. Waters and stay there. At once!"

· · ·

It was obvious, from Johnnie's scared expression, that nothing short of an earthquake would prise him away from Mrs. Waters until his fright at Kay's attitude was forgotten, and it was important to know how Kay would react to another mention of Megan and her death.

But Kay said nothing for a long time. Not until Miss Mings asked bluntly: "Want a sedative?"

Kay answered, "Sometimes I think I'd like to take something that would knock me out for a month."

"Need a holiday." Miss Mings looked pensively at the glass of iced water, then downed it herself, savouring the coldness of it. "When I come back we'll see."

"What?"

"A holiday. For Heath and yourself. When I'm back."

Kay blinked. After a moment she asked slowly, "Are you going away?"

"Wouldn't have said I was if I wasn't. I plan to leave Monday. Just prospecting around."

Kay smiled faintly. It was obvious she was remembering Stuart's employer sometimes drove away, to come back tired and contented, with a scatter of gold dust and a few semi-precious stones from her trips into the bush.

Kay said, "I hope you enjoy the trip, but Stuart and I couldn't go away. There's Johnnie, you see. We'll have a lot of planning to do because we can't simply pack him up like a parcel and send him back. It's not his fault either!" she burst out wretchedly, "We expected . . . have you ever thought how hard it is to throw away preconceived ideas and start all over again with something entirely different?"

"Think he's in need of medical help?" Miss Mings gazed into the empty glass. "This lying business I mean."

"Oh that . . ." Kay brushed the suggestion aside, "He's just trying to get attention that's all. I thought I was doing the right thing in not running after him like a fussy hen, but . . . I suppose Stuart's right . . . oh forget it!"

"He wanted me to give him his fare to Sydney. He wants to leave here straight away."

It was Kay's face that gave away thought this time. Her features moved from shock, to dismay and then horror, as though she was embarrassed, frightened that he might run away and appalled at the consequences that would follow.

She said, "What if he runs away!" in sharp panic.

Miss Mings said abruptly, "Tell you what—how about me taking Johnnie with me? You and Heath have never given him the chance to see the country. The boy loathes animals. Just a foible, but there's plenty of other things to get his interest. Prospecting around, say. It's only these last two years I've been able to sit back from working and get about and it's like a fever on me now. Let him find a bit of gold dust and he'll fever for it too. And there's camping out and cooking his own tucker. Never know, a taste of it might settle him down contentedly for a while.

"I was heading north-east anyway to the mountains. After he's had enough gold-panning we could run down to Sydney, see his dad, and then, if he flatly jibs at coming back to Quidong, he could stay there. Well?"

It was almost amusing to watch Kay's face. To see the shame in the silence that refused even a token observance of decencies by not protesting in any way; to watch the red in her cheeks turn to white and see her gaze sliding from the elder woman's owl-like eyes, in sheer humiliated embarrassed silence.

And there was sweet relief in the planning of going back to watch Johnnie; to sit in the shade by the window of the hall and watch him while pretending to sleep, with felt hat tilted low over forehead; to think that if all else failed there was the silent bush and quiet nights and solitary days, and that there would be just a woman and a boy alone in all that vastness.

· · ·

Johnnie's decision, late in the day, to crush down his fear and dislike of the police, and venture into Sergeant Coombs' office was not unexpected. What was, was his wild frightened dash from the security of the hall, into the police station.

Because a following wild dash might have brought question and surprise it was necessary to saunter after him, only to find, in amusement, that his dash had left him too breathless for speech and that he was holding on to the sergeant's desk in panting silence.

The porch of the police station was shadowed with creepers and out of sight of the sergeant who was studiously ignoring his small visitor as though quite aware he needed time to collect breath and wits and speech.

It would have been easy to go in and say quite pleasantly, "Coombs, the little wretch's taken my number plates. Turn him topside down will you and shake them out of him," and retire in triumph, except for the fact that Johnnie would then know the face of Megan's killer; that he might screech; and that Coombs might, just because he was a policeman, be prepared to listen.

It was better to wait and listen to Johnnie's slow panting and then to his swift, "I found some number plates off a car'n see I'm goin' . . ."

Coombs stood up, a little stooped, as though his duties weighed too heavily even for his vast shoulders.

He said curtly, "Number plates? Oh well, some fools'd lose their heads if those had screws. No one's reported a loss. You could have handed it to Mrs. Waters and she'd have called the number out over the loud speaker, but I'll fix it." One hand stretched out towards Johnnie. "Give. Might run to five bob reward if you're lucky, but don't count on it, mind."

Johnnie's small brown back stiffened. One foot shuffled behind the other and found solid flooring and came down bump; the other shuffled behind the first. Then he stopped. He said desperately, "There's not just one. There's two'n see I found 'em out in the scrub, hidden away where this fellow'd hidden 'em because they're false, see'nd he . . ."

"Oh no!" Coombs struck his hand against his sun-reddened forehead. "Oh no. I'm not playing. You take your tall tales somewhere else. Hey, wait on," he snapped out a hand to grab the boy's thin arm. "You've gone and pinched the plates off some car, have you?" He held out his hand again. "Give. I'll fix it so there's not a row . . . this time." His voice held warning, "but if you get up to any . . ."

Johnnie wriggled away, one foot shuffling urgently behind the other. He stood there a moment, silent. His face was out of view, but it was obvious which way his thoughts were scampering. He knew that as soon as the number plates was called Megan's killer was going to come forward and take them.

Then he shrilled, "Look, I was tryin' to stuff you, see. I reckon I'm sorry. I'll put 'em back m'self."

After a brief hesitation Coombs gave him a litttle push towards the porch. "On your way. But if I hear tonight there's a car missing its plates you're for it."

He went to the porch door to watch the thin figure rushing back to the hall. Then he turned, seeing his other visitor. A broad smile split his sun-reddened face.

He said, "G'day," then asked, "You hear that?"

"A bit of it. He's a terror, isn't he?"

"Terror! I've a stronger name for it. Mind you, the little beggar's not had much of a chance, but still . . . what can I do for you? Be sunset soon . . . be glad the two days are over. I'm always snowed under with extra work. Shouldn't grumble though, I expect. Your own job's not one I'd wish on myself. Be fine tomorrow, do you think?"

"I think so."

They turned to look at the sky. The top rim of the sun was

beginning to set, golden-orange, in a blazing cradle of red-streaked clouds over red earth that had taken on a deep purple tinge on the horizon.

· · ·

Johnnie was looking at it, too. The crowds were going, leaving only the tumbled wreckage of two days of fun behind them and Jess, he knew, after a spirited exchange with two other aboriginal girls, had walked off triumphantly with the topless red dress.

He was still thinking about that when he went to answer Kay's call. She was standing by Stuart and the two of them stood poker straight, their faces quite blank, but when he joined them Kay began, in that new, tight voice, "Where did you vanish to? I told you to stay here. Why did you go away?"

"I felt sick to my stomach," he said briefly. "We goin' back now?"

"Yes."

He slipped into the back and knelt on the seat, his gaze on the road behind as they sped back to Quidong. His whole body watched anxiously for the sight of a Felt Hat, but the road stretched emptily, because there had been no need to follow.

It was obvious where he was going and that he would be fed and be put to bed, and it was highly unlikely that he would attempt again that night to confide in Kay, or Stuart. He would use the night to plot out some method of getting to his father, and later, when he heard of Miss Mings' suggestion he would grasp it and wait. With each rebuff his self-confidence had sunk lower and lower, almost certainly, and with each such lowering he must have thought more longingly still of his father. It was almost certain that he would go on thinking until the idea engulfed everything else and completely dazzled him.

When both the cottage and Quidong homestead had settled into the silence of the night it might be possible to get the plates back and then there would be Johnnie alone to deal with; if not there was still the hope that he would go with Miss Mings and then there would be just a woman and a boy, and a boy could always suddenly disappear while an old woman foolishly slept, and never be found again.

· · ·

Johnnie had insisted on having his window down and had pushed a chair in front of his keyless bedroom door, but when he woke the window was up and the chair was gone and Kay was tugging at the sheets.

His first alarm gone he demanded, remembering the new idea the night had brought, "Could I call up Sydney today, huh? See, it's this way, if I could ring The Welfare they'd tell me where m'dad is and then I could get hold of him and say you wanted to be rid of me quick and how 'bout him comin' along at the double, see."

Kay's mouth tightened. That, she thought grimly, would be wonderful. She could imagine Bradford senior arriving in an un-pleasant mood, accusing them of cruelty, because once Johnnie let his vivid imagination run riot there was no saying where he would finish.

She said crisply, "No. You can write them, enclosing a letter for your father, Johnnie," she sat down on the foot of the bed. "We don't want to be rid of you. Please try to understand. We asked you here because we thought you'd be happy, but you don't like the country and we don't like the city, so it's . . . it's stalemate. Stuart's work's out here, so we can't move to suit you and anyway . . ." she fell into hopeless silence, then asked, "How would you like to go to Sydney with me and Miss Mings?"

"Now?" he yelled at her.

She said in a much lighter voice, "Don't be goosey. Miss Mings is going camping and she's offered to take you along and call in at Sydney on the way back, so you could see your father. If you say yes, I'll come, too. We'll have fun," she pressed when he didn't answer.

When he still remained silent, staring, she felt her nerves stretching out again towards breaking point.

She hadn't bothered to give close thought to what Stuart would say to Miss Mings' suggestion. She had only thought that it was going to be a heaven-sent chance to have a little peace and that he would say yes. Instead he had heard her out in silence, then had said coolly, "I'm not agreeing with that, Kay. Wait on," he had gone on swiftly above her startled breaking-in, "Just hear me out first. Johnnie's in our care. What's it going to look like when we fob him off with an old woman on a trip of that sort? He could get into heaven knows what mischief. We both know what he's like. What if he chooses to run off and hide? He could get into serious trouble out there in the bush alone with an old woman—and she *is* old, Kay."

"I hardly think she'd be flattered." She had tried to keep her voice light. "She can't be more than fifty."

"Perhaps not, but she's had a brute of a life. That prison camp for instance. And then coming straight here to spend years almost single-handed building up Quidong to its present level. What would happen if he was lost and never found, do you think? I think it would be the finish of our marriage. We'd never be able to look at each other again without blame, would we? If Johnnie was a complete devil it would be easier. But he's not. He has plenty of good points, but . . . we've failed to bring them to light, haven't we?

"I admit the idea's based on firm grounding. Most boys get a thrill out of camping out and a few specks of gold in a pan, as Miss Mings says, and he'd be thrilled. But it's out of the question to send him with her."

For an instant she had seen pleading in his blue eyes and heard it in his voice. "Don't you see, Kay, this is your chance? I can't leave my job and take him camping. But you can. You can show him we're really interested in him. Play the mother to him, the . . ."

At first the idea had simply appalled her. She had been looking forward to Johnnie's absence and to getting Stuart to herself again and trying to recapture some of the happiness of their first year together. Then she had realised that if the trip was a success Stuart would give her full credit for it, and there would be the self-pleasure in her own mind at having succeeded too. There wouldn't be the complete sense of failure to live with for always.

She repeated to Johnnie, "We'll have fun. You can pan the rivers for gold. Miss Mings has often found specks. And there are zircons, sapphires, plenty of other stones that people find out in the bush."

She went on talking of the gold and stones, knowing that he was interested by the shining look in his eyes, but he still said nothing.

Actually he was debating the wisdom of going. Ever since he had stayed out alone in the scrub all night, pretending to be lost, just to make Kay show some real interest in him, he had been scared of the bush. And the bush Kay was talking about would be far creepier than any round Quidong, he knew.

And there was the unpleasant fact that Felt Hat could follow them. But against that was the fact that there'd be Kay and Miss Mings with him, and he knew from previous expeditions that Miss Mings carried a rifle on her trips, so there would be, he thought thankfully, two women and a rifle to look after him, while if he stayed it might take a week or longer for a letter to reach his dad and in the interval he would be forced to go to school and anywhere else Kay and Stuart insisted he go, with the possibility that at any moment Felt Hat could get him alone.

And however bad camping out might prove, there was one shining thing to cling to—eventually he would reach his dad.

He said cockily, half dazed and dazzled by the way fate was stepping in to help him, "Well, I don't mind if I do, see."

CHAPTER SIX

At two o'clock on Monday they pulled up near the one storeyed hotel of a country town that possessed, at first sight, a bank, a post office, a garage, a scatter of shops, and nine dogs huddling in patches of shade.

Miss Mings gave a long sigh, letting her sun-browned hands drop laxly from the wheel to her lap. Then she said, "We're making good time." Her head twisted round to look at the back seat at Johnnie. "Hungry?" she asked.

"Uh-huh."

His alert grey gaze was still searching the road behind as it had searched through all the morning's journey. All day Sunday, while he had meekly stuck to the cottage and Kay, he had been thinking.

He had long ago discarded the idea of the plates being false ones. There would be no need for that, he had reasoned, unless the person came from a long way away. If he belonged in the district, false plates wouldn't do any good when the car itself might be recognised and from that he had gone into the question as to whether he had ever seen a green Mini in the district. He hadn't, he was sure. Minis weren't used round Quidong when anyone with a car used it for carrying all sorts of things, from parcels for a neighbour to chunks of wood that might come in handy for fences.

He had finally decided the green Mini belonged to the lady in red, which had posed the question of where the car itself had got to. He could swallow the idea that the lady in red was buried somewhere, but he couldn't swallow the idea of a grave big enough to swallow a car, even a small one.

At first he had thought of it being driven out of the district and left, but the idea had finally been discarded, because surely someone would come along sooner or later and ask what the car was doing there.

Then he had thought of the rubble piled in twisted disaster in the front cave and could have wept. He had known, with desperate certainty, that the lady in red and her green Mini were somewhere in there, but he had known, just as certainly, that no one was going to listen to him. They'd simply ring the district asking if anyone had lost their number plates—asking each person to pass the message on—till finally it reached Felt Hat and he simply took the plates off his own car and rolled up asking for the others.

If he didn't do that, Johnnie had worked out, it would mean he didn't have a car of his own and that he was one of the aboriginal stockmen, say, and for a while he had thought of doing it just to prove if it was or it wasn't, but the thought that if it wasn't he would then know the name and features of Felt Hat scared the life out of him. He had decided he didn't want to know. And there was the other thing he had thought of—that it was far more likely that Felt Hat was a white person, like the lady in red herself.

It had taken him a long time to decide that the best thing was to get his dad and let him settle it, and then had followed the problem of what to do with the plates. He had quickly discarded the idea of packing them in his case and taking them along, because he had known that Kay would root round among his things in search of items for washing and mending and she'd find them. Then she'd question and she wouldn't believe his answers and, he had come out in goose-prickles at the thought, she might turn him straight round and bring him back to Quidong, without ever seeing his dad at all.

He started, when Miss Mings poked him. Reluctantly he took his gaze off the road where he feared Felt Hat might suddenly appear and nodded to her, "Come along, boy. Probably be steak and eggs if you can stomach that in this heat. Bread and cheese if you can't."

The dining-room held tables covered with red checked baize on which purple glass vases of palely faded paper flowers drooped in discouragement. Johnnie eyed them without expression while Miss Mings advised, "Sit back and close your eyes till the food arrives."

She did it herself and so did Kay, though Johnnie had the uneasy impression that Kay was still watching him under her long lashes. Deliberately he closed his own eyes and promptly returned to fretting about the red dress. That it was evidence because it was the red lady's, he was sure, but when he had rushed into the homestead kitchen that morning to say good-bye to Jess the red dress had been on top of her cane workbasket and she had giggled at his silent, fascinated look and asked, "D'you think I'll look nice, Johnnie? I'm going to alter it to fit me. I'll do it for dancing next week." Her feet had begun to shuffle on the kitchen lino. "While Miss Mings's gone she says I can have fun—make up, she says, for me minding babies all Friday."

He had jerked, "You were mindin' the kids?"

"Yes. I didn't mind. I said so. I like babies. Little boys, too." She had giggled at him again, shaking her dark head. "Even bad ones, like you, Johnnie. You be good this time, Johnnie, or you'll catch it."

He hadn't bothered to listen. He had been realising that if she had minded the kids all Friday she was out of things. Not that he had ever, in imagination, put her under the Felt Hat, but he didn't trust dark skins. They scared him. There was the way the aborigines could track you and the way they knew things that had happened hundreds of miles away without there ever having been a telephone call or a letter or anything else.

He had wanted to warn her not to touch the red dress, but then Kay had come pouncing on him to drag him away. He said as the waitress, big bosomed and scant-chinned, dumped sizzling steak and eggs in front of them, "I just thought, maybe I ought to send Jess a postcard. I didn't have time, see, to say thanks for the cake she handed over."

Miss Mings asked with heavy humour, "What do you think they'd have round here to put on a coloured postcard?"

He grinned faintly. "Well, I guess there's not much, but I just sorta thought . . ."

Kay said crisply, "You can look around in the store while we get a few things."

The only postcards the store could produce were yellowed round the edges. He settled for a hideous frilled lizard and trotted off to the post office with it and fivepence for a stamp. Nibbling on the end of the post office pen he thought furiously, then began scribbling. After reading it through he frowned. Maybe, he reflected, he had better warn her to watch her step. There was no more room on the back of the card, so he used the lizard's frill for his warning, slipped the card into its dusty envelope and printed the address. Then he added "Private". Added a further "very" and crossed to the counter.

.   .   .

It was easy to ponder the wording of a telegram while listening to the boy asking, "When'll it get there, huh?" and the frizzy-

66

haired woman behind the counter slowly reading out the name and address and saying, "oh, tomorrow, maybe. That is, it might be put in the road box sometime late tomorrow. Depends on when they go down to collect it. That *mightn't* be for another day or so. Your girl friend, lad?"

It was a relief from days of tension to catch her eye and grin at Johnnie's red-faced horror, at his spluttering explanations of just wanting to thank her for a cake, and Jeez, he wasn't interested in girls, thanks.

It was easy to say lightly, still bent over the telegram form, "Kids're funny, aren't they?"

"You trying to tell me? I'm the eldest of ten and had to mother the lot. Maybe it's why I never married—I'd had enough. Oh yes, you can laugh, but after fifteen years of caring for nine kids and a grumpy father you feel you've had all the drawbacks of marriage already. It's a relief to cope with stamps and telegrams instead. You sending an urgent one?"

It was easy to say, putting down the pen, "I'm dashed if I can put all I need to say into a couple of lines. Might be better to ring tonight. Sorry I wasted your form."

"Not mine, the government's, and you're welcome. Want anything else?" She gave a wide, friendly smile, "Ta ta then."

.   .   .

Johnnie wished they hadn't chosen to camp out. He had never become used to the way the stars in the country looked bigger and closer than they did in the city. They seemed to hang just above his head and he knew that when the moon came up it would be huge and golden-orange, its light so bright it silvered half the sky, blotting out all the stars in the silvered parts.

And it cast shadows.

He looked uneasily over his shoulder. There had only been a couple of cars behind them all the afternoon, but he was still frightened, even with the golden camp fire where he and Miss Mings sat, with Kay leaning back against the side of the station wagon's dark bulk.

With something approaching feverish affection Johnnie remembered the dim, dark hotel with its smell of stale beer, where they had stopped just after sunset while Kay struggled to put through a call to Quidong. She had managed it at last and spoken to Stuart and had come back to say that he had been in touch with Sydney and Bradford senior would be waiting for their arrival the following week.

He knew by the sharp look she had given him that his apparent disinterest in the prospect was puzzling her, but all he could think of was all the days ahead till he saw his dad and the fact that Felt Hat could by now be coming after them, meaning to grab Johnnie round the neck and drag him away like a dingo with a new born calf.

He had already decided to cling closer to the two women than a tick to a bandicoot, but he wished that Kay wasn't acting so oddly.

.   .   .

It was a tantalising pleasure to sniff the air where the smell of frying sausages and potatoes mingled with the gum leaf fire and the tang of billy tea. It was faintly annoying to watch the boy gulp down the food when it was given him on a tin plate, and then scrape bread round it to mop up the last taste of sausage fat, while noticing that Kay Heath had merely cut her food into small pieces, and left it, to lean further back against the parked station wagon, closing her eyes.

When Miss Mings shot out, "Asleep, Kay?" there was no answer and she moved, going over to stand looking down at the younger woman and ask again, "Asleep?"

She turned then to grin at Johnnie who was watching. "What do you know, Johnnie, she's drifted off. You sleepy, too?"

"Uh huh."

"I'll fix our beds and tidy up," she told him, moving a little stiff-leggedly as though the drive had tired her quite a lot.

"Will I help?" he suggested.

"No, it's all right. You sit there. Have another cup of tea if you like. But don't scald yourself." She moved away into the darkness.

It was sheer relief and pleasure later to feel the boniness of his small arm under clutching fingers and hear his breath go in and out with long panting breaths as you bent down and asked: "Where have you hidden the green Mini's number plates?"

And then to add, at his desperate glance round, "You needn't look at her. She can't interfere."

He gave a little choked gurgle. He whispered frantically, "What have you done to her? What you done to her, Miss Mings?"

CHAPTER SEVEN

It shouldn't have surprised him, he thought dully. There was Felt Hat not having put in an appearance, and then Miss Mings offering him the trip. Johnnie was under no delusions about his reputation. He knew that most people would prefer sitting on an ant hill to tangling with himself.

If he'd only sat down, he berated himself wretchedly, and thought it all out he would have seen for himself it wasn't likely anyone as old as Miss Mings would have wanted him underfoot on a holiday. If he hadn't been dazzled by the thought of getting to his dad, and hadn't acted like a flea brain, jumping from one fright to another, he would have realised it.

But there was Kay, he remembered. He shot her a frightened glance and Miss Mings said, "You needn't look at her. She can't interfere."

He gave her a horrified look as he demanded to know what she had done.

She said impatiently, "She's not dead. I put a sleeping pill in her tea, so we could talk. I should have known Heath, with his rigid notions of what's right, wouldn't let me take you away alone, but it can't be helped. Where are the plates?"

Johnnie was completely silent. Only his wits were working. If you'd only thought, he was ranting at himself in growing fright, you'd have known that if the crummy old bat was really interested in you she'd have put you on the train. But no, she comes up with this offer and you fell for it like a mouse for bread and dripping.

And now he was sitting waiting for the trap to go clunk on the back of his neck. The idea reminded him brutally of the lady in red. That was what had happened to her, he thought, feeling sick again. She'd been hit to make her neck break. That was why there had been no blood to give away what had happened. Her neck had been snapped. Clunk.

And Miss Mings had done it. He turned his head slowly, looking at her. The firelight was dancing on her ugly brown face. One minute her eyes were lit up and then her chin and then her forehead and her long nose. He couldn't, somehow, fit her into the picture of that impossible Friday afternoon. It was just like trying to imagine her stark naked.

At the thought a queer little snorting sound started at the back of his nose, but then it fled again. He knew that things were suddenly quite altered. It wasn't him knowing about Miss Mings. It was a feeling in himself. Up to then there had been a kind of delicious horror in all his thinking—a half shadowy dream of him becoming a hero—that had blunted the edges of reality. That was gone now.

Miss Mings said again, "Well, Johnnie?"

His lips clamped shut. He could almost hear his dad saying, "Keep your flaming mouth shut."

She said, "Don't be stubborn, boy. Or are you just stricken dumb?" She tried again, "No good staying silent, I'm not going to hurt you, you know." Her big teeth showed for an instant as a white streak across her dark face. "You see, Johnnie, I'm a respectable and respected woman. Get that? And you're a detestable and detested brat. Nobody's going to believe your wild yarns about me, are they?"

Johnnie nodded his rueful appreciation of the point.

"So you see, there's nothing to be scared about. You tell me where the plates are. I collect them. That's your evidence gone. You know, you're rather a smart little cuss to have held on to them. Webber . . . stupid woman that . . . always claimed you had brains. But when I've the plates I'm safe, Johnnie. And you're safe. Get it? We just forget the whole thing."

Did she think he was that batty, he wondered with real interest. Or maybe she was like most adults who thought anyone in short pants had brains to measure. Let him open his mouth and he'd be about as safe as kicking a taipan. Not that he had ever met one, but he had heard plenty about it handing out a quick trip to Mr. Waters' glories of the future.

He knew quite well that once he spoke he was done for. He had a head, hadn't he? And a tongue and a hand to write with? So he could memorise the number and speak it or write it down and then if he and his dad yelled loud enough Miss Mings would be in

70

trouble. And he and his dad could go back sometime, couldn't they, and dig out the cave? She couldn't go and sit on it for ever like a broody hen to stop them.

"You're stricken dumb, eh?" She leaned forward. "I sent Kay to sleep so we could have things out. If you tell me now she needn't know a thing. D'you know, Johnnie, for a bit I thought you knew it was me, but knew no one would believe you. You just wanted the body found, but when it wasn't there you got scared silly and started making up hooded men so I'd think you knew nothing. But then you clung to those plates like grim death. Didn't trust a soul, did you—except the kids and they wouldn't help. Knew then you didn't have a notion if the person was man or woman, black white or brindle. Where were you anyway?" she suddenly shot at him.

"In the caves. Lookin' at you through them spaces 'tween the boards, see. There's another way in."

She didn't say anything. She squatted there, cross-legged, hands on knees, looking vast and terrifying, while her face seemed to be darkening in colour as though rage was twisting her, though her expression never changed.

Then, when she remained like that, he began sliding gently across the ground. He knew he could outrun her. Outdodge her, too. Of course he was afraid of the bush, but she was a worse terror, and not even the howling of dingoes under the stars in the distance stopped his sidelong progress. He was just flexing his legs, ready to jump up and run, when her hand whipped out.

She said, clutching him, "Well, Johnnie?" She pressed again, "Where are the number plates?"

"I put'm back in another tree, out there in the scrub, see. Right out," he stretched one arm in an effort to impress on her how far he had gone. "Near the caves. I could show you."

He had the dim hope she would start back to Quidong. If she would just give him one chance, he reflected, he could run and run and then walk till he hit some sort of town.

But when she spoke the bluffness and heartiness was gone from her voice, leaving it flat and without expression. "Don't lie to me, Johnnie. I've watched you. Night as well as by day. I know every place you've been."

Some of the cockiness returned to his voice with a brief, "Mean t' say you never kipped once?"

"It's a long time since I slept well. When I was sure you were sleeping I cat-napped, but I kept watching you through your window."

He thought of the great owl-face pressed against the moonlit glass, inspecting him, then demanded, "Then why'nt you get inside and look for the plates right then?"

"Because Kay wasn't sleeping. Kept coming in and brooding over you, stupid woman."

Johnnie felt his mouth fill up at the memory of Kay in her short, blue frilled housecoat, her long hair in two shining plaits over her shoulders.

"Jeez!" he whispered faintly to the dying fire. Fancy her coming and brooding over him. He hardly heard Miss Mings adding, "Too risky for me to get in with her awake like that."

He thought angrily, Yeah and by then you were all set to dangling m'dad in front of me like a fresh-scrubbed carrot, and get me all to y'self, you crummy old bat.

He began dredging in memories for vulgarity overheard in dark city alleys. The exercise of fitting the vulgarity to Miss Mings' features and figure and behaviour was something that kept his mind from going blank with fright.

But then she was thrusting her big face towards him again and saying, "I watched you. I know every place you've been. So don't lie to me. Where are they?"

The exercise in vulgarity brought inspiration. "In the little house," he said cockily and then snickered, "Bet you didn't watch me there."

But it wasn't funny, or even deliciously horrible. It was shocking and horribly frightening when she said in that flat voice, "Every time you went I went in after you and searched. So don't lie to me. When you were in the cottage I stayed on the homestead veranda. I could see you." She stood up, arching her back and rubbing it with her two hands, still watching him. "Be stubborn for tonight if you want. There's tomorrow. But it might mean Kay having to know."

That had a meaning that was supposed to scare him hollow, he knew, but he was too tired to work it out. He knew suddenly what was going to happen. Somewhere along the way of the trip he was going to be "lost". She'd say he'd run off and she hadn't been able to find him. There were plenty of kids, because Stuart had told him about them, who'd got themselves lost in the silent bush and been found too late or never at all.

She said briskly, "Bed, Johnnie. You can think things over. We'll talk again tomorrow."

Bed, he thought hopefully. That meant she was going to shut those owl-like eyes and he could sneak off, but she soon put an end to that idea. With her gaze still on him she fumbled in her case and came out with balled nylon stockings. She flicked them out between her hands and said, "I'm tying your ankles and wrists. Don't worry. Won't be too uncomfortable because they're soft and will flex a bit with your movements. Not enough to let you start playing tricks."

He backed away from her. She came after him gently at first, and then, as he turned and tried to run one hand snaked out and next thing he knew his ankle was twisted and he was knocked breathless, to the ground. He kicked up and out at her ankles, but she danced out of his reach. She kept that up, panting, as she tied his hands and then she had one knee in the small of his back and attended to his ankles. Then she rolled him on to his right side.

"There. Not too bad, eh? I'll put you in the station wagon and turn you a couple of times so you don't get too stiff."

He didn't say anything. He felt like a trussed chicken, especially with her talking of turning him, as though she was going to baste him in his own fat. He gave a whicker of laughter at the idea, then wondered why he hadn't, up to then, thought of screeching for help.

As though guessing what he was thinking she said, her voice bluff and hearty again, "No use yelling. Not a soul for miles and if someone happens along well, small boys and sausages often combine to make nightmares. Get it?"

"Crummy old bat!" he snapped at her.

He expected her to hit him. Instead she gave a jerk of laughter. "Don't be silly, boy. Heave ho," she slung him effortlessly and put him in the back of the station wagon. He could hear her moving about for quite a while, but he couldn't see her, but when he tried moving she was instantly there.

"Want to be turned?" she did it briskly before moving away again.

But now he could see her. She was putting her hands under Kay's armpits and dragging her, all sprawling legs and flopping arms. He gave a whimper of fright, screwing his eyes tightly shut.

• • •

Miss Mings woke him while dingo cries were still farewelling the stars. She was dressed right up to the felt hat with the green feather that she had donned the day before with her slacks and brown and white shirt. She set him sitting against the side of the station wagon, facing her as she squatted back on her heels.

"Well, Johnnie?" she demanded. "Where are the number plates off the green Mini?"

"Go crumb y'brains," he said wearily. "And fry 'em," he added for good measure.

He tensed himself for her boxing his ears, but she only gazed back with blank-eyed stare.

She said, "Knew you'd be stubborn. One of your traits, isn't it? Well I've planned for it. I'm going to untie you now." He knew his face had brightened. He couldn't stop it, but she thrust her own face close to his and said, "Then I'm going to wake Kay. Now listen to me. When she's awake we're having a cup of tea. Then we're moving straight on. Kay will drive. You'll sit in the back with me. One word for Kay either before or while we're moving, as to women in red, green Minis, number plates, or anything else touching them and . . . there'll be trouble for Kay, that's all."

She reached her hand down and the faint light of breaking dawn glinted on metal. "That's a rifle," she said in a flat, expressionless voice. "If you try to tell Kay or get help . . . I'll have to shoot her. She's not important to me. You are. Understand?"

He tried moving away from her, but one out-thrust hand kept him still. He closed his eyes tight, but her voice probed at him, "I didn't ask Kay to come. Heath's to blame, but she's here now, and if you make trouble or try telling her . . . I'll shoot her. I'll have to, because while you wouldn't be believed, she would be."

74

He managed, "If you kill her, Jeez, you'd be done for. They'd believe me then, wouldn't they?" He was yelling at her. "She'd be dead, see and . . ."

She didn't answer and after a moment he realised that of course he'd be dead, too. She'd "lose" them both and spin some story or other, but he was feeling so sick the fright simply didn't register.

She said flatly, "It depends on you, boy. There's Kay's safety and your own, both depending on you keeping quiet so Kay doesn't know. You tell me what I want to know and it'll be all right. I'll make some excuse to cut this trip short. Kay won't object. We'll go straight to the city and leave you. In fact, you can get up to some ghastly caper that'll give me an excuse to drop you like a hot coal. Get it? No one in the city will be interested in me. Kay and I'll return to Quidong and I'll get the plates from wherever you've put them, and destroy them."

His head was spinning. He wanted to tell her she was a liar. He didn't believe her. She'd never be able to let him go. Not when he could tell that number and maybe make someone, other than his dad, believe him. If he could only get Kay to help him, he fretted, they'd manage to get away. But then he looked at the rifle and simply felt sick again.

· · ·

Kay woke with the same tearing headache that had come over her by the fire the previous evening, but she hardly had time to think about it before Miss Mings' shadow was cast over her and the bluff, hearty voice was saying, "Can't hear a lark singing at heaven's gate, but the sun will soon be up, Kay. You've slept like a log. Went off in the middle of eating last night, so I just rolled you up and left you to sleep it off."

"Good heavens, did I?" Kay looked up at her in embarrassment. "Is Johnnie . . ."

"I rolled up Johnnie, too. We've all had a good night. No surprise you went off. It was a long day and to put it bluntly, you've been heading for a crack-up."

Kay pulled herself upright. She still felt desperately tired she realised, and she had no intention of taking Miss Mings up on the subject of cracking up. If the older woman expected a flood of girlish confidences over gold-panning the mountain creeks, she was going to be disappointed.

Her gaze went round the camp site, settling on Johnnie. What a pathetic little wretch he was, she thought in amusement. His felt hat was so broad-brimmed it made his thin body look like the stalk of a mushroom. She called, "Good morning, Johnnie," and frowned when he merely mumbled something.

Miss Mings said crisply, "Liverish. Splash yourself with cold water Kay, and there's lemon and soda in the glass. Sour, but the best thing for the early morning and a trip to come. Think you're up to driving today? My eyes are sore from squinting through yesterday's dust."

"Yes, of course."

Kay agreed readily, but she knew, as she obediently drank the lemon and soda and then a scalding cup of over-stewed, too sweet tea, that she would have given anything to stretch out on the back seat of the wagon and go on sleeping.

As she took her place behind the wheel, with Johnnie and Miss Mings behind her, she thought uneasily that the journey was getting off to a bad start. She was dopey, Johnnie was sullenly silent, and Miss Mings was already looking tired.

She drove swiftly along the main highway, concentrating on the road ahead and trying not to look in the mirror where she could see Johnnie's face reflected. He looked as though he had gone into a trance and all through the morning the only liveliness he showed was when they came in sight of some homestead or township.

They crossed a river just before mid-day. It ran sluggishly, dun-coloured, between dun-coloured banks, with a straggle of twisted trees and pale green scrub on either side. Kay glanced in the mirror, seeing that Johnnie was once more showing interest, staring through the window as though he were trying to print the river and the huddle of buildings away to the east, on his memory.

Kay called over her shoulder, "The river would be a good picnic spot, Miss Mings."

Johnnie looked up hopefully, but the elder woman shook her head. "There's a town not much further on. Thought we might get fresh bread there and iced drinks."

"Lovely," Kay gave a quick smile behind her and turned back

to concentrating on fording the river. Once away from it the land stretched flatly again, but dun-coloured now instead of the red earth of Quidong.

But the town they entered was almost a replica of the one where they had lunched the previous day.

She eased the car till they were barely moving, unconscious that Johnnie's hands were gripping tightly to the back of her seat. Miss Mings said, "Pull over into the garage, Kay. Get them to fill up and wait in the shade there. I'll take Johnnie to the store with me to choose some drinks." Her big teeth showed in a pleasant smile.

Johnnie left the car reluctantly. He looked hopefully at the garage mechanic who had come out at the sound of the car, but the mechanic had eyes only for Kay. She had taken off the tall-crowned red straw hat she had been wearing so that the sunshine gilded the crown of fair hair.

Before the man was in speaking distance he felt Miss Mings' hand close over his. He tried jerking away, but she held firmly and her expression, looking down at him, was a threat in itself. Once out of earshot of the garage and Kay, Miss Mings stopped.

She said quietly, in a flat, expressionless voice, "We're going into the store. I'm buying food. Remember this . . . you can be hit. Your arm can be twisted behind your back to teach you. Your mouth can be slapped shut. Your behind can feel my boot on it. Your voice can be drowned out by mine. Your babblings can be called lies by me. So," her voice bent down to his, "So don't try getting help."

The voice whispered at him in the hot sunshine, "You're a child. I couldn't do that to an adult without being questioned, but you're a child. A bad tempered, wicked, misbehaving brat who can have his mouth slapped shut, his arm twisted, his bottom kicked, his voice drowned out. And everyone will just nod and say it serves you right. Even Kay will say that if you play up. Get it?"

The face drew away and she dragged on his hand again.

She had it all her own way, he thought bitterly. It wasn't fair. Open his mouth to say she was a killer and she'd slap it shut with everyone looking at him and sniggering. Try to get away and she'd go after him and even Kay would believe her if she said he'd tried to lose her. Even if he bit and scratched and kicked it wasn't going to help.

.   .   .

They walked into the mustiness of the store side by side. The inside of the place was a jumble. He could see saucepans and towels and tins of baked beans and bags of flour. He could hear Miss Mings asking for soft drinks, "for the youngster," she explained, the bluff, hearty note back on her tongue again.

Johnnie moistened his lips with the tip of his tongue at the thought of the drinks. He eyed them, orange, raspberry, lime and cola, as they sat in a row on the counter. She went on asking for things.

"And how about biscuits? For the boy. You wouldn't have any cakes, would you?"

The sourness of the shop woman's face lost some of its vinegar as she said, "I baked this morning. If you like I'll give you a bit of fruit slab?"

Johnnie watched it being cut. The woman said, "Still a bit warm. That much be right for you?"

"Fine. What do you say, Johnnie?"

Inspiration came, in a jerked, "Say, can I use the outdoors?"

He thought the sour woman was going to direct him out the back, and a great well of relief rose in him, because Miss Mings wouldn't be able to follow and once away from her he wouldn't stop running for a week, he promised himself, but Miss Mings said reprovingly, "You can use the public one when we go back to the garage."

But she wouldn't let him, he knew. He tried desperately to think of something else and then light dawned. His left hand was free. It went sliding gently outwards. He kept his wide grey eyes on the vinegar woman as though he couldn't see the faded little man at the far end of the counter. His hand closed and slid back to his side and into his pocket. He knew the man had seen him.

In a minute, he thought, dry-mouthed, there was going to be a row, and The Cops would be sent for. Johnnie knew what happened when you shoplifted even a packet of sweets. It was a case for The Cops.

But the man made no move. Johnnie felt sick dismay sliding back

78

over him. He wondered if the man was going to stay quiet because Miss Mings was spending so much.

He heard her say, "Don't know where we'll finish up, so I'd best stock right up."

His left hand slid out again sideways at the desperate thought this might be his last chance. If they didn't stop again in a town he might never get away. Or Kay either. He added another small bag of sweets to the first, so that his pocket was bulging, but the man still didn't do a thing.

He saw with despair that Miss Mings was paying for the things. Then the man moved, coming forward to pack the things in a cardboard box. He was a little man with balding head and brown sun spots on his pale skin. He said, "Lady, I don't like having to tell you this . . . but your lad's stolen something off the counter."

Miss Mings jerked round on him. For a minute he was so terrified he was nearly sick. She looked immense, towering over him, her big face flushed and her eyes glinting down on him. Then she held out her hand. She said, "Give whatever it was to me."

Her hand slid down, yanking at his pocket. To the pair behind the counter she said, "I'm sorry. He's not mine, thank God. I'm helping his foster mother look after him. He's a child welfare proposition." Her voice dropped to a confidential murmur as she leaned towards them, "Father's in prison unfortunately. Thieving from building sites. And the foster parents are about to send him back."

Johnnie suddenly lost all control. He shrilled in despairing panic, "She's a liar. She killed someone. She . . . she kidnapped me, see. She . . ."

The slap across his mouth wasn't hard. It was the way she took careful, slow, deliberate aim at him that frightened more than the sting. Then she went on talking. He heard the sour woman murmuring, "You can't trust them and all this pandering just makes it worse, if you ask me. I don't envy you, that's all."

The man started carrying the box outside without looking at him, walking down to the garage in silence. Then Johnnie grabbed at the arm where a tattooed horse pranced amongst thick black hair. The arm he clutched was sweaty and his hand slipped away as he babbled, "Look, I'm not stuffin' you. She's kidnapped me, see. She . . ."

"Oh, for heaven's sake!" Miss Mings gripped his shoulders, swinging him away from the man, who had turned to stare at him. She said, "He has the imagination of a devil. As for antics. It's only a few weeks since he had the whole district roused looking for him. He'd just marched into the scrub and stayed there to frighten the wits out of everyone. That's one of the things made the foster parents give up." She pulled on Johnnie's hand, dragging him relentlessly to where the station wagon was waiting. "You know Caragnoo, by the way? I own Quidong station there. The foster father is my manager. An orphan himself, poor devil, and wanted to share his luck with some other deprived kid, but . . ." she shrugged.

The man trudged stolidly along beside her, nodding.

Johnnie could see Kay had stepped out of the wagon and was waiting for them. The mechanic was hovering round her, talking. Miss Mings ignored him as she called, "I'm afraid Johnnie's disgraced us, Kay. Shoplifting this time."

For one minute the world round Johnnie was a ring of faces. Miss Mings' blank and expressionless; the bald man chewing on something, staring at him; the mechanic with open mouth and startled blue gaze; and Kay, red faced and furious.

Kay, looking down at him, cried passionately, "Johnnie, how *could* you! That's . . . oh . . ." she pressed one hand to her forehead. He could see that her eyes were filled with tears.

There was nothing more said as the box was loaded in with their luggage and he was put into the back seat beside Miss Mings. Kay slipped behind the wheel again and the station wagon turned back on to the road. Johnnie, looking back, could see the mechanic and the bald man's white apron. The two of them were standing, arms folded looking after them.

And they wouldn't do a thing, he thought desperately. Even if the bald man had been a bit suspicious Miss Mings had settled things by saying who she was; by calling on Kay that way. And later . . . despair made his body droop bonelessly in the seat . . . if they were asked they'd say he had tried stealing. That'd give Miss Mings an excuse to say she had smacked him and he had run away into the bush. Yes, and that Kay had followed. And both of them had got lost.

CHAPTER EIGHT

MISS MINGS', "You're going too fast, Kay," had pulled her up sharply as the car had roared down the highway in a cloud of dust. She had jammed down on the brakes and the car had gone into a long skid. Then she let her hands slide off the wheel. She sat there, feeling herself shaking all over.

She threw back over her shoulder, "Take no notice. Please! I'll be all right in a minute. It was just . . . funnily enough, I've never before known him to steal anything."

"Temptation under his nose, that was all. Like me to drive? I'll take Johnnie in front and you can stretch out on the back seat."

The offer was tempting, but Kay shook her head. She knew she wouldn't be able to sleep and the road was so unevenly graded she would merely be banged about. "I'm all right again. Do I just keep on going?"

"Yes. There's a creek down here if it hasn't dried up since I was last around." Miss Mings smiled broadly. "Never can be sure in this country, can you? Plenty of shade round it, too. We'll picnic there."

Kay didn't answer. The thought of food was revolting, but she would have given anything for a cup of amber tea. She drove on, wondering if Miss Mings would be offended if she said bluntly that in future she wanted to make her own tea. It would have been easy to say, if she didn't have to remember that Miss Mings was Stuart's employer and that she and Stuart had to go on living at Quidong.

Things were already bad enough with their foster child saddled on her in this way. She told herself she should never have agreed to the trip. She should have known that almost at once Johnnie would make a complete fool of himself.

She bumped the wagon gently over the tussocky ground to the little creek, under Miss Mings' guidance, then stepped out. Miss Mings did, too, on the opposite side. She said briskly, "Come along, Johnnie, and don't sulk."

The next minute the door beside Kay opened. He shot out and started for the scrub with a furious energy that sent dust spurting

81

up behind him and knocked Kay flat against the side of the wagon.

He heard both of them yelling, but he kept on, head down, his felt hat taking the sting out of twigs and branches as he went. Then he fell. The next minute he was hauled up and looked into Kay's furious face.

He said desperately, "Run! You too! She's bats. Come on . . . come . . ."

But she had grabbed him tight. She started to shake him and went on shaking him till he was breathless and sobbing and her own breath was coming in long jerks. Then she fell away from him. She knelt there on the ground beside him and covered her face with her hands while he simply stared and Miss Mings put her hand down on his shoulder, pressing down and down till he could feel his knees buckling.

Kay's hands dropped away from her face. Johnnie expected to see long streaks of tears on her cheeks, but there weren't any. Her eyes had that same glassy look about them and her face was white under the suntan. She said quite evenly, getting up, "That was sheer temper, and unforgivable. I'm sorry, Johnnie."

Miss Mings said, "If you were heading for the city, Johnnie, you were facing the wrong direction. Come along back. At the double, boy."

He stumbled ahead of her towards the wagon. Kay didn't look back, and when they caught up with her she said quietly, "I don't feel like food, Miss Mings. I'm sorry I'm acting like an hysterical fool, but . . . I'll be all right soon. If you don't mind I'll lie down in the back of the wagon while you and Johnnie eat."

"Good idea. I'll tell you what," Miss Mings had reached into the wagon for her big shabby purse, "I've some pills here. Take one and stretch out and sleep the afternoon away. One should be enough. If you're not used to taking them one should knock you straight out. Use them myself sometimes. They don't leave any after effects. Here you are."

Kay looked at the white tablet lying on the palm of her hand. She murmured thanks, while Miss Mings got out the insulated water container and poured a glass for her, but she knew she wouldn't take the pill. Stuart had been right about Miss Mings being too old to cope with Johnnie. His last caper had shown that.

But for herself catching up with him he would by now probably be lost. Miss Mings had merely puffed and called far in the background of the absurd race.

And heaven knew what Johnnie could get up to in one whole afternoon while Miss Mings tried to drive on and Kay herself slept. He was probably expecting punishment for the shoplifting, of course, she reasoned, and that was why he had tried to run away, but with running away on his mind he could try it again.

No, she wouldn't take the pill, she thought regretfully. She would simply lie down till they started moving again.

She said, "If you'll just get out what you need I'll stretch out," and when Miss Mings nodded, ordering the boy to drag out the packed box, she was able to slip the tablet into her pocket and simply drink the water.

She let Miss Mings settle her with a cushion under her head and said, "Call me if he plays up," and closed her eyes.

. . .

With Miss Mings walking right behind him Johnnie lugged the box away under the trees. The station wagon was almost out of sight when she said curtly, "Put it down there."

A moment later a hard, thrusting hand shot into his back, sending him sprawling on to his face. He felt her hands and the nylon stocking at work round his legs again and tried hitting back at her, but she simply knelt on him. Then she dealt with his hands and finally lugged him over to prop him against the trunk of a tree.

"You asked for that," she said briefly. Her eyes, he saw in panic, seemed to be bulging out of her round face. She was angry, he knew, but her voice was muted when she went on, "Know that you played into my hands back there in the township?" She gave a brusque laugh. "Don't know what I mean, do you? I thought at first I might get you to talk without too much trouble. Foolish of me." She ignored him then, digging into the box with eager hands. "Let's see what we have. Bread . . . looks nice and crusty. And a piece of tasty cheese. Can't stand those strong smelling ones. Put me in mind of dead dingo. And a tin of peaches. Like peaches?"

He nodded wordlessly. He was finding it hard to cope with her changes of mood from bulging-eyed anger to affability.

83

She went on, "And the fruit slab. Looks good. Can't beat a countrywoman for a good fruit cake. And I suppose you'd like the red drink?"

She set the things on one sheet of plastic film and spread another over to discourage the flies. Then she cut off one slice of bread and sandwiched it with oily butter and a thick wedge of cheese. She sat there cross-legged, opposite him, slowly savouring it.

He could feel his mouth watering and his stomach churning in anticipation. She was going to keep him tied up all afternoon he supposed, and was going to feed him piece by piece. He was too tired and hungry to wish more than that she would hurry up. Breakfast had only been a cup of tea and he had been too scared to ask for more. But she went on savouring her way slowly through the bread and cheese. Then she opened the tin of peaches, forking some of the golden rounded halves on to a tin plate. Afterwards the fruit slab engaged her attention.

She said then, "I shan't bother boiling the billy. Water will do." She poured a cupful, drinking it slowly. "Hungry?" she asked.

He nodded, watching her cut off another slice of bread. She pulled off a corner, tossing it a few feet away. He hadn't seen the birds till then, but immediately there was a flutter of wings, a harsh cry and the bread was gone. He stared silently at her.

She asked, "Where are the plates? Tell me that."

He licked his lips. "I hid them Saturday. In the boxes of jumble. The junk bits. I packed 'em for Mrs. Waters, see."

"Liar! You had them when you left for Quidong that evening. The way you clutched yourself gave that away." She grinned at him. "I tried all day to get you alone, but you played it canny, didn't you? No use lying though. I watched you, remember. By day. By night. I know where you went . . ."

"If you do, why don't you just search where I was?"

She didn't answer, and his grey eyes narrowed. He wondered if she was as big a liar as himself. He frowned, wondering how she expected to know when he did tell her the truth, if he ever gave in.

He said at last, "I put 'em under a big stone. At Quidong."

"Liar. That would be madness and you're far from being mad."

She threw another piece of bread to the ground and again it vanished to the sweep of wings and a shrill, harsh call. She said, "I

84

thought for a while the other boys would take them off you and I could have walked in and got them back. I even thought of demanding them off you, but I wasn't supposed to know about them, was I? And I was afraid of uproar and you knowing who it was . . . why didn't you give them to Coombs?" she snapped in sudden anger.

Then she shook her head impatiently. "Don't wonder he disbelieved you. Last show day a mob of toughs took the plates off every parked car and switched them. Took us all weeks before we were sorted out. People had gone hundreds of miles with one number at the front, another at the back, and them owning neither."

She gave a sudden shout of laughter that scared him more than her previous anger.

She jerked out, "The plates! Where are they?"

When he didn't answer she began pulling bread off the slice and tossing it to the birds. She held his gaze till the bread was gone. Then she asked the question again. When he remained silent, she said, "You'll be sorry before I've finished."

She upturned the tin of peaches over the ground. Then she began to crumble the fruit cake.

Finally she opened the bottle of soft drink and carefully, still looking at him, she poured it on the ground.

She said, "You may have one cup of water."

.   .   .

Kay blinked one eye open and rolled over, putting her feet to the floor of the station wagon. The sun had moved on and now it was over the shading trees and shining straight through the windows on to her. She felt hot, sticky and desperately tired and suddenly frantically hungry.

She glanced at her watch and realised the other two must have almost finished their picnic. But there would be something left if she hurried over before they packed up, she thought hopefully. She couldn't after all the embarrassments of the day, ask Miss Mings to unpack and wait while she satisfied her now raging appetite.

She couldn't find her shoes, then realised Miss Mings must have packed them away with the rest of the luggage. She leaned over the back of the seat, fumbling among the boxes and cases, but suddenly the craving for food was so great that she simply gave up the search and went running, with little dancing steps because the hot ground burned through her thin white socks, towards the other two.

She could hear Miss Mings' voice. It stopped just as she came in sight of the picnic spot. She could see Miss Mings' back and Johnnie's hat-shadowed face opposite, but her gaze was held in fascinated astonishment at the waste of golden fruit and thick syrup flowing over the ground from the upturned tin in Miss Mings' brown hand. Kay's stomach knotted with greedy anticipation. She was so hungry she could have scooped up the fruit from the ground and stuffed it into her mouth.

She was going to run forward and protest when Miss Mings spoke. She said, "You'll be sorry before I've finished."

For a moment Kay simply couldn't connect the voice, cold and thickened with words slurring together as though the speaker was almost too enraged to speak properly, with Miss Mings. Her gaze went flickering round the spot, looking for a third party.

And then she realised that Johnnie was tied up. For a minute she felt only astonishment, then rage washed over her.

He's tried to run away again, she thought furiously.

Then her gaze and her thoughts jerked back to the oddness and unreality of Miss Mings' actions. The elder woman was crumbling rich fruit cake over the peaches. Then her fingers stretched and arched greedily round the neck of the soft drink bottle and red bubbling liquid ran over the ruined food.

Then Miss Mings put the bottle aside. She said, in that strangely thickened voice, "You may have one cup of water."

Her head, in the felt hat, went nodding forwards and backwards. She repeated, the words slurring, "One cup of water and nothing else."

Kay saw Johnnie wrench anguished gaze from the food. He looked upwards, saw her standing there and gave a little snuffling cry of what sounded to her like terror.

Miss Mings turned slowly. She said, her face blank, "Thought you were asleep."

Kay strove to keep things unemotional. Whatever she did she knew she mustn't lose her temper. Miss Mings was old. And definitely, by the look of it, a bit queer into the bargain. But she was Stuart's employer, so it was impossible to say outright what she felt at the sight of Johnnie tied up; of the ruined food; of the elder woman's callousness towards him.

"I didn't take that pill because I was scared Johnnie would play up again and prove too much for you," she said evenly. "I see he has been, but Miss Mings, even if he tried running away again . . . he did, didn't he? . . . it doesn't justify this. It's . . . it's abominable!" She bit her lip, forcing down a rising tide of disgust as she looked into the round blank face. "I suppose in your day depriving a child of food was normal punishment, was it?" She tried to smile, but her mouth wouldn't co-operate. "But we don't do it now. We know it's not even a sensible punishment, and though perhaps tying him is best, if you were scared he'd dash off again, can't you see he's right in the blazing sun?"

Miss Mings said flatly, "You spoil him. That's been the trouble. You're afraid to tell him off or lift a hand to him because he's not yours and you keep asking yourself, 'Would I whack him for that if he was my own boy?'"

There was so much truth in that that Kay remained silent. At last she said, "At any rate I can't let you do this sort of thing. Is there any more cake? Or some fruit? I'll untie him and we'll give him something to eat and . . ." She suddenly turned back and said desperately, "Miss Mings, this holiday just isn't going to work out. It's been a complete mistake, hasn't it? Johnnie's too much for you and . . . will you drive us back? Or even to the nearest railway or hotel? I can send a message to Stuart."

Miss Mings said, "No."

Kay tried to ignore the cold finality of the word. She was completely bewildered at the elder woman's odd behaviour. Bewildered, and sickened, as she looked from the ruined food to Johnnie, like a hunched-up gnome in the blazing sun. She went to hurry to him and Miss Mings called, "Stop!"

When Kay looked at her she said, "Tell you what—I'll drive *you* to the railway. You leave the boy to me. You and Stuart have muddled yourselves so, you don't know where you are with him. There's plenty of sense in the sort of discipline my generation had handed out to them. Made men and women out of us, didn't it?"

Women with a sadistic streak who wanted to give children the same as they'd received themselves, Kay thought in disgust.

She said, "I couldn't do that. We'll both have to go back. I'm sorry to upset your plans, but honestly, you must agree, that we can't go on now. Johnnie, to put it mildly, will try every trick he knows on you to get even for this."

She nearly added, And I wouldn't blame him.

She turned away towards Johnnie again and took two steps. Then abruptly her right ankle was gripped, and twisted. She was reminded of cattle in the branding yards being thrown to the ground by one expert twist of a stockman's wrist, as she fell with breath-destroying force on to the ground, on her side.

She heard Johnnie scream. Shrilly, like a small animal seeing death in an eagle-hawk's claws above it, but she was so winded she couldn't move. When she was able to pull one knee under herself and force herself upright she turned her face, bewildered, dust streaked and scratched from twigs, to the other woman.

For a moment she wondered if she had caught her ankle on something and imagined that quick, expert twist. Then Johnnie whispered, "You're all bleeding. All down your arm."

She stared stupidly. She had fallen on to her left side, on to the edge of the peach tin, she realised and blood was dripping down her arm from a jagged cut.

She said stupidly, holding out the arm towards the other woman, "I cut myself."

But Miss Mings made no move to help her. Kay went on gazing at her, as she said, "Put your handkerchief around it."

Something in Kay concentrated stubbornly on the cut, and on normal things, refusing to look closely at what had been done to her, and why. She said, the stubborn concentration showing in her voice, "I need the medicine chest. It needs disinfecting and washing."

When there was no answer she went on with that same stubbornness, "Look how I'm bleeding. Why don't you do something?"

"Because I've other things on my mind. What to do with you for one. Didn't think you'd see reason and go off leaving Johnnie with me, but it was worth a try. Didn't have much hope of keeping things from you, either. The boy's too pig-headed. Pity you didn't believe him, Kay, but I suppose hooded men and gallons of vanishing blood were a bit too much for anyone."

Johnnie's voice whispered shockingly across her dazed consciousness. "It was true. Not the hooded men, or the blood neither, but the lady in red was. She was real. And she got killed'n she got put in the caves."

"So you know that. Worked it out did you?" Miss Mings stared at him, then turned back to Kay. "The boy has something of mine. See if you can make him see sense. Will save you both a lot of grief if you can."

Kay knelt there, the sun beating down on her unprotected head. She said, "It's not true."

"Don't be a fool. There's a dead woman in the caves all right. I thought I'd planned everything. Everyone was at the show. Even if the noise brought someone who could have questioned what I was doing? Owned the place, didn't I? And no one could have shovelled out the rubble without my permission. I burned her papers. Couldn't burn her clothes of course. Lighting a fire that big in mid-summer would have brought people investigating the smoke. So I stuck them in the jumble. Just a faint risk there, but not much. By the time anyone started looking for Megan her clothes would have been worn out on other women's backs.

"And then the boy saw me, and stole the number plates off Megan's car. I'd left them in a tree. Meant to move them in a few days and take them out east somewhere right away from Quidong. "Couldn't take them home. Jess's a snooper. I couldn't think of a place to put inside where she mightn't stumble on them. Couldn't use the outbuildings either because of the stockmen and Stuart constantly poking around for bits and pieces. Couldn't even leave them in the car. Webber was borrowing it because her own was in the workshop. I thought the tree was safest."

She thrust her head towards Johnnie. "Where're the plates?" she jerked at him.

Johnnie looked back, wide-eyed. He was wondering what she was going to do to Kay. He was safe he knew, till he told what she wanted, but Kay . . . she'd said she'd shoot Kay.

He searched through memory for some insult to throw at Miss Mings. All he could think of was Mrs. Sparrow who had lived in one room of a tenement near him for a while. He had once heard two women talking about her habits.

He said huskily, "I bet y'never change y'underwear!"

He expected Kay to smile and he tensed himself ready for collecting a blow from Miss Mings, but neither of them reacted as he had expected. Kay stared dully at the drying trickle of blood on her arm, beneath the handkerchief and Miss Mings just nodded and said, "When I was in prison camp I didn't have the chance. Come to that, after a while I didn't have underwear. I learned then to appreciate having good things. And food." She repeated the word. "I learned what doing without food can do to people. Even cocky and courageous people.

"So if you want to eat from now, Johnnie, you'd best tell me where those plates are. And you," her voice thrust into Kay's dulled consciousness, "if you want to eat, persuade him to speak up. Now get up! Hurry up."

Kay dragged herself to her feet. All she could think of to say was, "You can't possibly get away with this."

Miss Mings got to her feet, the rifle held pointing towards Kay. She asked, "Who's going to stop me?"

Kay realised there was no answer to it. It was useless to say Stuart, or someone, would come searching for them. He wouldn't until the time of Johnnie's appointment in the city was over and the welfare people rang Quidong. Afterwards it might take a long search to find them, and tracing along he would find that Johnnie had tried shoplifting and that she'd been upset.

She thought, She'll say Johnnie ran away again and that I followed and both of us were lost and she'll get away with it because no one could possibly guess the truth.

Then her gaze slid to Johnnie as she wondered, panic-stricken, if he realised that both their lives were in his hands. Did he realise that once he had told where the plates were they would both disappear?

He's got to hold out, she told herself. He's got to fight down the craving for food and be quiet. Then she wondered how on earth she was going to make a nine-year-old stick to that.

Miss Mings said in her ear, "Pick Johnnie up and carry him back to the station wagon. Hurry up. Put him in the back seat.

Hurry. Go on. Hurry up." The rifle moved in a vicious little jab towards her.

Kay was suddenly acutely conscious of the burning ground under her shoeless feet, and the throbbing pain in her arm. She asked, "What about my arm?"

"It's stopped bleeding. Forget it. Pick Johnnie up."

Kay stumbled back to the station wagon with him. He felt far heavier than the four stone odd that Stuart claimed he still weighed. At the thought of Stuart she found herself wondering what he was doing then. It was a profitless exercise that stopped when she had obediently put the boy on to the back seat of the station wagon. He had said nothing all the time she had held him. As she put him down she whispered urgently, "Keep your mouth shut!"

His head jerked up and she looked into surprised grey eyes, not realising that she had sounded like his father, but there was no chance to say anything more because something struck her viciously in the midddle of the back. She fell forward, half over the boy who gave a faint, startled cry.

Slowly she inched herself up, staring back over her shoulder. The owl-like eyes were bulging at her behind the round-rimmed glasses.

"Don't try that again. If you speak to him tell him to speak out. Try anything else and you'll pay for it."

It was her boot, Kay thought confusedly. Her boot, in my back. She looked down at the sturdy, thick-soled, lace-up shoes. There was something indecent in the fact that the woman with her blank ugly face could have kicked her like that.

Miss Mings said, "Get back and pack up the food and bring it here. Hurry. I'll be right behind you."

Kay asked commandingly, "Where are my shoes?"

She expected the other woman to glance down and give her a chance to grab the rifle, but Miss Mings continued staring at her face. "I don't know," she retorted. "Do as I told you."

Kay went. Slowly. So slowly that something hit her already aching back and Miss Mings warned, "That was a small piece of stone. Next time you slow down it will be a bigger one."

She stood over the girl while everything was packed. Then Kay walked back acutely conscious both of the rifle behind and Johnnie's frightened grey eyes in front of her.

She put the box into the back of the station wagon, locking the tailboard in position in a silence of helpless fury. She didn't dare look at Johnnie any more. That he must be ravenously hungry, scared stiff and exhausted, she knew. But he had to hold out.

Obeying Miss Mings, she slipped behind the wheel of the station wagon again. Her headache had come back, reminding her of the pill Miss Mings had given her. Her gaze narrowed against the glare ahead Kay wondered if she could use the pill on Miss Mings herself. Then her thoughts slipped away to the previous night. That was why she herself had fallen asleep so suddenly she thought bitterly. A sleeping pill.

She bit her lip, trying not to think what Johnnie might have gone through while she had lain there, sleeping. No wonder he had merely grunted in answer to her good morning. All that surprised her was that he hadn't started screaming to her for help. But of course, she realised, Miss Mings must have told him she'd shoot his foster mother if he let out so much as a murmur.

She tensed as ahead of her she saw a small blue car, but immediately Miss Mings said behind her, "Don't try it, Kay. If you do Johnnie will pay for it. Get me? He has to speak out so I can't make him incapable of that, but I can hurt him."

"He's a child. Have you forgotten that?"

"No. If he were an adult I'd have tried rough measures on him before this, but a kid can take only so much of physical rough-housing, while starvation . . ."

"Don't you realise," Kay threw over her shoulder, "that he can tell you anything? That you can't be sure, unless you go back to Quidong first, that he's told you the truth? You can't keep dashing from Johnnie in the bush to Quidong."

"I know approximately where the plates are." The voice came in that flat unemotional tone Kay had come to dread. "I'll know when he lies. And a person always tells the truth in the end. I found that out in Malaya. The Nips never knocked us about. If they wanted something they just starved us. Sooner or later you told the truth. Kept screaming it out over and over when the first time didn't bring you any food. You kept saying it even in hysterical half-consciousness."

Kay trod on the brakes. She was shaking so desperately she

couldn't have driven on. Her whisper stroked desperately at the hot air, "You couldn't. Oh, you couldn't."

The only answer was a brief vicious jab at the nape of her neck. "Drive on."

Kay looked at her shaking hands and thought, "I can crash the car. I'm shaking so much that it will look reasonable. And it'll give me a chance . . ."

But there was nothing to crash into. The world stretched ahead of them, dun-coloured, empty except for a few stark trees far from the road, and the purple tinge low in the eastern horizon where the ranges lay.

She set the car moving again. Twice cars passed them going in the opposite direction. Each time she tried to signal desperately with aching eyes and silent mouthing, but both times the drivers went by with a smile and a wave.

By late afternoon they were in the foothills and the world had changed again. The earth was chocolate brown, rowed with lines of vegetables near small homesteads, and green-yellow where cattle grazed on grass. Kay drove more slowly, tired eyes alert for some chance of help, but every time the homesteads grew closer together, or traffic joined in behind them she was ordered to turn off on to secondary roads.

She began to wonder if Miss Mings had any idea where they were really heading. The sun, going down in a flush of pink and black-streaked clouds, was on their left when Miss Mings said abruptly, "There's a garage ahead. Stop. The gauge is pretty low. Get them to fill her up and we'll take a can of petrol as well."

Kay licked at nervous lips. She tensed and the voice behind warned, "Remember, any trouble and Johnnie will be hurt. This is sure to be a one-man place, too. He can be shot and a hold-up faked if necessary. Remember it."

The garage was on the intersection of a highway and two second-ary roads, one looking like a mere lane leading into sunset distance. The garage was a bright, new looking place and Kay's spirits rose as she turned in and pulled slowly up to the pumps.

She let her hands slide into her lap. She could see someone through the glass of a door opposite and in a moment he came hurrying out. A little dark man with a cheerful smile. One man,

Kay thought ruefully. Just one, and not another soul in sight.

She turned towards him desperately, wanting to mouth the word Help, yet not knowing what he could do even if he got the message, because he would try to question her and there was Miss Mings and the rifle to stop that. Then she thought that Miss Mings might only make fun of her, and then later on, if Stuart came this way, he might learn how she had mouthed and how Miss Mings had turned the appeal aside. Stuart, she thought, with a tug at her heart so painful she gasped. If they could hold out till he came . . . but she knew it was useless to think of him coming at all.

Miss Mings wouldn't wait that long, she thought, still trying to catch the man's eye and failing, because he was filling the tank while talking to Miss Mings of the weather. Miss Mings would remember questions would be asked if Johnnie didn't turn up in Sydney on time. She must be sure Johnnie would have given in before then, and then both Johnnie and Kay would disappear. It would be so easy. A pathetic, distraught elderly woman stumbling from the bush to rouse a search party with a story of Johnnie running away and his foster mother following and never coming back.

She had a sudden horrible memory of a recent story she had heard of two bushwalkers stumbling on the skeleton of a woman who had disappeared two years before.

She looked over her shoulder and saw that Johnnie was sitting hunched-up, his bound hands and ankles hidden by the light rug Miss Mings had put over him. His head, with its huge-brimmed felt hat, was bent.

She spoke, so loudly that the sound seemed monstrous, "Could we have a glass of iced water if you've any? The little boy hasn't been well."

She saw Johnnie's head come up. His gaze met hers and a faint grin touched his mouth. She wondered if he was realising the man would wonder why he couldn't reach for the glass, or whether the grin was one of relief for even a cup of water.

Her stomach knotted at the thought and suddenly the hunger that had been ignored came raging back at her so savagely she felt ill. Then she realised the man was saying, "Sure. Like a couple of cokes for yourselves? We've got them on the ice." He jerked his head towards the bright red of the automatic dispenser near the office door.

Miss Mings said heartily, "A good idea. Don't uncap them though. We'll drink them later."

Her gaze mocked Kay's as they sat silently waiting till the man came back. Kay thought of the fact that not even a bottle of coke was allowed and the hard knot of hunger returned full force.

The man put the bottles on the front seat beside Kay, and went to hand the filled glass in through the open back window. Kay tensed and Miss Mings said, "I'll take it thanks. I'm not having it thrown in your face. The little imp's been playing up the whole trip. Here, Johnnie," she put the glass to his lips, "Don't you touch or I'll smack. Just sip."

She turned back to the man as the boy drank greedily, "Know any tips for handling a pugnacious nine-year-old?"

He laughed. "Like that? Got one myself and the best tip I know is one over my knee and the strap."

Miss Mings laughed with him. She handed back the empty glass. "Thanks. We'll be moving again. Want to make camp before night-fall. Off we go, Kay—straight ahead."

So that was that, Kay thought. It seemed impossible the woman should get away with it, but she had done so. And abruptly a hand reached over the seat and the two bottles disappeared. Miss Mings said, "You can't win, Kay."

Kay said nothing. She was thinking of Stuart, tracking them, finding the garage and listening to the story of how Johnnie couldn't even be trusted with a glass of water for fear he'd throw it in someone's face. If anyone tracked back over their journey after she and Johnnie were lost everything was going to point steadily to Johnnie's running away, beyond control.

She was so deep in thought she almost missed Miss Mings' curt command and had to stop the car and reverse into the narrow lane the other woman had pointed out. Once on it they bumped slowly upwards. The sun had almost gone, leaving the whole western sky streaked with orange and red and black and pink. The dull green tracery of trees now crowding in on them was changing to darker green, some of the trunks merging into shadows, some becoming stark and white against the dimness of their surroundings.

She realised suddenly that for a long time the air must have been growing cooler. Now it was actually quite cold. Two parrots, blue and red streaks of colour above the darkening trees, flashed over the car and were gone and then she was out on what seemed to be the top of a ridge.

In the fading light ridge after brooding ridge of tree covered mountains spread out before her, fading into valleys and arching up to spread broodingly over valleys beyond. The very immensity, the silence, of it scared her beyond belief. Out there, she thought, anyone could be lost and never found.

Miss Mings said, "Go on. The track winds down again. We're camping near the bottom."

It was almost dark when she directed Kay into bumping the car gently over a fairly clear area to stop under the shadows of trees. The place was quiet and the headlights picked out only trees.

Miss Ming said, "Get out. Pack up Johnnie and leave him sitting against the side of the wagon. Leave the car lights on. Get out the food. The water. The blankets. Leave the tailboard down and fix two of the blankets for Johnnie's bed. Hurry up."

She added, as Kay moved stiffly to obey, "Don't talk to him unless you're seeing reason and mean to persuade him to talk."

Kay nodded. She put Johnnie down and on sudden impulse brushed her parched lips against his cheek. The worst of the afternoon's agony had been concentrated on the fact that at mid-day she had been the one to corner and drag him back. If he had escaped then, her mind had twisted and turned and upbraided her, he might now be safe.

He said softly, "Jeez, you getting soppy?" but he rubbed the cheek against her for a brief moment before she left him and went back to obey instructions. It was as she hefted out the heavy insulated water box that she acted. She turned, dropped and flung it all in one movement and then gaped stupidly at the speed with which the elder woman dodged. But speedy as she was the heavy box caught her arm. She gave a shrill scream that was drowned in the shattering report from the rifle.

The scream of pain that followed came from Johnnie. He screamed again and even as Kay was calling to him, scrambling desperately towards him across the dark earth, he became silent again.

CHAPTER NINE

MISS WEBBER had kept up a non-stop rattle of conversation throughout the meal. Stuart was half glad of it because it stopped him from having to make conversation himself, but he had been too tired to appreciate either her over-bright efforts to entertain him or the meal that had started with some peculiar iced soup and gone through an elaborate chicken dish to a sickly sweet. He would have preferred Kay's cold roast any day of the week, he had told himself, and then at the thought of Kay, he had felt strangely bereft.

It was stupid to feel that way, actually, considering that in the past few months they seemed to have been at polite loggerheads, but the cottage didn't seem the same without her and he had missed, with an intensity that had surprised and faintly dismayed him, watching her about the usual activities of each morning and evening.

As Miss Webber led him firmly into the sitting-room he was wondering how soon he could decently make an excuse and go back to the cottage. She had probably expected him to be brilliant company from the trouble she had taken over the meal and he had let her down. He had let Jess down too, by the look of it, he thought ruefully allowing himself to be settled into a chair opposite Miss Webber. The girl had served the meal in sulky silence far different from her usual smiling attitude. Probably, he realised, she had expected while Miss Mings was away to spend her evenings out with Jackie Light.

He said, realising that silence had descended on them and that his hostess was hovering over the record player, "I hope Jess didn't have a date tonight that I ruined by coming up?"

"What?" She half turned, then laughed. "So you noticed that scowl. That Johnnie! It's his doing. He played a trick on her and she's so furious she nearly ruined the dinner."

He frowned. "Johnnie?"

"Yes." She had put on a record and was swaying gently in time to the music. Then her small foot began to tap eagerly on the polished wood floor. Her eyes were bright and expectant and he mentally groaned, but to sit there stolidly when she obviously expected him to dance would be no payment for the dinner.

He inched himself out of the comfort of the chair and she kicked aside the two rugs, then came forward to him, still gently swaying her plump body. She said, "Just a silly joke. Do you know where I'm going for the Christmas vacation?"

She was back in full spate, eyes glinting and mouth smiling, as he dutifully propelled her round the floor. She kept putting on more records and coming back eagerly to dance again, but at length he called a halt with a faintly apologetic, "I have to be up before dawn tomorrow."

"Poor man," she patted his arm, "but one thing you had a decent dinner tonight and not some tinned thing. Oh, don't try to make out you didn't eat out of tins last night, because I just wouldn't believe you. I know what men are when they're on their own, poor dears."

She talked all the way to the screen door of the veranda and he was half way to the cottage before he remembered Jess and remembered, too, the disturbing thought that had popped into his head when Miss Webber had mentioned Johnnie playing a joke on her.

When he went back to the kitchen door he could see her at the kitchen table, with a red dress and her work-basket in front of her. She turned when he knocked and came in, her dark face still sulky.

He asked gently, "What is it, Jess? Miss Webber said Johnnie's played a trick on you? He hasn't . . . taken away something of yours, has he?"

Her face cleared a trifle. "No." She hesitated then suddenly thumped the dress in front of her. "It's my dress. He's spoilt it all now."

"You mean he cut it? Dirtied it?" He reached out a hand.

She shook her head, "He wrote me a postcard. Says as the dress was on a dead woman." She shivered.

He looked at her, frowningly. He knew how the aborigines hated to touch something that had been on a dead person and it seemed an odd spitefulness for Johnnie to think up, especially as he had seemed quite fond of Jess.

He asked, "Why, how did he say that happened? Where did the dress come from anyway?"

She pouted, giving the dress a little push, "I bought it from the jumble, and was going to alter it. It's a lot too big, but so pretty." Her hand reached out as though to caress it, then moved back again. "Look," she jumped to her feet, "I'll show you. That Johnnie— he's nasty, that one. And after I baked him a cake just for him, too." She thrust a postcard into his hand.

In Johnnie's small writing he read, "Dear Jess, the red dress you bought belongs to the lady that's dead in the caves. She was killed and put there with her car and I've found the number plates off it and I'm going to tell my dad, but the red dress is a Clue and you mustn't cut it up, but hide it away and don't say anything to anyone till I've seen my dad."

Surprisingly it finished, "I am, yours sincerely, Johnnie Bradford."

Jess suddenly giggled. "You turn over. That Johnnie!"

Stuart turned the card and saw the black words around the lizard's frill, "Watch out Felt Hat doesn't get you."

He was suddenly overtaken by laughter. Then he sobered. Damn Johnnie, he thought wearily. And nasty of him too, the little wretch.

He said lightly, "You know you don't believe Johnnie, Jess. Now do you?"

"He spoilt my dress," she said petulantly with a push for the dress in front of her, "I don't like it now."

Stuart sighed, reaching in his pocket. "Will it make things right if I pay you for it and take it away? But you're being a fool, Jess— for one thing if there was a dead woman in the caves all the boards would have had to be taken off. Go down and feel them and I bet you they're as firm as the rock around them."

He walked back to the cottage with the dress bundled under one arm, wondering what on earth he was to do with it. Johnnie and his dead woman, he thought in disgust, but Felt Hat was a new one, and a more reasonable horror than the two hooded men of his previous story.

As he pulled off his things and got ready for bed he thought that it was the first time he had known Johnnie to be spiteful. He lied certainly, but not with the intention of spiting anyone. Then he yawned, standing by the open window, folding his arms round himself and luxuriating in yawn after yawn. Jess must have done something to flick the boy on the raw, he thought sleepily. Or maybe there'd been no spite in it at all. That was it, of course. He had just meant to get Jess scared into going down to the caves to peer fearfully between the boards.

He went to sleep chuckling.

• • •

Miss Mings' voice came gasping across the shadows, "What've you done?"

"It's Johnnie. You shot him! Bring a torch."

A moment later something was thrust into her hand. She knew the elder woman was pressing forward behind her, but for the moment Miss Mings was out of her thoughts. Her whole attention was riveted on the small huddled figure by the station wagon.

She could see, by torchlight, that the bullet had struck him across the forehead. There was a long bleeding furrow, but she said, "It's only shallow—a scrape," and knew sweet relief, but then she realised it wasn't the only damage. He'd been jerked sideways and had crashed with the side of his head against a jagged stone.

She should, she thought in amazement, have ceased to be surprised what the woman would do next. Her ankle was caught and twisted with that expert trick again and she was flat on her face. Before she could start trying to get up there was a knee viciously in her back and her hands were looped and tied.

Then her face was thrust down into the dirt. Miss Mings said breathlessly, "Lie still. I had those stockings in my pocket just waiting my chance. If you're wise you won't struggle while I rope your ankles. Every minute you struggle makes me a minute longer in helping Johnnie."

Kay was instantly still, but when she was tied she asked, "Can I move on to my back?"

"If you can."

Kay made the mistake of pulling her legs up under her and trying to get on to her knees, but without her hands to support her she fell forward on to her face again. Her face felt as though it had collected several more scratches by the time she rolled sideways, wriggling on to her back and then sitting upright, to stare towards the station wagon. She tried wriggling sideways towards it and Johnnie, but Miss Mings said sharply, "Stay where you are."

Kay began, "Is he . . .?"

"Oh, he's alive. Tough little beggar. He's out cold though. Thanks to you, damn you!" For a moment the owl-like eyes behind the round-rimmed glasses were turned on her.

Kay ignored that, demanding, "How do you know he's all right? The smack on the side of his head looks dreadful. How can you possibly know . . ."

"I'm a nurse."

Kay remembered her speaking of her doctor fiancé, of a medical mission in Malaya, but Miss Mings had never before spoken of training as a nurse. Kay found herself concentrating on the oddness of that, when Miss Mings lived in the outback where a trained nurse was someone valued beyond price, because usually there was one doctor and one hospital to an area covering far too many miles.

Then she said sharply, "That's not true. You're not a nurse. When that stockman was injured you never came forward to help. You can't know that Johnnie is all right."

"Hilary Mings isn't a nurse, so she couldn't come forward, could she?"

"But . . . but of course you're Hilary Mings. Don't be ridiculous." For a moment she wondered if the woman had gone completely off her head. "*Please*, Miss Mings," she begged, "tell me how Johnnie looks. I *do* know a bit of first aid. If you'll only let me look at him properly . . ." Her voice fell to desperate pleading across the silence, "You don't want him to die, do you? Not now, when you don't know where those number plates are." Then she demanded, "Why are they so important?"

"Because if they're found someone's going to ask who owns them. If they find Megan does they'll ask where she happens to be. They could find out she was heading for Quidong, I expect. Then they'd ask where she got to."

"Megan . . ." Kay murmured the name, then brushed it aside from thought. "Miss Mings, please let me look at Johnnie! Remember what I said about you not wanting him to die? If the number plates are so important Johnnie's important, too. If you'll let me look at him . . . you needn't untie my hands. Just let me look. *Please*."

"I told you, I know what I'm doing. I'm a nurse I tell you. Be quiet."

"You're not a nurse."

She saw the glasses reflected in the tail lights of the wagon again as the elder woman turned towards her.

"I'm a nurse," the answer came in a flat, thickened voice, "I'm not Hilary Mings you see. Hilary Mings died in Malaya. Now shut up."

Kay stared silently at the hunched back, at the hands moving about Johnnie, at the torchlight and headlights that made circles of light and patches of mystery beyond them. There had been such viciousness in the final words that she was frightened to ask any more. If the woman lost her temper completely there was no knowing what she might do.

The woman, she thought dazedly. That's who she was now. An unknown woman. Hilary Mings died in Malaya. The words kept repeating themselves round and round in thought, pressing and calling there to consciousness till she could have cried out.

Then the woman stood up. In the half shadowed, half lit world by the station wagon she looked monstrous. She said in that same thickened voice, "He'll do I think. Might be all to the good." She turned slowly, looking down with blank, owl-like gaze at Kay. "When he starts coming round he'll babble. They usually do. Always of the thing uppermost in mind. That'll be the number plates in Johnnie's case. He'll talk, and then I'll know."

Kay tried to speak and couldn't. Then the elder woman went on, "Don't try to make trouble. I might need your help to nurse, but just remember you're expendable. Get it? Try and make trouble and . . ." she reached for the rifle, reloaded, then said, "Wriggle over here."

She stood silently until Kay, breathless again, was close to the boy.

"Keep your eyes on him. If he tries moving call me. I'll be getting something to eat." She hesitated, then put the rifle down and bent. "I'm going to take your socks. If you do manage to get free you won't get far over this sort of country, barefoot. Don't try struggling. Just remember you're expendable, any time."

I want to live, Kay thought dully. I want to live. The urgency of that was all she could think about. She felt like laughing as she remembered that only a few days before she had exclaimed dramatically, "I wish I were dead," when thinking about the trivial problems she had had then.

She kept her gaze on Johnnie's face. Except for the bandage round his head he might simply have been asleep, but at any minute he might wake and try to talk. And you didn't, Kay thought in desperation, remember to lie when you were half asleep. You told the truth, and if he did that the pair of them would be finished.

She concentrated on willing him not to speak, not to wake; trying not to let thought of hunger pains be aware of the smell of warming tinned steak; of the smell of a gum-leaf fire and new made tea. She willed herself not to look around and see the woman savouring her way through the food and drink, but willpower abruptly gave way. She turned, gasping, licking at dry lips, seeing bread scraping round the plate to remove the last traces of steak.

The plate was put aside and the woman gazed at her across the gum leaf fire. "That was good," she said huskily. "In a little while I'll give you a scraping of something. No point in actual starvation now, because the boy will babble soon. If he doesn't a few hints, a good shaking, will help make him. I'll give you enough food to keep you helpful if I need you. Not enough to give you the strength to get far if you try getting away though."

Kay tried to return to concentrating on Johnnie's face and probable waking, but her hunger went on growing. She had to do something to stop thinking about it. She demanded, "Who are you? If you're really not Hilary Mings."

"I'm not. Once I was called Olive Donelly. I was a nurse, and used to a backseat life by the time Hilary Mings moved into the mission." She sucked greedily at the mug of tea. "But see how it finished up. Hilary Mings died. I didn't" She demanded, "Johnnie moved?"

"No. What happened to her? Hilary Mings?"

"Just lay down and died. Straight after the Nips moved out and we were free. Told you, didn't I, that happened to some of them. Hilary took imprisonment better than most of us, too. Funny to think of that. She was religious. I expect that helped. She got some sort of fever. I did what I could, but she died." She finished unemotionally, "I buried her. No one else to do it. Just a shallow grave. I didn't have strength for anything more. That's what lack of food does to you."

She suddenly grinned, the big white teeth making a splash of light across her shadowed face.

Kay felt hysteria welling over her. It was tiredness and shock and hunger and the incredibility of having mild Miss Mings suddenly turn out to be a wolf in sheep's clothes that made her start gasping with laughter and cry out, "Oh, what big teeth you have!"

The mug struck her full in the face. For a minute, after her startled cry, she felt nothing, then her whole face seemed to come flamingly alive with pain. She sat there, rocking herself, with little moaning sounds of self-pity.

The woman said in that thickened voice, "Count yourself lucky it didn't have hot tea in it." Then she demanded harshly, "What made you say that?"

"I . . . don't know," Kay gasped, still rocking herself. "Yes, I do. It was you, turning out to be a wolf. In sheep's clothing you know. Why did you hit me?" She wept, the tears coursing down her pain-wracked cheek.

The woman ignored the question. She said, "Sheep . . . Hilary was a bit of a sheep come to that. That was what Megan said, you know. That's why I got angry and hit you."

Kay went on rocking herself. She didn't even try to make sense of what the elder woman was saying. Then she was told, "I'm making you a sandwich. I'll feed it to you."

She came across and suddenly jerked Kay's head back. Her face came close, with the owl-like probing gaze. Kay shrank away, but the hand held her firmly by her hair.

"You're not hurt. Just bruised. Here," bread touched her mouth. "Eat it. Not like that." There was suddenly disgust in her voice, "You're not an animal."

Aren't I? Kay wondered vaguely. Yes I am. A frightened scared, terrified animal who wants to live, but knows it's going to die.

But obediently she chewed carefully through each mouthful,

knowing there would be little enough to follow it and for clear thinking she needed food. For action, too.

Then the woman said, "Wriggle yourself back over there. I'll put a blanket over you. You can sleep for a while. Then I'll ask you for an hour while I sleep. But don't try to be clever. I wake easily. If Johnnie starts talking I'll come awake again."

Then he mustn't wake, Kay thought wearily, and was appalled at herself. She told herself, as she stretched out on her side and felt the blanket covering her, that she hadn't wished Johnnie to die. That was an appalling idea. But he mustn't wake up. Or if he did he must wake clear-headed so he wouldn't tell where the number plates were.

But that, she was sure, wasn't likely to happen.

I'm not asleep, she told her weary body and mind. I mustn't. If he starts to talk I've got to get to him and make him be quiet; do something so he won't tell. I'm not to sleep, she whispered, and even while whispering it she knew she was going to do it just the same.

.   .   .

She woke only when the woman shook her awake. She cried out complainingly because her head felt a monstrous size of pain and her stomach immediately began craving food. Both facts were almost unbearable, but when the woman said, "Wriggle over to Johnnie and keep your eye on him. If he moves call me, and I'll wake at once," she nodded and pressed her aching body into the movements necessary to carry her to Johnnie's side.

Miss Mings lay down on the other side of the wagon, so that her face could be seen beneath it and her ears could hear any sound from the other side, Kay realised.

She sat there trying to think of something to do. If she wriggled round say, and knocked the gun to the ground and then wriggled it with her feet into the far scrub . . . then she discarded the idea. She could never get far before Miss Mings woke, and a quick search would soon find the rifle because it was too big to hide easily. And even with it gone remained the fact she was bound hand and foot.

In stories, she thought tiredly, there was always a handy stone to cut the prisoner's bonds. Then she remembered the stone that had caused Johnnie's injury. She wriggled gently backwards, her bound hands groping, and instantly came a sharp query, "What are you up to?"

"Easing myself into another spot. I've cramp, and pins and needles."

"I don't believe it. The stockings have a bit of give in them. They can't be too bad."

Kay remained silent, but after a while, she could hear soft breathing, and her hands went groping for the stone. But it was no good, she realised a long time later. She was running with sweat, and her heart was thudding in sheer pain. And the nylon just slid over the stone, or snagged for a moment and then slid away again. She would never, in a full night of work, manage to cut through the stockings that way, she realised.

And the woman knew what she had been up to. That was the most frustrating thing of all. She came, a darkly seen figure, round the wagon and said, "That was stupid. I could hear you panting and gasping and working away. Wriggle yourself back over there and lie down."

CHAPTER TEN

IT was close to dawn when Kay woke again and instantly her thoughts were concentrated on her stomach. It was ridiculous and undignified and smacked so of self-pity that she felt tears of mortification pricking under her lids. And then she realised that Johnnie was talking.

She could hear a faint murmur and then the woman was asking, "Johnnie, tell me where you put the number plates from the green Mini."

Kay screamed. She went on screaming, hoarsely, determinedly, till there was a rush of footsteps and the woman was looming over her. Sheer desperation drew up her legs and struck her bound feet viciously upwards, but the woman dodged with that effortless speed that had so amazed Kay the previous night.

The one effort had taken all Kay's strength. She lay there, shivering, waiting for a blow or something worse, but Johnnie had stopped murmuring, she realised thankfully, then thankfulness died away as she remembered that soon he might be talking again, and she wouldn't be able to scream every time. The woman would simply gag her.

She was still thinking of that when the woman went away again without doing anything to her. Kay could hear her voice wheedling at the boy, but he didn't speak.

After a while she could hear the clatter of dishes, and smell another gum leaf fire. The faint breeze that had sprung up overnight drifted the pungent smoke and smell of billy tea tantalisingly to her nostrils.

She was allowed a slice of dry bread scraped with oily butter and a cup of over-stewed, over-sweetened tea, but she found herself savouring each mouthful in grateful enjoyment until she realised she must be looking like the other woman. Then she gulped at the rest of the tea, not caring when she was promptly upbraided again for behaving like an animal.

Then her feet were untied, and a hand under one armpit hauled her ruthlessly to her feet.

She was told, "I'm untying your hands. Then you can, as Johnnie would say, use the outdoors," The voice was mocking. "But just remember I've the rifle aimed at you and that you're expendable. You nearly died this morning," she was told unemotionally, "You made me furiously angry, but I remembered I'd need you to drive the wagon, while I kept Johnnie still in the back. Anyway he was only babbling about m'dad," the voice mocked again on the last word.

"How is he?" Kay asked.

"All right, I think. He's tough. Go on. Get moving. Then you can have a clean up and get behind the wheel."

"Where are we going?"

"A creek. I've been there once. It's right off the track, but the wagon can take it. Bumpy though, which is why I want you to hold on to Johnnie."

"If it's bumpy you might kill him," Kay protested heatedly. "If you're really a nurse you must know he should be kept quiet and still." ·

"I know what I'm doing. I'm a nurse all right. Use that water. Hurry up. The towel's there. And don't try throwing it. I'll shoot at once. Get that?" In a minute she added, "Time's up. Get behind the wheel."

For one brief minute Kay hesitated, but for the life of her she could think of no way out. If she ran into the scrub she wouldn't get far in bare feet and there was the fact that a rifle bullet could bring her down with no effort. She had seen the woman shooting several times and knew exactly what a crack shot she was.

As she walked slowly to the wagon she had the uncomfortable feeling the other woman was laughing at her; had read her thoughts and known her conclusions and was amused.

Kay hesitated by the back seat. Johnnie was lying there. He looked smaller than ever and the white bandage made his face look sallow under the tan. Then a swift prod in her back sent her round behind the wheel.

Miss Mings slipped into the back seat. She said, "Go as gently as you can. Reverse up the track."

. . .

Dawn over Quidong was red in the east, with a rim of white on the far western horizon, with purple-black grey-edged clouds spreading out from it.

Stuart came to the cottage door feeling the hot air pressing down on him, so that immediately he stepped outdoors his skin pricked with sweat. He stood there, hat tilted to the back of his dark head, appraising the weather, deciding the day would clear over Quidong. The storm would work itself out in thunder and lightning and downpouring rain somewhere in the arid plains of the far west. And when the sun came out again the plains would bloom for a day or two with flowers, before they died under the sun and the place was desolate again.

He let his gaze fall from the sky and saw that Jackie Light was patiently waiting for him, squatting back on his heels beside the bay mare tethered to the one soaring gum of the home paddock.

Jackie called, "G'day, boss," with a flashing smile that showed his teeth, stark white against his dark skin. "You have any rags I could have?"

Stuart smiled. He had long been accustomed to the perpetual cry of the aboriginal stockman. All of them tried to outdo one another with gleaming saddles, and shiny-bright harness that reflected back the sun's harsh light in head-splitting glare. Many of them went in for polished fancy boots as well, but he had put his foot down at Quidong over the wearing of the big, jangling spurs that many of them wore.

It was common to see them, with a moment to spare, bringing out rags and polish and getting to work against the fine coating of red dust that came down over everything in next to no time.

He was about to refuse, not knowing what Kay might have put aside for the men and what she had selected for the house cleaning among any rags in the cottage, when he remembered the red dress and jacket. They were no good to Kay he knew. He had never seen her wear that harsh shade. Always when she chose red it was a rose-red. Besides, he couldn't imagine her choosing to parade in another woman's cast-off's.

But to his surprise and annoyance when he collected the dress and came back to toss it to the aboriginal, Jackie shook his head, making a little dance step from it as it lay on the ground between them.

"That one no good," he said flatly, and kept repeating it.

Stuart said impatiently, "I suppose Jess has been telling you of Johnnie's postcard? You know his yarn's as tall as a hundred foot gum. You were with me Friday evening anyway when he was talking about hooded men and gallons of blood."

The young man gave a soft chuckle, but he made no move to pick up the dress and in exasperation Stuart bent, picked it up and tossed it through the open door of the cottage, before slamming the door and moving away.

"You go to hell then," he remarked with grim affability and Jackie chuckled, his white teeth flashing, as the two of them mounted and rode off into the far paddocks where bullocks were being rested before taking the overland trek to the eastern saleyards.

It was two hours before the little irritating scene of the morning came back into his thoughts and then he was only annoyed because it persisted in niggling at him.

Scattering the ashes of the small smoko fire he mounted the black stallion again and promised himself that he could go and check on the boards over the cave, just so he could point out to Jackie and Jess they were firm as rocks and that being so Johnnie has foxed them and they were a couple of fools.

The promise made, he immediately forgot the whole thing.

.   .   .

The mountains brooded silently under a lowering dark sky as Kay eased the station wagon round the winding track that was leading, she was sure, into one of the valleys. Wherever she looked there was only the track, the mountains, the lowering sky and the vast closure of trees on either side.

If it rains, she thought, we can't stay out in it. It would look too odd later on to say that we'd camped out in the middle of a downpour in these mountains. We'll have to go back to civilisation and find a hotel.

She threw hoarsely over her shoulder, "It's going to rain isn't it?"

"Perhaps. We'll be all right in the station wagon."

"It will look odd, if anyone comes along, and sees us sitting in the wagon in the middle of a downpour," Kay retorted shortly.

"No one's likely to come along in the middle of a downpour, stupid. They'd be under shelter."

Kay sank her teeth viciously into her lower lip, but she hardly felt the pain. There was such a rising tide of fury in her body and brain that it scared her. If she wasn't careful she was going to lose all control and do something completely foolish. Then, with a nervous pulse beating wildly in her throat, she remembered that she was only alive now because the woman had needed her to drive. If the woman intended to camp by this creek where they were going, until Johnnie talked, then Kay wouldn't be needed any more.

Then she thought desperately, she can't possibly do without sleep. If Johnnie gets worse she'd need me to help. If he started struggling, someone will have to hold him.

Then she remembered that if he started struggling he might well start talking, too.

She remembered the pill then. It was still in her slacks pocket where she had slipped it the previous day. She tried, searching desperately through memory, to dredge up what she knew of sleeping pills and head injuries. Did you, she wondered, give tablets like that to someone with a head injury? You wouldn't give a full tablet to a child, she was certain, but half a tablet might be safe. That should keep him quiet for a while.

Then she wondered if the tablet would be so wrong for him that he died. Looking down at her hands on the wheel she could see they were shaking. They looked like a stranger's hands, too. The nails had dirt under them and the flesh was scratched and bruised.

What if I killed him? She asked herself again, then realised there was no chance to give him the pill anyway. He wasn't conscious and even if he came round it was unlikely the woman would let her give him anything.

And she was highly unlikely to let Kay near her own food, so giving the woman the tablet was out, too.

She threw over her shoulder as she turned another curve in the track, with careful slowness, "Why did you have to kill that woman?"

The answer came abstractedly as though the elder woman was bent over Johnnie. The track was so winding that Kay didn't dare take her eyes off it to look over her shoulder, as she was told, "She knew I wasn't Hilary, of course."

"But . . . did it matter?" Kay asked vaguely, "I mean, everyone accepts you as . . ."

"She could prove it. Hilary Mings had small teeth. That was what Megan was looking at all through coffee, though I didn't wake up to it. She was obsessed with teeth. Had her own out when she was fourteen. I suppose you could call it morbid interest in other people's dentistry. Should have remembered it, but I didn't. Then she leaned forward over the coffee cups and asked, 'Have you got false teeth now, Hilary?' "

"I still didn't wake up. I said, 'No, thank God.' "

"Then she squinted at me and said, 'Then how does it happen you've got great big teeth like that?' That's why I lost my temper with you last night. You sounded so like Megan. She pointed out that Hilary had had small neat teeth and it wasn't feasible her teeth had lengthened and broadened with the years."

"You mean, you and Hilary Mings and this Megan were all friends at one time? In Malaya?"

"Prison camp. Megan Dale was visiting Malaya when the Nips came in. Had a sister somewhere. Megan was rounded up with the rest of us. She had plenty of time to look at our teeth, damn her. I thought she was dead, actually. She vanished when the Nips went. She wasn't around when Hilary died, I do know."

Her voice had grown slower and remote, as though she was losing herself in memory, but that she was still sharply alert to present surroundings was made plain as she abruptly ordered Kay to take the left-hand fork of the now dividing track.

The going was worse there, but they were still heading downwards, Kay realised. The bush seemed to press closer on either side, but there was no sound except the engine and the bumping as they moved on.

Kay said slowly, "But it was all so long ago. If . . . why didn't you say she was mistaken?"

"To be honest, it was so funny, so hideously funny, I roared with laughter. Think of it. Then she told me something I'd forgotten, if I'd ever truly thought about it. Hilary'd broken both her ankles when she was a teenager."

Kay remained silent, frowning at the track ahead.

The woman burst out, "I was a fool to go. She wrote me as soon as she landed out here. Perth that was. She went home to Canada after Malaya. She had no family left. Like me. The sister died in Malaya. She just drifted round, as far as I could make out. Then came out here. Hilary told us both about Quidong and her people. Megan had only the barest idea where the place was, but she wrote to Quidong, asking if Hilary was there, or where?"

"I thought it best to answer, in case she came snooping around. She kept writing and hinting I ought to invite her over to talk about old times. A fool of a woman. Fancy anyone wanting to talk about those days! I could see she'd turn up if I didn't do something, especially when she went to Sydney. I told her I was going to Sydney too and if she liked I'd take her to lunch. I thought that would finish her. It was nearly twenty years and Hilary had been about my build and with dark eyes, too. I forgot about the silly fool's obsession with teeth. If I'd remembered I'd have had the lot pulled out years ago."

She said with sudden violence, "I should have remembered! And there was Megan grinning at me and saying I was Olive. Told her she was crazy, but she reminded me about Hilary's ankles and said they'd show in an X-ray if one was taken. I told her no one was likely to start X-raying me and she said Hilary's cousins would see to it if they knew. She had cousins in England. A whole mob of them. They send me cards at Christmas and letters now and again. That's why a trustee was put in at Quidong when the Mings couple died. If Hilary didn't turn up the place would have gone to the cousins."

She didn't say anything more and Kay sat silent, her gaze on

H   113

the track ahead. She had followed the woman's jerky speech with only part of her mind. The rest had been working on the problem of what she was going to do and she had come to a decision to crash the wagon.

If it was put out of action it would have to be left there on the track. It wouldn't be possible to push it far enough into the thick bush to hide it. And then someone would come along... surely people used the track quite frequently? ... and they'd see the car. They'd see it had crashed and report to the police. Probably the police would finally ring Quidong and they'd make a search in the surrounding bush. Wouldn't they? her thoughts pressed.

And if her luck held, the confusion of the crash would give her a chance to overpower the woman—to knock her out and flee into the bush with Johnnie. It might take a while for them to get to safety, but that was better than being slowly starved while waiting for Johnnie to speak.

She could see the trail ahead of her snaking away downwards. She decided that as they rounded the next curve the station wagon would go into a skid and into the trees. She sat tensely, waiting.

And then Johnnie spoke.

CHAPTER ELEVEN

JOHNNIE said quite clearly, "M'dad'll know."

Kay sent the wagon spinning crazily down the twisting path. It was the only thing she could think of doing. She didn't dare dwell on the thought that she might be causing graver injury to Johnnie with all the swaying and banging. All she could concentrate on was the fact that once he was capable of telling where the plates were he was going to die, and so was she.

She could feel a cold vicious thrusting at the nape of her neck, but she knew the woman didn't dare shoot. If she did the station wagon would career off the track and probably finish the lot of them. She went on and on till sheer dizziness and sickness forced her to slow down and finally stop.

Waiting, she felt complete exhaustion sweep over her, then suddenly she doubled up, fighting a savage attack of cramps. It was sheer hunger she realised. She had eaten practically nothing since Sunday, yet had driven hundreds of miles, been attacked and tried attacking in return and lived through an intensity of emotional beating. Sunday she had been too tense to eat much. On Monday she had missed breakfast and picked at steak in the dreary country hotel at lunch-time and had had nothing that evening. And tea on Tuesday morning . . . she found herself going over and over each item of food with a deliberate savouring of memory that reminded her acutely of the woman.

She had nothing for Tuesday's lunch, a sliver of cheese between bread for the evening meal and bread and tea that morning, she remembered.

When waiting brought no retribution she wondered in sudden startling, cramp-easing hope, if the woman had been knocked out during that mad, crazy dash down the trail. She whipped round, staring.

The owl-like eyes were staring back. The woman's face was red, as though she had sat too near a fire.

Kay saw all that. Then a hand whipped out and struck her

face, fingers outspread, thrusting her back so viciously she thought for one minute her neck was going to snap.

The woman said, "I'd shoot you now if there wasn't a chance someone might happen along. Turn round. Drive on."

Kay turned slowly. Now to add to her injuries her already bruised face was aflame with pain again and the back of her neck hurt intolerably.

She managed to get the station wagon moving again as she asked, "How is Johnnie?"

There was no answer. She went on repeating the question louder and louder till she could feel moisture on her face and knew she was crying, but there was still no answer, so as part of her punishment she had to drive on not knowing if he was all right or if she had hurt him further.

A long time later she was told, "turn over there, between those trees."

Kay drew the station wagon to a gentle halt and looked doubtfully ahead. There was no track. Just bare earth, fallen twigs and short, blackened grass, and trees.

She was told, "You can get across it. Go slowly and you'll find there's plenty of space between the trees. I'd prefer getting right out into the bush away from any tracks at all, but it can't be helped. Can't afford to leave the wagon when it'd be found by hikers or someone probably. They might think it a stolen car, abandoned, and report it."

Kay remembered her plan of crashing the wagon somewhere on the track with a feeling akin to disinterest. She turned the station wagon between the trees and went ahead slowly, twisting and turning. As she had been told it was easy enough. Some time in the past year or so there had been a fire there that had cut a wide black swathe through the bush where hints of grey green were now poking in hopeful growth once more. Winds and time since the fire had carried up the ashes and left only the earth and the stark, blackened holes of trees, that like the earth, were spreading overhead now in new leaves.

She found her spirits sinking even lower as they bumped on. The place was depressing. Even when the faint glint of water was picked up under the lowering sky it made things no better. The water was only in view for a short length, before disappearing in enclosing bush at either end.

Obeying instructions she came to a stop where the water trickled away into mystery somewhere east. The woman said, "Always knew it'd be handy to mark all my trips on the maps. Marked this place eight months ago."

Kay asked, "How is Johnnie?"

There was no answer to that, but the woman said, "We're camping for a while. If anyone comes along don't try any tricks. Act normally so they'll go away thinking Johnnie had just a small accident and we're staying put for a couple of days. Get it?"

Kay's spirits soared up again. She can't do away with me, she told herself. Not yet. If anyone comes along she must have me here, because it might look odd, after we're lost, if someone comes forward and speaks of seeing her and Johnnie but not myself. I have to be around until we're lost.

"Yes," she agreed, but said in swift mockery, "Of course they're going to think it quite reasonable, aren't they, that I should be tied up."

"I've thought of a way of coping with that. You can't win, Kay, though that was a good try last night."

Kay thought in amazement, she sounds quite pleasant. It was worse than the red faced fury, when she turned slowly it was to see the creased, ugly brown face she was used to. It was suddenly incredible that the woman wasn't Miss Mings; had killed someone; intended to kill two more if she had her way.

She asked in sheer bewilderment, "Why did you have to kill that woman . . . Megan . . . Megan . . .?"

"Megan Dale."

Kay rushed on, "I suppose she wanted money to stop her telling the English cousins, but couldn't you have . . ."

"I gave her plenty of money and she spent it. The Mini was one thing she bought. Sealed her fate as you might say. If she'd bought a bigger car I couldn't have run it into the cave—I'd have had to have thought up some sort of accident. When she had the car she had a new idea. She was going to live with me. She wouldn't listen to reason."

117

"Would it have been so hard to take?" Kay asked bluntly. "Harder than murder?"

"She drank like a fish. That's why she had no friends left to worry about her. Even her husband divorced her years back. I couldn't have trusted her one minute. Anyway she kept making cracks about my big teeth and remembering things about Hilary and coming out with, 'Remember how . . . oh, what's her name? . . . used to do this or that?' and then laughing. She'd have let the truth out."

"And then Quidong would have gone to the English cousins?" Kay challenged, "But you've had . . . how long is it? . . . nearly twenty years there. You've had a lot out of it."

"I put my soul and my backbone and everything else into it. It was worthless when I reached there. When they told me in hospital in Malaya the Mings pair were dead I thought I'd be stepping into something worthwhile. And don't look at me like that. The English cousins were comfortably off. Hilary'd often said so, and I'd always had a backseat out of life up to then. So I came and found I'd lied for nothing.

"But it was scratch myself a living there or somewhere else, so I stayed. I've made it what it is, but you don't think that'd count if I was found out now, do you. It'd still be fraud on my part. They'd take it all off me right down to the last rug on the floor and the last calf out in the paddocks.

"It's only this last couple of years I've been able to relax and taste a bit of comfort. D'you think I was going to hand that over because of Megan Dale?"

"Didn't you think the cousins might pay you for all the work you'd put into the place? Wasn't that worth a try?"

"And what if they'd said no? Wonder if you'd be so high-minded if it'd been you. But I'm not here to talk to you. Get out. Hurry up."

The rifle jabbed at her viciously again, but it was an effort to move. A cruel effort to move stiff muscles, to stand upright and feel cramps trying to double her up again, and to walk, barefooted, over the stony ground, at the woman's ordering.

She should have been prepared for it, she thought furiously the next minute, as her ankle was grabbed and she was tossed with that quick expert stockman's throw. She had never before realised, too, how easily she let tears flow. She could feel them running down her cheeks again in sheer exhaustion and bitterness as a knee landed viciously in the small of her back and her arms were dragged backwards.

Then she was released.

The woman said,"I've tied your arms above your elbows. That allows your hands a bit of play, but not enough to let you play tricks. You can roll over and sit up and wriggle over to a tree and prop yourself up. I'm going to put a cardigan round your shoulders. Then if anyone comes along you'll look quite normal.

"But remember this. You try throwing the cardigan off, say, or screaming for help, and it won't be only you who'll suffer, but the person whose help you're striving to get, too. Don't misunderstand me. You don't think I'd let them walk off and summon help, do you?"

Kay rolled over, blinking up at her. She said, laughter bubbling at the back of her throat, "You're quite crazy. How could you dispose of a group of hikers, of . . ."

"You wouldn't get a group here, stupid. Groups are greenhorns mostly. They keep to the better known tracks. Mists can come down like lightning in these valleys. You'd only get experienced bushmen round here. One or perhaps two. I never saw a soul all the time I was around here eight months back."

"And how," Kay wriggled upright, "could you stop even one person? Are you going to fill these mountains with "lost" people? And a hiker might have left word to say he'd be back the same day. If he didn't turn up," the words tumbled over each other in her efforts to make the woman see reason, "they'll send out a search party and . . ."

"Ever heard of accidents? They happen here frequently. A chap falling, say, on that stone. Over there in the creek." As Kay jerked her head round to look the woman went on, "And then he fell face forward into the creek say, unconscious, and was drowned. Just an accident. And we wouldn't be here when he was found. You just can't win, Kay."

Kay licked her lips and tasted dirt. Her face must be filthy she thought resentfully.

Then the woman said, "Get over to the creek and wash your face. You can manage that by inching your hands up and down and bending your face right down. Go on. Hurry."

The water was cold. It smarted on her bruised skin, but she splashed it gratefully but awkwardly because of her bound arms. She was still kneeling there when she heard the woman asking, "Johnnie, where are the number plates?"

Kay hadn't known it was possible to drag herself upright so quickly and then run. Water was dripping from her face and hands as she sped across the ground, unconscious of the stones ripping at her feet. She stopped, and thrust out one foot all at the same time. The bare foot caught the woman on her just turning face. She went backwards mouthing unintelligibly and Kay launched another kick at her and another.

It had been an attempt of sheer desperation and it failed. Her bare feet weren't capable of heavy damage, and her legs had been extremely hard to move at all. The two wild kicks exhausted her so much she simply went teetering off-balance for a moment, away from the woman, and then she collapsed.

For one moment she thought the butt end of the rifle was going to be used on her face. The woman towered over her, still mouthing. Her glasses had been knocked askew, and were looped round one ear only, hanging down her face. There were leaves and twigs in her greying hair and a great smudge of dirt on her brown face where Kay's foot had caught her first.

But she didn't look ridiculous. Only terrifying.

She held the rifle high, the heavy butt-end jabbing down towards Kay's face, then abruptly the rage went out of her lined face. Deliberately, still watching the younger woman, she hooked the round-rimmed glasses back into place, then reversed the rifle's position.

She said in that flat voice, "If it wasn't I couldn't explain your face away if someone happened along, I'd teach you a lesson for that." Then she slowly nodded. "But now you know how weak you are, don't you? Two kicks and you're done. Think how far you'd get out in the bush. Have a good look round you, then picture yourself out in it, barefooted, with your arms tied so you've no hopes of releasing them, and remember you couldn't take to the tracks even, because I could run you down with the wagon.

"Go on back to the water. Wash yourself and use the towel I tossed you. Then get over to the tree. I'll be watching you every minute."

Kay crawled, exhausted into complete obedience, but she wasn't thinking of the exhaustion, of her hurts, of washing, or even of the woman's enraged face. She thought only that Johnnie must have stirred and perhaps opened his eyes. That was why the woman had called to him that way. He hadn't spoken but if he had been conscious enough to hear the woman's voice he might have taken in the scene that followed and been reminded of his position.

She began awkwardly patting the towel over her flinching skin, knowing the woman's gaze was going over her. Kay's movements became slower and slower. She went on desperately patting as though she was trying to ease the pain in her face, while all the time she was wondering what Johnnie was doing.

Because when she had turned from the creek she had seen him. The station wagon was parked with its tailboard to the bush at the far end of the clearing, the headlights pointing towards her. And for a moment she had seen Johnnie's bandaged head round the side of the wagon as he had slipped round behind it.

She wondered desperately how long it would take him to get right away into the bush. She went on patting her face till suddenly the woman demanded, "What do you think you're doing?"

"What? Drying my face, of course. Did you think," she asked with wry humour, "That I was dancing the dance of the seven veils?"

But the woman didn't break into that shockingly good-humoured smile that occasionally still crossed her face. Her gaze narrowed. Then abruptly she whipped round. Kay tried to get up but the woman was striding back to the wagon, had glanced inside and then started to run.

And Johnnie, Kay realised in despair, must have only gone a few steps before collapsing, because the woman was bending on the edge of the bush, and scooping him up.

She had put the rifle down for a moment, but her gaze still watched Kay as she carried the boy back to the wagon and settled him on the back seat. She warned, "Don't try anything. Or Johnnie will pay for it. I knew he wasn't badly hurt. He'll keep coming round for longer and longer periods. I should have kept him tied of course. Your antics made me forget.

"And you knew, didn't you, that he was out of the wagon?" She gave that sudden apparently good-humoured smile. "You can't win, Kay. He couldn't have got far in any case. Get back to the tree over there. And behave yourself."

* * *

Stuart Heath rubbed the black stallion gently along its spine, making a soft, soothing little sound of tongue against teeth. The stallion he had broken to cattle work himself four years before and sometimes he thought that it knew his thoughts long before a tug on reins, or pressure from his knees, turned them into commands.

He went on stroking, the big horse standing quietly, nuzzling gently at his shoulder. Then Stuart's hand stopped as he became conscious of being watched. He looked up and saw Miss Webber's plump figure, in a navy and white dress, in the doorway.

"Hello there," she came teetering down the steps in her absurd heels. "I just popped in to do a little tidying up for you. Miss Mings told Jess to do it but I said no, because though I really hate to say it, those aboriginal girls can't keep their fingers out of other people's pies. And I thought to myself what if they have private letters and papers lying around? After Jess saw them they wouldn't be private any more."

Stuart sighed, then abruptly grinned as he remembered Johnnie saying sagely once, "M'dad says neighbours're like flies—once settled in y'kitchen it's hard to get rid of 'em."

He said feebly, "Good of you, but I was intending to flick a duster around now and again."

"Oh you men!" She gave his shoulder a little pat, then asked absently, "Has Kay a sister? I was just looking through that photo album and there's a lot of Kay with a blonde girl and I wondered, because Kay never said . . ."

With the rueful reflection that Jess might have pried, but certainly wouldn't have questioned him afterwards, he said, giving the stallion a final pat. "No. That would be one of Kay's friends you mean. She was Kay's bridesmaid."

"Oh?" She looked disappointed, then trotted at his heels as he strode towards the cottage, "And what is Jess's dress doing on the floor?"

He stopped, frowning, remembering the promises he had made and promptly forgotten.

"I bought it off her to make up for the upset. I tried fobbing it off on Jackie this morning for cleaning rags but he said he wouldn't have it. It's funny the way you've only to hint something is off a dead person and they'll shy away from it."

"Cleaning rags!" She sounded outraged. "There's perfectly good material in that dress and jacket. Really, you men are impossible sometimes. Kay would get several cushions out of it. The skirt is so wide and it's cut on the cross in two pieces. Just you wait and I'll show you how it could be cut and . . ."

He looked at her in sheer exasperation, but she was pushing past him, still in full spate, and abruptly he said, "I'm sorry. I can't stop now. There's a job I had to see to for Miss Mings," he added vaguely as he saw her disappointed face. "Thanks for the tidying up," he added, and clattered out to the shed where Kay's ancient car was housed.

It was killing two birds with one stone, he thought in faint amusement as he headed for the caves. He'd put an end once and for all to Johnnie's ridiculous stories and by the time he got back Miss Webber would surely have taken herself off.

The light was beginning to fail when he reached the end of the track. He parked the car there and stood looking about him as he rolled a cigarette, remembering the Friday evening and himself and Jackie rooting around in furious silence.

"That Johnnie!" he murmured and wondered how the boy was making out and whether he had already found a small bit of gold dust to make his eyes glitter.

That reminded him of the day he had held Johnnie up to the front cave, after removing one of the boards, and had shown him what it looked like inside. He remembered the boy's awe-stricken look with something that he realised was close to wistfulness.

Still standing there, he wondered why he and Kay, so eager to

123

help and so sure they could, should have flopped so dismally. Of course Johnnie had been a disappointment. He admitted that he had dreamed for too long of a fair-haired sturdy youngster he could have moulded into the beginnings of a man of his own kind. He grimaced at the thought. Self-love, of course, he thought in disgust. You couldn't mould anyone into your image, and it was wrong to try. Johnnie would grow up into the sort of man he'd been destined from his beginnings to be, and it had been simply foolish to try and foster in him a love for things that scared or bored him.

His eyes on the boarded-up cave entrance, he suddenly remembered the job he had to prise off the board before showing the cave to Johnny. He had sweated over it, cursing for what had seemed like ages.

And afterwards, he remembered, the bolts had been a little loose in the rock and he had brought down a bit of cement and cemented them back in securely.

He gave a little nod. So that put paid to Johnnie's yarn without even testing the boards. No one could have removed them all without long hours of work prising out bolts and chipping away the cement from the ones he had removed himself. No one would have dared hang round the place doing that when at any time Quidong's owner or stockmen could have turned up and demanded to know what was going on.

It wasn't even remotely feasible , that someone had killed a woman there and then had worked through the long sweaty job of getting the boards away from the cave mouth. In fact it made as much sense as the Hooded Men and gallons of blood.

He suddenly laughed, the sound sending up two birds to wing above him in the darkening sky.

You were a fool to come, he told himself as he turned back to the car. You didn't believe Johnnie's story anyway, so why did you bother to come out?

CHAPTER TWELVE

THE long afternoon dragged into evening that came with merely a darkening of the still lowering sky. Johnnie didn't stir again and when Kay asked huskily at last, "How is he?" concentrating on the answer in an effort to dull the pain that had come out of the weary discomfort of her pinioned arms, the woman said shortly:

"He's all right. The effort of getting up like that and trying to walk knocked him flat again. He should come round tomorrow."

She went across to the two hurricane lamps she had left ready by the wagon ready for the evening. She bent down to them and for an instant light flamed over her lined, brown face. Then she picked up the lighted lamp and came across to Kay. She set the lamp down a little way from her and said, "I'll give you a cup of tea in a while. The lamp's so I can see you. Don't try knocking it over. You might think a fire would bring help, but I'd be gone by then, and Johnnie, too. I could always say you'd knocked over the lamp and I couldn't save you, couldn't I?"

Kay said nothing. The disappointment of seeing Johnnie brought back and tied up had stayed with her all afternoon. She had been holding onto the fact that if he woke and was conscious of things he might escape before the woman was aware what was happening, but now it looked as though she intended to keep him tied except when she had her gaze on him.

Kay said slowly, "Johnnie needs food. If he was in hospital they'd have some way of seeing he got nourishment, wouldn't they?"

"He's all right. Shut up."

Kay could smell soup warming. She tried to ignore it, but finally the woman crossed to her and said, "I decided to give you soup instead of tea. Here. You can manage it even with your hands bound if you bend your mouth down."

Kay clasped the mug eagerly, jerking it up and her face down with a little eager, muted cry of sheer relief.

The first sip nearly scalded her mouth. She gasped, but hunger was greater than the chance of scalding and she bent her head again, quite aloof from the woman's disgusted, "You look like a dog. Snuffling and choking and spluttering over some offal."

But she lost interest in the warming drink for a moment when the elder woman went on, "If he hasn't come round tomorrow I'll help him round with a few slaps and a good shaking."

"You might kill him."

"Rubbish. He's not that bad. If it were possible for a nine year old to will himself into unconsciousness I'd say he's done it. I can't waste too much time, though. I've got to get back to Quidong as soon as possible and get those plates and destroy them. And before that . . ." she broke off.

Kay nodded. Before that, she thought, drinking again, she has to deal with Johnnie and myself and go through the mockery of rounding up a search party for us. Then she'll go back. And Stuart, she thought wearily, would take all the blame on himself. He'd never forgive himself.

The mug slipped and she only just managed to save it. She blinked up at the face that seemed to be looming over her. She tried to cry out the knowledge that she knew the woman had drugged her; tried to upbraid herself for not remembering the woman had sleeping pills and might use them to keep her quiet. Then the struggle for speech was wiped out by the monstrous thought that now in the dark Johnnie could wake and talk and she could do nothing at all to stop him.

.   .   .

There was a scurry of movement, a flash of small, light-coloured body near the caves. Automatically, Stuart whirled in search of the gun by the black stallion's saddle, then he remembered he had neither horse nor rifle, but only Kay's old car. He stood idly smoking for a moment, wondering if there were any other rabbits about. It was the first he had seen around Quidong for some time. The stockmen claimed the wiping out of the rabbits was why the dingoes were now so bad in the district, attacking even calves.

Perhaps, he thought, there was a burrow somewhere round the caves, even another entrance to the caves themselves where the rabbits were breeding, and in next to no time they'd be back in full force.

The dusk was deepening but it was still light enough to see the entrance of any burrow about him, as he walked slowly round. He came up against the caves entrance and stopped, looking at the boards, then, leaving his cigarette between his lips he stooped, tugging at the bottom board. It moved slightly, but held, but when he went on tugging the steel bolts slid out and the board came away.

He stood looking at it, frowning. Then he reached to tug at the next one. The board moved, and like the bottom one a few vicious tugs were enough to heave it on to the ground.

Johnnie? he wondered. Were the loose boards the boy's doing. Then he tossed the idea aside. It would have taken a tough-muscled adult to shift the boards the way the bolts had been put into the surrounding rock.

Abruptly, with long strides, he went back to the car, rummaging in the glove compartment for the torch Kay kept there. He went back with the same quick strides to bend down and flash the torchlight through the opening.

Then he grinned and started to laugh.

So that was it. The frail wonder of the roof had given way at last and come crashing down, and the jolting and jarring had worked the bolts loose. Johnnie had almost certainly been hovering around when the roof had gone and he hadn't been game to tell because he had been in forbidden territory.

But he had used his knowledge in the end to help scare Jess.

Impatiently he reached for the boards, easing them into position and pressing the bolts back. He'd come out with some cement as soon as possible, he promised himself. Though it was now impossible for anyone to get into the caves except by the tiny hidden entrance, someone might get the boards off and poke round in the rubble and bring a landslide down on himself. It was better to be safe than sorry. He pressed the last bolt home with a little pat of the flat of his hand, then flicked off the torch and went striding back to the car.

·   ·   ·

The cottage door opened, and Miss Webber's plump figure was silhouetted against light. Stuart gave one despairing glance heavenwards, then said feebly, "Still here?"

"I had an idle half hour and Jess won't have my dinner ready yet and I thought you might come up with me?"

"Thanks, but I've book work to do tonight."

"It wouldn't take long for you to pop up with me . . ." then her voice trailed off, "Oh well, you run along and have a bath or shower or whatever you want and I'll finish this unpicking before I run along. See," she held up what seemed to him a huge red flag, "I thought I'd unpick it and then Jess can wash it and it will be all ready for Kay to cut and machine into cushions." She gave him a look of disgust, "and then you won't be tempted to use it for rags. And look," she called him back as he was striding towards the bedroom.

He stared down at the four little silver buttons in her outspread hand.

"They're real silver," she told him. "Somebody's pet set of buttons that she put on the jacket, and I must say she's not very handy with a needle," her tone was disapproving. "They were just . . . cobbled on, you could say. And pink cotton instead of red to match the jacket, which is just slovenly, you must admit, but you'll have to ask round whose dress it was, because she'll want the buttons back, though really as they were sold with the dress, I don't know how the law would look at it . . ."

She fell into pensive thought and he made his escape into the bedroom, firmly closing the door, but she followed him to call through the panels, "but anyway she'll want them back."

"Why? Probably she broke one of the first set of buttons and dredged up something from the attic to stick on instead."

"Oh you men! Of course she didn't. They're real silver I tell you and quite pretty too. They're a pet set. I used to have one myself—I used to think they brought me good luck to tell the truth, but this is the sort of set you'd take from one worn-out thing and put away till you bought something else that was special and then . . . she'll be wanting them back I'm sure. Anyway the dress is practically brand new. I suppose it didn't really fit and she put it out for jumble in quite a hurry and forgot the buttons, but she must be terribly upset . . . shall I take them t Ellen Waters in the morning and ask her to find out who owns them?"

"Yes. If you would."

"They're antique I think, because I'm sure you couldn't buy a solid silver set like that these days, which reminds me, Johnnie's left his precious shell collection that you gave him in his room, which means he must intend to come back, don't you think? I can't help feeling that this trip will be the making of him because I think he rather admires Miss Mings, don't you?"

"I suppose so."

"I think he does, and with her taking such an interest in him he'd naturally feel flattered, wouldn't he?"

"I suppose so." He sighed, wondering whether walking out to her in his birthday suit would get rid of her.

Her voice flowed on, "I said to myself when I heard about the offer that it just goes to show, because I'd always put her down as someone . . . well, it's not nice to say . . . but someone who only does things for some chance of gain. Like me, you know. I met Miss Gavin—the teacher before me, that is—in town before I first came to Quidong and I must say she was quite bitter, poor dear, when I told her I was going to board here. She said she'd boarded at Prescotts and in the wet season she was often bogged down there for days at a time, with no hope of reaching the school or anything else.

"And she said to me, 'But of course you're Farley's marmalade, aren't you?' and I am, you know. My grandfather that is, but to tell the truth he's not a scrap interested in his grandchildren, but I've never dared say so, with Miss Mings insisting on nothing but Farley's preserves on the homestead table.

"I must admit too, that I think she openly agreed to board me because she thought I might invest a bit of money in Quidong, which makes things a bit uncomfortable, as I'm sure you'll agree, so it was quite a surprise . . . oh!"

Stuart grinned at her through the gap in the doorway. He said lightly, "I'm afraid you'll get a surprise in a moment. I can't find my bathrobe, so . . ."

. . .

129

She had left the buttons on the table, he saw wearily, as well as half the unpicked dress. That meant she would probably be as half the unpicked dress. That meant she would probably be sitting up when he came back the next evening. Suddenly the sheer pain.

He tried not to think of her, fingering the little buttons and reflecting it was odd the owner hadn't already asked about them. Then he slipped them into his pocket and bundled the dress onto a chair. He'd drive into Caragnoo after a scratch meal, he decided. It would fill in an evening completely empty for him without Kay and he would give the buttons to Ellen and the dress as well. He knew Kay would dislike the harsh red, but she would probably make cushions out of it rather than hurt Miss Webber's feelings and then he and Kay would have to live with the wretched things.

He was tired of Miss Webber, he decided grimly as he opened tins and heated food. She meant well, but lord, how she talked. But her babbling that evening had thrown a new light on Miss Mings. He had often wondered what had made the elder woman suddenly offer to board the new schoolteacher and continue to board her when she often looked completely irritated by the other woman's talking.

Then he laughed, reflecting that Miss Mings wouldn't get any gain out of her offer to Johnnie, unless a headache could be called a gain.

．　．　．

Kay knew that someone was shaking her, but her body and mind were so tired they refused to respond to stimulus. Only when water touched her face did she reluctantly open her eyes.

Then sharp consciousness returned. She knew that her arms were free. She flexed them, trying to spring upright, but her tired body protested and immediately the women's voice warned, "Don't try any tricks. I left you untied last night so you wouldn't get too stiff. You can go across to the water and clean yourself up. Do your hair, too. You look a mess."

"Johnnie?" she asked hoarsely. Her throat felt like sandpaper and her tongue seemed strangely swollen.

"He woke for a while." At the sharp jerk of Kay's gaze upward the woman laughed. "He didn't say what I wanted, but he's getting round to it. I gave him some soup and he went off again. I'll heat some more soup and leave it in a thermos ready if he wakes again."

Kay moved sluggishly, under the threat of the rifle. She knelt by the creek, gaze searching for some sharp stone her fingers could grasp and hold and throw into that blank, lined face. But as she knelt there the rifle touched the nape of her neck, then moved away again.

The woman seemed capable of reading her thoughts Kay reflected bitterly as she was told, "Throw something at me and I'll shoot you immediately. Yes, I mean it. I'd rather have you around for the time being, dangerous as it is, just in case someone happens along. I don't want it reported there's a woman of my description round here, with a boy, but . . ."

"But without me. Oh I understand all right," Kay said flatly, raising her dripping face and looking over her shoulder. "But I'd like to know how you intend to explain away my face." She touched it gently.

"I'll cope. You can't win Kay. Wipe your face and fix that hair of yours. And here," something fell beside her with a faint whispering sound. "Clean shirt and underwear. Can't have someone wondering afterwards why your case was never unpacked and your things never used, can I?"

It was so completely callous, so assured, that Kay simply stared blankly. Then deliberately she turned from the other woman and made herself go through the movements of fixing her hair, undressing and dressing again.

She was fastening the zip on her slacks when her ankle was caught and she fell again.

I'll never learn, she thought in wild hysteria, that sent bubbling little cries onto her tongue. Damn her, I'll never learn to be ready for her.

When her arms were tied, the slacks were zipped up for her and she was dragged over to the tree of yesterday and left looking down at her bare scratched feet.

"Bread this morning," she was told in another moment. "And a scrape of jam for a treat. And tea."

"Which I expect you've drugged."

"Think I'm that stupid? If someone happens along I don't want both you and Johnnie dead to the world. Here, you can handle the bread and jam yourself. God," the tone changed to sharp disgust, "what a gulping, guzzling animal you are."

Kay looked up. She asked quietly, "I wonder what you looked like in that prison camp?"

"A good point that."

Kay thought confusedly that the woman would never cease to surprise. She sounded affable again. Kay took advantage of it to ask, "What did Johnnie say last night?"

"Nothing much. But he kept mentioning church. That's where the plates are I'm sure. I had him under my eyes from Saturday morning till we left. Even had my meals where I could watch the cottage. He didn't come out, and he wouldn't have left them in his room where Jess or Stuart could find them when cleaning up.

"I tried all Saturday to get him alone, but it was no good and I didn't dare walk up to him and simply demand he hand over the plates. He'd have made an uproar and though I was sure he wouldn't be believed I was afraid someone might notice the number on the plates, then notice my own later on, and I was scared, too, that if someone came asking about Megan having been at Quidong, or if she was ever found, that someone would remember Johnnie and the plates and who had taken them off him. I couldn't risk it. I kept trying to think of every eventuality," her tone was brooding, "maybe I tried too hard. Maybe I should have grabbed the plates when he went to Coombs, but then I was afraid again . . ." she fell silent. After a moment she went on, "But even when I had the plates there'd still be his memory and the way he might talk to his father, or to the others, and once I'd grabbed the plates he'd have known who Megan's killer was. He'd have been doubly hard to get hold of, and if he'd kept squawking about me and the woman in red and then disappeared . . . I couldn't risk that."

"I can't spend too long on getting him to talk though. If he won't . . . well I'll have to find them by myself, but how the devil am I going to explain away ransacking the church and vestry? They could be under or behind the altar for all I know or anywhere else. Sunday afternoon you dressed him up in those grey pants Stuart bought him, and a shirt and tie and took him into Caragnoo to Ellen Water's Sunday school in the church."

Kay remembered. The Caragnoo church was big, considering the size of the district. And old, because the pioneers had built it with their own hands. She tried to think of somewhere Johnnie could have put the plates.

The woman said, "I followed you in and sat right at the back. Afterwards the other kids went away and you cornered Ellen on the front steps. I'd gone outside by then, expecting Johnnie would come out with you and Ellen, but he didn't. I went in by the side door and he was in the vestry then. When he saw me he ran away to you. He had a good ten minutes to himself, though. I'm sure that's where they are. He wouldn't have left them in the cottage or the homestead or the outbuildings with people poking around all the time. He did go into the garage Monday morning before we left, but I keep that bare as a board, and I could see they weren't there and I searched the wagon too. No, they're in the church or the vestry. It's safe enough for the moment. With Waters away and the relief man coming only every three weeks the church is pretty well deserted . . ." then abruptly she demanded, "Got any idea where they are?"

"Of course not."

"You could guess."

"I can't. I'm too tired to think anyway."

She said seriously, "That's tiredness and the lack of good food. Here's your tea. Don't guzzle it, girl. You're disgusting."

Kay ignored her. She was thinking of the big, gloomy church, and the vestry. The vestry was lined with cupboards, she remembered, and the church had pews. Johnnie could have even screwed the plates under or on top of something.

She let the woman take the mug from her, then she sat, while the sun came up and birds wheeled and cried above her; while ants investigated her bare toes and were kicked away; while she thought and thought and realised that unless help came soon or she and Johnnie managed to escape, she was one morning nearer death and oblivion.

.   .   .

She was realising the lack of food was hampering her even in clear thought and that as time went on she was going to think not only less, but less coherently, when Johnnie moved and called out.

The rifle was instantly jerked up. The woman said, "One sound from you, Kay, and I'll finish you."

Kay nodded. She knew the woman meant it and perhaps, she prayed desperately, Johnnie wouldn't talk or else he would come round to full consciousness and realise he had to stay quiet. But if he did start talking . . . she dropped sideways, her hand trying to reach towards a stone. She could throw it, she thought. And hit the woman and take her mind off Johnnie for a while at least, and by the time she returned to him he might be quiet again. That would give him a little more time—time in which help might come for him, even if too late for herself.

But she knew, as her hand closed round the stone, that it was useless. With her arms tied that way she could never throw it more than a pitiful few feet.

I'll have to scream again, she told herself. And keep on screaming until she stops me.

Johnnie wasn't talking yet, she realised and suddenly the woman called, "What are you doing? Get up. Move over there to the thermos. He's threshing around and I can't leave him. Bring the thermos over. You can manage that. Hurry up. But don't try to play the fool. I'll try to get some soup down him and he might relax and talk. Go on. Hurry, damn you!"

Kay moved with a speed that surprised herself. From somewhere energy had come rushing back. Even as she scrambled to her feet and went across to the thermos and dropped down to her knees she was reaching in the pocket of her slacks. Her hands could just manage it and the pill was still intact, which seemed surprising after the way she had been continually crashing to the ground, but when she tried to break it she realised it wasn't going to be possible. The pill simply refused to break across at all. She was still trying, her fingers slippery with sweat, when the woman called sharply, "What are you doing?"

The pill slipped and went into the flask, from which she'd unscrewed the cap. She knelt there, terrified, then the woman was rushing at her, "What are you doing?" she was demanding.

Kay bent her head, raising the flask, pretending to drink. Then it was snatched off her, and she received two savage smacks across her aching face.

"Thief!" the word was spat at her. "Thieving food from a child."

Then she became quiet again. She said quite evenly, "That's how it was in Malaya. You lost all decency." She turned and hurried back to the wagon and thrust over her shoulder, "He's quiet again, anyway."

Kay drew a long breath of relief, and slowly her spirits started rising again. If only Johnnie didn't wake again, she thought hopefully, the woman would probably drink the soup herself. And then she'd fall asleep, she thought exultantly.

But if she tried to give it to Johnnie, Kay would have to tell her what had happened. She knew that. She couldn't possibly risk Johnnie swallowing the soup with a whole sleeping pill in it. Of course, she realised, he might only take a spoonful, but still . . .

Then she realised what stupidity she had shown in any case. She had been intent on keeping Johnnie quiet so he wouldn't babble in half consciousness, but people, she remembered, talked in ordinary sleep, too and sleeping pill or not Johnnie was quite capable of babbling.

She dragged herself to her feet and went slowly back to the tree again. She sat there, her gaze watchful as the woman recorked the flask and put it down and then went back to the rifle and seated herself there, blank faced.

Soon, she thought, the woman would get hungry. And the soup would be waiting. She held fast to the little bit of hope.

CHAPTER THIRTEEN

STUART jerked out of a dream in which he and Miss Webber were dancing in the caves while the roof fell in, to give a shout of laughter as he remembered the dream's absurdity.

He was towelling himself dry when the extension from the homestead rang and he went to answer it. The cottage wasn't in direct connection with the exchange and to receive or send outside calls it was necessary to go to the homestead. It was an item that had irked Kay quite absurdly, he remembered, as he barked a hello into the house phone.

Even at that hour of the morning Miss Webber sounded archly bright, he thought sourly.

She said, "Ah, I caught you. Sleeping in, this morning? Ellen Waters rang me because she's going to Sydney. They had to open the exchange especially last night to get a message through, poor soul." Her voice dropped and the archness and false glitter were suddenly gone. She sounded a little tired as she said, "He's going. Mr. Waters, I mean."

He made a sound of shocked dismay and she went on, "They say there's no hope. And do you know poor Ellen can still think about tidying up ends till she comes back and I suppose settles up for good, because you wouldn't think she'd go on living out here all alone would you, and I don't think she has a soul except some aunt or other. But anyway, she wanted me to tell you that before the exchange closed last night she rang just about everybody but nobody knows about the buttons—and I don't know why you drove in like that, because I was going to take them when I went to school this morning. So it seems the dress must belong to someone who only came for the day, but Ellen's left the buttons in the red box on the writing desk in Mr. Waters' little study and she says if anyone enquires off you her girl will give them to you."

Stuart sorted through the spate of words, collected the important information and gave brief thanks for the message, then firmly hung up as she started to talk again.

His face was sombre as he began dressing. He hadn't particularly liked Jim Waters, who had always seemed a pitiful misfit in the outback, but he had a deep liking for Ellen Waters who had borne more than her fair share of her husband's job. And Kay, he remembered, was extremely fond of her. There was Miss Mings, too—her friend for a dozen years.

He wondered if there was some way of getting a message to Kay and Miss Mings. If they knew the elder woman would almost certainly agree to them going straight to Sydney and supporting Ellen through the crisis and burial. It didn't look as though Ellen would have any other friends to support her. Johnnie probably wouldn't raise any objections as he'd see his father the sooner.

He knew that Kay had taken her little portable radio with her. He stood there wondering if it was possible to put a radio call out for someone, and if so how anyone went about it.

Coombs will know, he realised abruptly and went back to finish dressing, phrasing a message to Kay in thought—one that wouldn't make her think something was wrong with himself, but the thought that she might indeed panic and come rushing back to him if she feared he was in trouble and needed her, was suddenly a comforting glow in his heart.

.   .   .

Miss Webber, he saw with relief, was already on her way to school as he walked up to the homestead. She started to slow down, waving to him, but he waved back and detoured away, arriving at the homestead by the kitchen door.

Jess merely nodded to his request to use the phone. He could hear the bell sound for a long time before the policeman answered and he sounded short-tempered, but when Stuart had had his say he said, relief in his voice, "Glad you thought of it. She needs someone, though she has her chin cocked so high in the air it's painful. Gibley's wife is driving her seventy miles to pick up a private plane from a property there. She'll be in Sydney tonight. If your Kay and Miss Mings are with her it should help a lot. I can arrange about a message and the police'll keep an eye out for the car if you think that's an idea? O.K. It's a Holden station wagon, isn't it? Fawn or something like that? And what's the number? Oh well if you don't know I'll soon find out. Any idea where they are?"

"Only the vague address of somewhere in the eastern ranges, but Kay has the portable radio and she's sure to tune in sometimes during the evening. They'd have nothing else to do out there except listen or talk, once it's dark."

A chuckle came over the line. "Not even a chance for young Johnnie to go pinching any more number plates either. He'll find his style cramped out there."

Stuart murmured, "I dare say," then said sharply, "What? What was that about number plates?"

"I suppose I'm letting several cats out of several bags but you can't whop him, so what's the odds. He came sneaking in here on Saturday looking scared half to death and tried to spin me a yarn about finding some number plates out in the bush. I sent him off with a flea in each ear and a promise of trouble if he didn't get the plates back on the car they belonged to. Remember last year? Oh no, you wouldn't, you weren't there, but I can tell you it was a fine do . . ."

"Did he actually have the number plates?" Stuart broke in. "I mean, did you see them?"

"Eh? Oh he had them down his jersey. He was holding his middle as though he had a pain. Keeping them safe."

Stuart sat beside the silent phone for a long time, rolling a cigarette over and over between his fingers long after the tobacco was rolled in the paper. He was remembering Johnnie clutching himself on Saturday and the oddly meek way he had allowed Kay to boss him around all the following day.

Suddenly he called, "Jess," and when the girl's smile showed round the door, he demanded, "Where's Johnnie's postcard? Have you still got it around?"

She pouted. "That Johnnie! I stuck it up b'hind the tea caddy." She shook a dark finger at him. "You wait'll he comes back and I give him my tongue."

He smiled at her. "Be a good girl and let me see it, will you?"

But when the postcard was in his hands the unease that had

gripped him for those five minutes slowly evaporated. The story was ridiculous of course. Women in red and men in felt hats and murder and stolen number plates weren't the sort of thing that ever happened. Then suddenly he remembered the silver buttons that Miss Webber had claimed might be antiques. And the practically new red frock. He thought of the loose boards and wondered if the roof coming down really would have jerked the steel bolts out.

Suddenly he thought of something else—why had Johnnie gone voluntarily to the policeman, when he was scared to death of what he termed The Cops?

He went on sitting there a while longer, then he slipped the postcard into his pocket and went down to where the black stallion was waiting him.

.   .   .

Stuart left the horse tethered at the end of the caves track and went slowly to the place where Johnnie had claimed the woman in red had died. He felt faintly ridiculous as he bent, peering at the ground. He felt more ridiculous as he poked round in the scrub close to the spot. There was nothing there. No signs, except in faded, shredded litter of some long-ago picnic that anyone had ever been there.

Impatiently he strode back to the cave mouth and began removing the boards. When they were all on the ground he bent closely over the bolts, fingering them, twisting them so that they shone dully in the sunlight. There were faint traces of cement still to be seen, but his gaze was thoughtful and worried as he stood up again, looking into the blocked cave.

He stood, moving his arms as though lifting something, his gaze measuring. Then he nodded. The cement traces were on the wrong bolts altogether. They were on the bolts that had held the top boards. And he hadn't removed those at all. It had been one in the middle he had removed to let Johnnie see inside.

So someone had definitely removed the boards at some time, then replaced them.

He looked at the rubble, shaking his head. Anybody could have removed them. Some fools who'd found the boards a challenge perhaps. But if that was so, why bother to replace them?

It would be reasonable for the boards to be left on the ground or tossed into the scrub.

And he couldn't move any of the rubble he knew quite well. Move one piece and another would come sliding down. Keep on shovelling and probably the whole roof would simply collapse. It would take a team of men working carefully to see if there was anything there in the cave, and more than a team of men to probe the water that lay beyond it.

He'd never get anyone to take it on, he knew. After all the story was ridiculous and based on the word of a boy who was a confirmed liar. But there was Johnnie, scared of The Cops, and avoiding them like the plague, going to Coombs and talking of number plates found in the scrub. Why had he done that?

He'd known about the loose boards, too. Then Stuart realised Johnnie could have seen someone remove them a long time before. And seen them put back. And then he'd woven a story about them of course. Kay . . . what had Kay said? Something about the boy's yarns always having a basis of truth in them somewhere.

But that reminded him sharply of something else she had said —that Johnnie's last story hadn't sounded like him at all—that his stories were never meant to be found out as lies, while the tale of Hooded Men had been so impossible no one would have believed it.

Then he remembered that on the postcard Johnnie had changed that. He had spoken of one man. A man in a felt hat.

"Oh damn Johnnie!" he swore suddenly, ground the cigarette out beneath his boot and went back to the black stallion.

· · ·

"You again?" Coombs sounded affable this time, as though his bad temper had cleared with the morning skies. "No, I haven't done anything yet. Hasn't been time, but I'll fix it, don't worry, and if Kay's listening in tonight she should ring you first thing in the morning. They can't be too far off the beaten track, you know, because they wouldn't be likely to leave the station wagon and hike through the bush."

"No, I know. What I rang about was—did you see a woman at the show on Friday who could fit in with this description? She was driving a small green Mini, and she must have stood out among the locals because she was wearing a bright red dress with an enormous skirt, and no top. It had a jacket with silver buttons. She might have worn that during the day, or not."

There was a chuckle over the line. "You aiming to have a bit of fun while Kay's gone? Saw her once and fell for her, eh? Oh all right, keep your wool on," he added as Stuart began heated protests. "No, I didn't see her."

"Could you make enquiries as to who did see her then? It's important I get hold of her. She's lost something fairly valuable. Ellen Waters made a few enquiries round here, but no one seems able to help, but someone must have seen her, surely."

"Can do. If she's not known locally she's probably a visitor at some outlying place. Shouldn't be hard to pick her up, but it might take me a bit of time."

Stuart said shortly, "Do your best. As soon as possible. And, thanks a lot."

．　　．　　．

Kay could hear footsteps long before anyone came in sight. She tensed, lifting her head almost unbelievingly, her gaze sidling towards the woman.

Instantly the rifle swung her way. The woman said softly, "Remember, Kay. I'll use it. And if necessary this person'll meet with an 'accident'. Get it?"

Kay nodded wordlessly, but there was still renewed hope in her body as the steps came closer. Someone was whistling too. Tunelessly.

Then the man appeared.

Kay raised her eyes, her gaze fixed greedily on him, then hope evaporated. He was quite alone, and he was little more than a boy. A gawky looking youngster with fair, close-cropped hair and a prickle of fair beard on upper lip and chin. His bony knees poked out almost pathetically from the shelter of wide-legged grey shorts above thick woollen socks and heavy soled boots. He was wearing a zip-up weatherproof jacket and the heavy rucksack on his shoulders bent his thin body forward so that at first he didn't see them. Then he caught sight of the wagon under the trees and looked up alertly, a wide grin breaking across his face.

"Why, hi there, everyone," He had a pleasant voice, light and gay and eager.

Kay tried not to hear it. She had a horrible mental picture of him lying face downwards in the gently moving waters of the creek.

She jerked, "Are you alone?" and felt the last vestiges of hope slide away from her at his look of surprise then quick, "Yes. Gosh," he looked at the station wagon, "I didn't know you could get a car down here."

He wants a lift, Kay thought with another surging of hope that was quickly dashed when the woman said, "It was a bit bumpy but I wanted to get away from the beaten track, and the creek water's clean here."

"Mind if I borrow some of it?" he grinned at her.

Kay watched him slip the rucksack from his shoulder, then bend, scrubbing over his face, and then drinking from cupped hands. He said over his shoulder, "It's pretty murky further along. I've been following it from the mountain shoulder over to the east, by the falls."

"When are you finishing up?" the woman asked.

Kay tensed. Oh let him say he's expected somewhere, she prayed. Today. Tonight, quickly. Or she might kill him. She's crazy enough for anything.

Her breath relaxed in a long sigh when he said, "I'll be hitting the trail further along the creek, then I'll move up again. Actually I'm running late. I promised to meet the rest of the crowd at dusk. They said the valley was too rugged and went up over the falls and I must admit they were right—I nearly gave up half way."

The woman said affably, "Sorry we haven't the billy boiling, but if you care to wait around . . ."

She had to say that, Kay thought. It was the bush hospitality that had to be offered in case he thought they were eager to get rid of him.

"Thanks all the same, but I'll move on in a tick," his smile flashed out again. "To be honest, I'm not a tea addict anyway. Comes of steeping myself in coffee while studying."

"Study, do you? What?" the woman asked.

"Science. This is the vac before the end of year exams you know. I stewed myself silly last year and nearly failed. This year I thought I'd get into the exam room with clear wits at least." He stood up, then smiled down at Kay, "and as a medical student let me solemnly advise you not to caper round in bare feet out here."

She knew she was supposed to respond with some light mocking rejoinder, or perhaps produce her shoes for him to slip on her feet, so he could make some laughing remark about Cinderella, but she couldn't respond. She simply gazed at him hopelessly, and saw something like disappointment slide down over his expression. Then he squatted down, leaning back on his heels. "Good grief, you've had an accident, haven't you? I mean, your face . . ."

Kay licked at her lips. She tried to croak out something, but the woman was ready before her. She said, "Looks nasty, doesn't it? Her foster son did it. Threw his dinner into her face, plus the plate, and then hared off into the bush. He'd been getting the rough side of our tongues for a previous piece of mischief. And we took this trip for a holiday!"

She has it all her own way, Kay thought, closing her eyes, and unconsciously echoing Johnnie's bitter thought. All her own way. Now there's someone else to talk later on of Johnnie misbehaving, and trying to run away.

The youngster's glance had fallen to her hands, she saw. She followed it, seeing the light playing on her wedding ring. The sight of it brought weak tears flooding back into her eyes and because she didn't dare let him see them and question them she closed her eyes again.

The woman went on, "Little beggar's resting at the moment. He fell flat on his face in the middle of that dash into the bush and skinned his forehead. Was a dashed good thing he toppled, really, because poor Kay was flat on her back covered with gravy, and can you see me doing a sprint through the bush at my age?"

The poor old soul! Kay thought in wild amusement. The poor old soul! And he can't realise what part she's getting ready to play.

She opened her eyes and tried to speak. She was going to ask

143

him, as a last resort, to look at Johnnie. As a bush-walker he might know quite a lot of first aid. He might know enough to know Johnnie's stillness was more than sleep. He might say the boy needed hospital care and offer to get the police rescue squad out to take Johnnie out. The woman couldn't refuse that or laugh it off, or even just say she'd take him out in the wagon, because the youngster would offer to go with them.

But the words remained unsaid. She realised that if that happened he would die. He'd finish up face downwards in the creek as the woman had threatened. She would never allow him to interfere or carry such a message out of the valley. Then they would move on somewhere else and know nothing about the student being found and no one would know anything about them, either.

She watched in dull despair as he began to ease the heavy rucksack back onto his shoulders. Then she said huskily, "There's some hot soup if you'd care for that." She wondered if he could see the urgent pleading in her eyes. Her whole body was tense with that pleading prayer that he would agree when she said, "If you've a thermos you could carry it along with you and have it later on down the trail."

He hesitated. Kay didn't dare look at the woman. She was sure the pleading could be seen by suspicious eyes searching her expression and then the woman would wonder and perhaps he would never get away.

Kay urged, "Do have it. It . . . it was made up for the little boy only you see, he wouldn't have it, and . . . we're not hungry ourselves that . . ." the words trailed off into silence. She knew she would never be able to say anything more. She felt exhausted both with the effort of speaking and silently pleading with him.

And the woman suddenly cleared her throat.

The harsh sound seemed like a warning.

Then he said, "I'd like that and I've a thermos all right." He began to ease the rucksack off his shoulders again and undid the straps, delving inside to hold out a battered black flask.

Kay opened her eyes that had closed in sheer blessed relief. She saw the woman's hand close over the thermos and in a moment the steam was rising between the two flasks as the soup was poured.

She heard the woman ram home the cork in the black flask

and then say, with that bluff affableness that now seemed like a mockery, "There you are, son. Like some bread and cheese, too? Bread's a bit on the stale side I'm afraid. Meant to make a damper tonight."

He shook his head. "Thanks, the soup will do fine."

Kay leaned back against the tree. She couldn't force herself to say good-bye. All she could think of was that somewhere down the trail, if he remembered . . . and surely he would remember? . . . he would drink the soup. Then a wave of sheer sickness engulfed her at the thought that perhaps he had only accepted it to please her. That he wouldn't drink it at all and maybe it would finish soaking into the earth of the quiet bush.

She fought down the sickness and closed her mind on the mental imaginings that pressed relentlessly, mocking her faint hopes. She concentrated instead on the picture of him stopping somewhere on the trail and drinking and then . . . she could remember the woman saying that day that now seemed years ago, as she put the pill into Kay's hand, "If you're not used to them one should knock you flat straight away." So if the boy wasn't used to pills like that he would fall asleep there in the bush and probably sleep until dawn.

He wouldn't turn up at his appointment at all and his friends would report him missing. They had almost certainly worked out the route for him to take when he hadn't wanted to climb the falls. So they would know approximately where he should be. She knew what happened when someone was lost. One party started from his point of leaving and another from where he should have arrived. So there would be two parties, at the first crack of dawn. One going over the falls and coming west. One heading east. Probably the latter would soon stumble on him, sleeping, or he'd be moving by then towards them, wondering what had happened to him.

But the other party . . . she clung fast to the faint small thread of hope. They would come on from the falls until they came to the campsite by the creek. She refused to think that the other party might possess a walkie-talkie and tell the others he was found, so that they would turn back, the journey uncompleted.

It would be the rest of the hikers, and perhaps someone living near the falls, who could be quickly roused and sent down, who would come at first. People who wouldn't possess walkie-talkies as a normal course of events surely, her tired mind went on reasoning. It would be only if the first search failed to find the student that the alarm would be given and the expert rescue squads, with their equipment, brought into action.

She sat there, eyes closed, clinging tightly to that frail thread of hope that depended on so many possibilities coming true. Two parties, she willed, one coming east, one going west and neither with a walkie-talkie. Two parties. With at least two strong men in each, she prayed silently.

At first she had hesitated to offer him soup, simply because she was hoping the woman would drink it herself. But the woman hadn't touched it at lunchtime, and if she offered it to Johnnie Kay knew she would have to speak up. And if Johnnie didn't drink it it was more than likely the woman would simply give it to Kay herself in the evening.

Abruptly the woman demanded, "Why'd you offer him that soup?"

Kay's eyes flew open. She moistened lips that seemed suddenly tight with a tightness that refused to form words.

The woman had come closer to her, and was peering down at her, brooding over her darkly like the mountains themselves.

She repeated sharply, "Why'd you press that soup on him?"

"I . . . I just thought of it. You said . . . act normally, so I tried to. You said I was to act normally. So I tried to." Suddenly, though previously she had found it impossible to speak, she couldn't stop the words flowing. She went on repeating herself over and over again.

The woman said shortly, "I'd like to believe it, but there's something odd about you. You were acting as though you'd been struck dumb, and then . . ."

She moved away, to finally sit down half way between the girl and the station wagon where Johnnie lay. Her round eyes, behind the round, dark-framed glasses, were fixed on Kay.

Kay closed her own eyes, unable to bear the scrutiny.

For a while there was silence, then abruptly the woman jerked, "You played the fool with that soup when I told you to get it for the boy. You got the cap off and the cork out. When I yelled at you

you held the flask to your mouth. I thought you were drinking it . . ."

Kay said, "I was. I told you I couldn't help it. You said that was what happened in prison camp too, people not being able to control themselves and . . ."

She stopped, exhausted again, knowing the woman was still watching her.

It was some time later that the woman suddenly rose to her feet. She said, the flat, thickened note in her voice again, "What'd you do with that pill I gave you? Don't pretend you don't know what I'm talking about. You told me you never took it. What'd you do with it?" She strode forward, the rifle coming up in a swift ugly arc.

Kay babbled, "I threw it away. Under the bushes there. In the water. I don't remember. Why ask me that? You've given me millions of pills since then, or it seems like it. In bits of food. I threw it away."

"I don't believe you. You had it somewhere. And when Johnnie woke that time you slipped it into the soup. Didn't you? You wanted to keep him quiet. You could have killed him. Know that? Well he didn't get it. But you remembered, didn't you? I suppose you hoped I'd take it myself. Then that youngster came. Now you think he'll flop somewhere and search parties will come out."

She gave a sudden thin sound that might have been laughter. "Too bad, Kay. We're moving on."

CHAPTER FOURTEEN

THE woman said, "I'm going to untie your arms. Try any tricks and that's the end of you. Won't make much difference to me. I'd rather have you drive, but give me an excuse and I'll finish you now and bury you out in the bush where no one's ever likely to find you. I had plenty of practice in Malaya at burying. I helped bury all those who died. You know, if I could have got Megan out here that's what would have happened to her, but she wasn't one to agree to a camping trip."

For a moment her owl-like gaze seemed to be looking into far distance that brooded as solitary and cruel and dark as the mountains, then a strange little jerk started in her shoulders and travelled down her body for a couple of minutes.

Looking at her closely Kay saw that the round eyes and the cheeks were sunken. She looked tired and ill.

But that's going to help her just the same, she thought bitterly. When she pretends to stagger from the bush, crying of two lost people and herself searching for them, she'll be fussed over and cosseted and believed.

Then the woman said, "Anyway, I'm going to let you drive. But no tricks. You do as you're told. Get me? I want to keep a watch on the boy. I'm beginning to think he's shamming. Tomorrow I'm getting to work on him. I've got no more time to waste."

Kay whispered, "Couldn't you take him to a doctor?"

"Don't be a fool."

"If he dies . . ."

"Then I'll have to rely on my own wits to get the plates back some way, that's all, but I hope to heaven it doesn't come to that."

Kay asked, "Where are we going?" trying to shut off the callousness of the woman's planning with the desperate idea that she might leave behind some clue to their whereabouts.

"You'll see," she was told. "I've packed the wagon. Now stand there while I make sure you've tried no tricks like scribbling with your fingers in the dirt."

Kay said with sudden mockery, "It's the only thing I never considered."

The big teeth showed in a smile.

"Getting slow-witted? You needn't tell me. I know all about the effects of little food. Kneel down. Go on. Hurry up." The rifle jabbed at her. "I'm not having you making a dash for liberty as soon as the knots are loose. It will take you time in your condition to get to your feet. Go on, kneel!"

Kay knelt awkwardly and felt the knots loosened. Then the woman moved away. She said, "Wriggle the stockings down your arms and off. Move over to the wagon. Put the stockings on the back seat. Don't talk to the boy. Don't touch him. Then get round behind the wheel. Hurry up."

There seemed so many instructions that Kay had to stand there and struggle with them, sorting them out and then slowly beginning to obey. She was surprised that the woman didn't yell at her again to hurry, then she thought that perhaps the woman had once had instructions yelled at her that her dulled, starved wits hadn't been capable of coping with. So she knew.

That was the damnable part of it, she thought. The woman knew everything. Just what lack of food did to a person. Just how much a person could perform and do on little more than a slice of bread. She knew the bush and its paths and its dangers and silences. She knew how to cope with every emergency that threatened her. And she was well fed, quick witted and nimble, Kay thought in resentment that lingered on the idea of food and became a fury that shook her body.

But she obediently put the stockings on the back seat with only one glance at Johnnie. He didn't move or speak and to her anxious gaze he looked strangely unreal with his small features looking sunken and sallow.

Then the rifle moved and obediently Kay went to get into the front seat, knowing the woman had slipped into the back behind her and that the rifle was pointing again at the back of her neck.

She was told, "Start up. Take care. Take it slowly. Back the way we came in."

The orders were repeated.

Kay found it much harder to go back than it had been to drive to the creek. She found herself slowly, dully, groping with the question of whether that was because she was so much more exhausted and so less able to hope for a miracle or whether it was the bitterness of leaving the place where help might arrive in the early dawn, that was slowing her.

She was only dully grateful that the woman didn't try hurrying her. When they were once more on the track she was told to go up again.

·   ·   ·

Long before dark on the Thursday evening Stuart had convinced himself that he was a fool and had simply wasted his time, but there still persisted, as he woke the following morning, the astonishment that Johnnie, so afraid of the police, should ever have dared trying to play a trick on the sergeant.

He went up to the homestead with dawn still waiting on the birth of pink clouds and gold light in the pale eastern sky and breathed a sigh of relief at Jess's information that Miss Webber was still in bed. He had to wait patiently then for ten minutes before the exchange was open for the morning, then he rang Coombs.

The policeman sounded sleepy and cross again. "I'm going to grow a beard," he growled over the line. "Every morning I get half shaved and someone rings."

"Get up earlier then, before the exchange opens." Stuart chuckled. "Thanks for the call. I heard it, and Kay or Miss Mings should ring in some time today. I'm leaving a message with Jess to pass on to them. Had any luck with my other request?"

"Your girl friend? No one remembers seeing her. If she'd been a good looking bullock now . . ." he gave a shout of laughter. "But she must come from out past Black Top."

"The other side of Quidong from Caragnoo?"

"That's right. As you'd said Ellen Waters had asked round here about her I didn't think I'd get far. I rang my opposite numbers in each direction asking who owned a green Mini, but they couldn't help, so I started on the pubs on the off-chance they'd know who had visitors. The pub at Black Top say a woman in a topless red dress called in there Friday for a drink. They'd never seen her before and she was on her own, but she drove a green Mini." He added smugly, "Can't say I didn't do you proud, can you?"

"No. Thanks a lot."

"That all you're going to say?" Coombs sounded outraged. "What's the story? Your lady friend asked for the Quidong road. That's what the chap in the pub says. What about that?"

Stuart remained silent. He was telling himself that it was wildly impossible that a woman in a red dress, driving a green Mini, had actually been on the Quidong road that Friday afternoon a week previously.

Johnnie couldn't be right, he thought in desperation, then sudden relief welled over him again. Of course he wasn't! The little pest had been round the caves all right and had seen the woman in red arrive there and probably play out a love scene with someone from the district who had thought of the caves road as a private spot on showday.

He remembered again Kay claiming the boy always had a basis of truth in his whoppers. He had seen the woman in red and the green Mini. That was correct. And a man in a felt hat, too probably. And he had woven them into a drama of his own creation.

He started to laugh.

$$\cdot \quad \cdot \quad \cdot$$

On Friday morning the station wagon was parked under trees at the end of a trail that had proved to Kay a nerve-wracking ordeal of constant twistings and turnings, bumpings in and out of potholed earth and side-pressing bush that had scraped several times either side of the station wagon.

When the journey had been completed the woman hadn't waited for Kay to get out before pinioning her again. She had leaned forward as soon as the engine was cut off, dragging the girl's arms back and tying them with swift efficiency, before ordering her out.

Then she had eaten. She had savoured her way steadily through a surprisingly hearty meal. Kay had averted her gaze, not because of hunger, but because the sight of the woman eating richly with thoughts of the future causing her no concern at all was revolting.

Half way through the meal the woman said, "The scratches on the station wagon don't matter. They'll help my yarn. I can say I drove up and down every trail calling and calling and went through the bush on foot."

After she had finished the meal she had tried rousing Johnnie again, but he hadn't responded and finally, her forehead creased in impatient, angry lines, she had brought a cup of overstewed tea to Kay. When the girl had shaken her head stubbornly she had said impatiently:

"Think I've put a pill in it? Well have the bread. I've smeared it with peanut butter for you. And I'll cope with you later."

Kay had taken the bread greedily, and then too late had realised the pill had been crushed and put in with the peanut butter.

It was suddenly so absurd she had gone to sleep giggling weakly.

But this time the pill hadn't kept her out for so long because she woke with dawn and then had to devil dulled wits, gazing about her, before she realised that they had come to this new place the previous dusk. And then she looked at the pearl grey of dawning sky and thought that by now there were probably two search parties, one going west, one east, and the thought of it was so unbearable she gave a little cry.

The sound brought the woman and a mug of scalding, oversweetened tea, but Kay drank it thankfully.

Then the woman said, "I'm going to see if Johnnie's shamming or not. I've wasted enough time. It's Friday . . ." she stood there a minute, silently. "I can't wait much longer. There's the Sydney appointment for one thing . . ."

Friday, Kay thought. Just a week since Johnnie sneaked away from the show and went to the caves. It was funny really that the woman hadn't considered that Johnnie, with his hatred of bullocks and horses, might sneak away, but then, she realised, the woman had probably never known Johnnie went near the caves. She would have expected that his foster parents kept him well away from them.

That made her think of Stuart and the way he had told her she hadn't kept an eye on Johnnie.

Then suddenly she cried out. She tried to stand upright, and failed, and then she struggled forward on her knees, because the woman was bending over Johnnie, shaking him, slapping at his cheeks, calling to him over and over again.

She cried, "No!" just as Johnnie said: "The church." He whispered it twice more and was silent. Kay lay where she had fallen, ears straining.

Then the woman said dully, "He's not shamming after all. He's just repeating it, damn it. Over and over again. When I mention the church he repeats it and that's the lot." She ordered, "Get back over there. If I had stimulants of some sort—drugs I mean . . . but I never dreamt of this. It's your doing!" For a moment she looked broodingly at the girl. Then she shrugged, "But he should come round soon. Or start talking."

"He'll die," Kay said. "He'll die and you'll never know where they are unless you search and search and search, and what if someone finds them first and thinks of Johnnie being lost and remembers his story and perhaps . . ."

The woman said shortly, "Don't get my goat. Get it? You think I'm keeping you alive in case someone comes, don't you? To show we're still one big happy family. That's true enough, but I could drug you to keep you quiet, but for one thing. If Johnnie comes round, I want you awake. If he won't talk I can't give him much rough-housing, but I can do a lot to you. You needn't start shaking. A few threats will make him start behaving I should think. Threats and the offer of a good meal. I'll give you a spit of water afterwards to clean up, but we'll have to go easily with it. There's no water round here I know of and the fill-up I collected at the creek won't last too long, and I can't afford to waste petrol roaming around looking for water."

She went away again and Kay closed her mind on the appalling callousness of what the woman had told her. She caught instead on the word "water" and began to worry at it like the dogs after one of the big goannas that sunned themselves, mottled of skin, against the mottled bark of the gums near Quidong.

She thought at last, If I manage to spill the water she'll have to find some more, and the oftener we're out on the trails the more chance there is someone will see us.

Her thoughts closed round the idea, clinging to it tighter and tighter, repeating the words round and round.

.   .   .

At mid-day, with the dust of moving cattle filling his mouth and nose and eyes and throat, trickling under clothes and sticking to sweat-sodden skin, Stuart suddenly remembered that the woman in the red dress no longer had it. If she had been wearing it that Friday, he suddenly asked himself, while the cattle dogs worked at the protesting bullocks' heels, how had it come to be in Saturday's jumble collection, still with the silver buttons on the jacket.

And then he returned to the other question—why had Johnnie, scared of the police, gone trembling-kneed to Coombs to talk of finding number plates in the bush? Number plates that he had claimed, on the postcard, belonged to the green Mini?

He sat there on the black stallion, rolling a cigarette, the heat of the sun striking through the back of his shirt, remembering the previous Friday evening when Johnnie had rushed out of the cottage to greet him, wide-eyed with apparent terror. It had been that terror, he remembered, that had made him, in spite of Johnnie being the world's worst liar, say to Kay, "I'm always afraid he'll tell the truth one day and we won't know," and go out and search.

He might, he remembered, even have questioned the boy further, only Johnnie had started babbling of hooded men and that had been that. Remembering, he thought again of Johnnie changing that story on the postcard to one man in a felt hat.

With cigarette smoke dribbling into the dusty air he went on thinking, remembering too, that the boards had been removed, a job that had surely taken hours of patient work. And then they had been replaced.

.   .   .

The big policeman said bluntly, "Nuts!"

"But look . . ." Stuart began.

Coombs nodded, popping another biscuit into his wide mouth and tossing one to his visitor before leaning back so that his chair teetered alarmingly on frail back legs. He mumbled, "I'm lookin'. You've got a woman in a car who drove this way and left her red dress behind . . . maybe. Might be anyone's red dress. And you've got Johnnie—who tells more lies than a politician—talking of a woman in a red dress being killed and tossed down the caves. And you've got a fall in at the caves and those boards being removed—some time. When? This month? Last? How'd you know old Miss Mings didn't find them on the ground and pop them back meaning to bring some cement down some time and fix them properly? Or what do you say to her knowing about the cave-in and taking the boards off to have a look."

"She'd have mentioned that and either way she would have created merry hell about the loose boards. She had a horror of someone fooling around there and being hurt and suing her for damages."

Coombs chuckled, "A bit of an old tight wad, but who'd blame the old girl. She's worked like a nigger for everything she has. But I'll tell you something you've forgotten—remember that mob of chaps who came out about six months back and wanted her to let them go down the caves? She said no and they came in here and complained. They were scientific students or something—the type that bumbles round a cave and tells you later on that was where Adam tore off Eve's fig leaf and done her wrong, because they've found the leaf."

Stuart grinned. "I remember. They'd written to her and been knocked back, then they turned up to try again. She said afterwards they probably thought her some old dear in lavender and lace and came out to charm her."

"Uh huh. I told them the caves were on her land and dangerous, and unless they got a government O.K. some way that was that. They hung around for a couple of days, asking if anyone had heard of other caves. What d'you bet they sneaked back on the quiet, lifted the boards and had a private dekko?"

So that was it, Stuart thought disgustedly. Johnnie, trust the brat, had almost certainly gone there one day after school and seen the scientists.

Then he asked, "What about the red dress? If she was wearing it that Friday, how did it come to get into Saturday's jumble? It was nearly new. Do you mean to say she saw the jumble box and promptly changed her dress and tossed the red one into the box?"

Coombs reached for another biscuit. "Are you tryin' to turn me into a blasted 'tec? All right, I'm game to solve that one, too. She came along to meet her boy friend and he told her she looked a real old galah and she was so mad and disappointed she tossed the dress in the box, having bought it to impress the chap in the first place. My old lady went to her mum's last year and came home with a hat to make a bull shy." He nodded grimly, then laughed. "That finished in last year's jumble and one of the black gins has worn it ever since."

"It's a week since the woman was here. You'd think she'd have remembered those buttons and written to her boy friend to get them back, wouldn't you?"

"How do you know she really wants them back? They could have been some she picked up somewhere. Oh all right, all right, they're antiques or somethin', but I'll solve that one, too. She was passing here on her way somewhere else. And she means to go home again through Caragnoo, so she means to stop off and ask about her buttons in person. Any more questions?"

"No." Stuart stood up. "You think I'm a fool, don't you? You're almost certainly right and we both know Johnnie's imagination is a riot, but I still can't see why he came near you with that story of finding stolen number plates. It's not the sort of thing I can see Johnnie thinking up as a piece of fun—he's scared to death of policemen."

Coombs nodded. "Oh I agree with you there. He was pop-eyed with fright, but he was almost certainly made to feel pretty inferior by the other kids. Kids can be murderously cruel when they're roused, you know. Ten to one they all know he's scared of the police—what d'you bet some of them dared him to tell me a lie that I'd believe and act on? He'd have done it all right to put himself on a level with them again. Think so?"

Stuart nodded, cramming his felt hat back on his dark hair. He said shortly, "Sorry I wasted your time."

"Sorry you wasted yours, but I say," he was grinning again when Stuart turned, "Have you asked round if anyone else got a postcard? Ten to one half the kids—anyone who'd be likely to be taken in by him—got a card telling of wild adventures on the trip east. Probably he filled in an hour while old Miss Mings and Kay were resting, with using up a bundle of cards."

Then he laughed, shaking his head ruefully, "That Johnnie!"

．　　．　　．

Jess gave him a smiling greeting as he came into the homestead at dusk. Her dark eyes were glowing with curiosity as she burst out, "Mrs. Heath's gone and rung. Miss Webber took the call and she won't say what Mrs. Heath had to tell, but . . ."

Stuart had already rushed past her, the day's tiredness and dirt and worry forgotten. Kay had rung. That was the important thing. She was all right.

He hadn't realised until that moment how deeply uneasiness had lain on his mind. The knowledge came with a sense of decided shock, but he brushed it aside. Kay had rung. That was all he could think of. But Miss Webber was in her bedroom with the door closed and he had to hang round, impatiently smoking, until she came out.

He said, before she could start talking, "What did Kay have to say?"

"It wasn't Kay," she shook her head and his wild feeling of elation plummeted away to nothing.

"Not Kay," he repeated, hardly able to believe it.

"It was a youngster and I had to reverse the call because he went on talking and he said he had no money. I only hope I did the right thing because Miss Mings is really quite . . . well stingy, actually . . . about things like that. Why sometimes I swear she practically breathes down my neck while I talk, to make sure I pay for the call. But this was about Miss Mings herself really so . . ."

"Kay," he broke in loudly. "What about Kay? Who was it ringing?"

"If you'll just let me tell you, I *will*," she said with a look of mild reproof. "This youngster—Alex or something he said his name was—said he had been hiking and he came across the party by some creek or other, only he wasn't sure it was *our* party, only it was two women and a boy and the youngest woman was called Kay. He asked me that first—was Mrs. Heath's name Kay. Then he asked if she had rung us up, and I said no. Then he told me he'd seen her and would like to go on talking only he didn't have any money for a trunk call. So I reversed the charges."

Stuart turned away from her. Her mouth, opening and shutting and babbling away, was intolerable to look at. He wanted to hear about Kay and she wouldn't tell him.

But he swung round again when she said, "You're not going to like this, but . . . Johnnie's been playing up."

He asked shortly, "How?"

"He threw a plate and his dinner into Kay's face. This Alex says her face was all bruised and she looked absolutely exhausted and her manner was quite odd. He couldn't explain how. He just repeated that she looked odd and quite queer, but I don't blame her for what she did, just the same, and I must say the youngster has taken it very well, when after all it might have caused quite a disaster, because he might have wandered around half drugged and fallen over a cliff or something, mightn't he?"

"What are you talking about?" he snapped at her.

She blinked, stiffened, then said, "If you'll be *patient*, Stuart . . . you see, this Alex saw them and Miss Mings told him about Johnnie. She said that after hurting Kay, Johnnie had tried running away, but he had fallen over and hit his head. Johnnie had his head bandaged and was having a little sleep, this Alex said."

Stuart was suddenly furiously angry. Damn the brat, he thought in a gust of rage that surprised and shocked him, but it was the thought of Kay with her face bruised, with a look of exhaustion, if the young chap was to be believed, that was enraging him.

He listened dully as Miss Webber rattled on, "And after that Kay suddenly begged him to have some soup, as they didn't have the billy boiling. She said it had been made up for Johnnie, only he wouldn't take it and would this Alex like to put it in his flask and carry it with him? So he took it and a while later he drank it and he went straight to sleep!

"It was dreadful, you must admit, though I don't blame Kay. I expect she was so tired that she thought a sleeping pill was the best thing for controlling Johnnie, for fear Miss Mings got angry, but she shouldn't have forgotten about putting it in, should she?

"But this Alex was astonished, because up to taking the soup he'd felt quite bright, and it was the way he went straight off to sleep frightened him. He said it was just like the previous year, when he'd been studying too hard and taken some sleeping stuff, and he was knocked right out for twelve hours, only this stuff seemed even worse. His friends laughed when he walked out of the bush this morning and caught up with them, but they all got worried when he explained what had happened, because, as he said, anything that would knock him out like that would be far too strong for a little boy.

"Only I don't think the others really believed him, because finally they took the dregs in the flask to some chemist or other. And this Alex was right! It was frightfully strong sleeping stuff.

"So," her plump bosom rose and fell in a long drawn breath, "he was telling his friends about the party and they told him of the call they'd heard last night for a party of two women and a boy and they decided to ring to see if Kay or Miss Mings had already rung us.

"When I said no, he said he and his friends would go back to the creek. He said that probably the party had had an early night last night and never heard the call, but he was frightened Johnnie might have been given some of the drug last night and if he went on sleeping Kay and Miss Mings mightn't realise something was wrong until too *late*. As he said, no one in their right senses would give a powerful drug like that to a little boy, so they must think it was some sort of quite harmless pain-killer for his head.

"And then he said that they might be all right at the moment, but that at any time, if Johnnie got a headache or felt out of sorts, they might give him a dose still believing it a harmless drug. He was worried because Miss Mings said something about them maybe moving on from the creek today. He said if he and his friends found they were gone, they'd ring us again tomorrow.

"To see, of course, if Kay had rung. If she had we'd have warned them. If she hadn't—had had another early night say,—he could try to find them. He said it was Saturday tomorrow and there'd be a lot of bushwalking clubs round the tourist areas—though not where Kay and Miss Mings and Johnnie are, because it's very rugged there. But he said that with the wagon Miss Mings would have to keep to the fire trails and tracks and only go off if she found a clear way somewhere. So," she drew a long breath, "he suggested that if Kay hadn't rung by the morning he ask some of the clubs to come to the area and they could go up the trails and tracks and they'd soon find Kay and warn her."

Stuart stood silently smoking, his expression blank, but he was frightened, and knew he was frightened and that his imagination was trying to run riot, trying to picture Johnnie unconscious and Kay unconscious too. Had the youngster said that Kay looked exhausted? That her face was bruised? If she thought the drug was harmless what more likely than she should down a considerable dose to ease her face and make herself sleep? What more likely, into the bargain, that Miss Mings, tired out herself, mightn't also down a dose.

He knew his skin was pricking with cold sweat. He looked at the fingers holding his cigarette and saw with stunned amazement that they were shaking. He wasn't frightened, he realised. He was terrified.

Then he looked at the clock. If the hikers were going back to the creek, he reflected, they must know they could get there before dark. And it was dark now. They'd be at the creek now. They'd be with Kay, he tried to reassure himself, only to ask that rioting imagination the question as to what if Kay had moved on?

But if she had moved on, he told himself, she must be all right. And so must Johnnie, surely—they wouldn't dump him, still sleeping, into the station wagon and drive away, surely. And Miss Mings must be all right, too.

Then he realised that it would only mean they were all right at the time they had moved on. What if, after a little while, Johnnie complained of a headache? Or if they were now camped somewhere else, feeling tired, deciding to give themselves a dose and be sure of a good night?

But in that case, reassurance came slowly back, the bush-walkers would be brought out in the morning. The youngster had said, hadn't he, that the party would have to stick to tracks and fire trails and that they would be easy to find?

His gaze on the clock again he thought hopefully. If Kay doesn't ring in the morning, if I don't hear her voice, there'll be people all round the area searching for her tomorrow.

He asked, "What time did they expect to reach the creek, did he say?"

Miss Webber laughed. She said, "Oh, but he's not going. I told him, of course, not to bother his head about it."

CHAPTER FIFTEEN

"You told him what?"

He knew he was shouting; that he was towering over her and that his face must betray his rage; that she was backing from him in alarm, but he repeated, "You told him what?"

"Really, Stuart . . ." abruptly she put out her two small hands and pushed him, hands flat against his chest, away from her. "Don't be ridiculous. I told him, and you ought to realise it yourself, that there's not the slightest cause for alarm. Kay doesn't take sleeping tablets. I know, because when Johnnie lost himself she almost collapsed and I suggested getting some sleeping stuff for her when she told me afterwards she simply couldn't sleep for worrying about Johnnie trying to vanish again. But she said, she hated the stuff and considered it habit-forming and she wouldn't take it even once.

"But Miss Mings *has* got sleeping tablets. Terribly strong stuff. And she worries about them. She won't give anyone even half a tablet—I know, because I tried once. She explained quite gravely that I might have an allergy to the drug or have some undetected heart ailment or anything and that her pills were dangerous. Jess is a terrible snoop you know and Miss Mings used to worry that Jess might get hold of one and be hurt by it." A slow blush came into her cheeks. "You know," she confessed rapidly, "I think she even imagined, after she refused me that time, that *I* might stoop to taking one, too. But she had the habit of carefully counting the pills every night. She kept a little book with a note of how many she took and how many should be in the bottle. Why, it was quite a fetish, you could say, with her and it got worse after the day she found Johnnie up here rummaging through her room. No, I know she didn't tell you—she told me it was just curiosity and she wouldn't have minded, except for those pills. Afterwards she was always worrying about him getting hold of the bottle.

"I explained that to Alex and pointed out Kay must have

thought the tablets were aspirin or something similar and taken one without bothering Miss Mings, to give to Johnnie, then forgotten it. But Miss Mings took those tablets nearly every night and she counted them *every* night, and being so worried about Johnnie getting one, I imagine she would count them even more carefully out there with him. So if some were missing last night she would have made a terrible fuss. If Kay or Johnnie had taken one she would have driven them straight out to a doctor.

"I told Alex he needn't worry his head because by now Kay would know what the tablets were; if neither Kay nor Johnnie had taken one it was all right and if they *had* taken one they would have visited a doctor long before this. You see," she smiled at him, then patted his arm. "My, didn't you get in a panic!"

Stuart flopped into a chair. He remembered his riot of imagination. He remembered the prickle of cold sweat and his frantic shouting at her. He started to laugh. Then uneasiness came slowly creeping back. He asked, raising his gaze to hers, "Are you sure that . . ."

"Of course I'm sure. You just stop worrying. They're all right. Perhaps they'll miss the call again tonight if they have a nice early night again, but it can't be helped, can it? And you know, everything must be fine again, mustn't it? I mean after Johnnie's naughtiness they must have had a little talk with him and everything was smoothed over, or else Miss Mings would have packed him into the station wagon, wouldn't she, and driven him straight out and on to Sydney, to get rid of him. I mean, she wouldn't stay on in that wild sort of place if she thought he was going to keep running away, now would she?"

"Of course not." Relief rolled over him again. It was all right, he told himself as he went back to the cottage. Kay had behaved foolishly, of course, in taking the tablets, but perhaps she had been afraid to make a fuss and ask for medicine. She might have seen Miss Mings take the tablets but not realised what they were for, and she had taken one herself perhaps, for her aching face, and decided to give Johnnie one too for his head.

Perhaps, he thought, the well of relief growing deeper and

wider, that was what the youngster had meant when he had said Kay acted oddly. Perhaps she had just taken one of the pills and had been on the verge of sleep.

For a moment faint uneasiness crept back at that idea, then he dismissed it. Miss Mings would have discovered the loss of the pills that evening. If Kay had taken any, Miss Mings would have acted.

A faint trace of uneasiness remained, to grow as he asked himself what if Miss Mings had failed for once to count the tablets? What if Kay had taken a couple and gone to sleep, after giving Johnnie one, too? What if Miss Mings had taken her usual tablet and so dropped off as well, not waking until morning.

Then he laughed at himself. Go on like that, he reflected, and he could keep asking questions and needling himself for a year. Miss Mings wouldn't have let the other two sleep all through the following day. She would have known by the look of them, surely, that something was wrong.

No, it was all right, he told himself. There'd been a fuss with Johnnie, and it had been smoothed over. Miss Webber was right about that. And there might have been trouble, but for the hiker coming along. As it was there was no harm done. Kay might ring in the morning. If she didn't hear the call she might still ring. Just to speak to him. They might go out to a township for fresh food and she might take the chance to call.

He wondered, in sudden exhilaration, what she would say if he suggested a holiday to her. They might even go to Sydney, if Miss Mings left him free. They could take Johnnie about a bit. The kid was proud of the city and loved it. He'd probably get a kick out of showing them around and they'd all see each other in a new light.

He went on contentedly planning.

．　　．　　．

It was the early hours of the morning when he woke, with the question burning and probing into wild uneasiness—why, if Miss Mings had discovered the loss of some of her tablets, had she done nothing about the hiker? Kay must have admitted to the elder woman what she had done. Why hadn't Miss Mings driven out to find out if the man was safe? He might have, as Miss Webber had suggested, gone staggering around and fallen to injury or death, for all Miss Mings had known.

So why hadn't she done anything about it?

She couldn't have tried finding him—that would have been sheer foolishness, but she could have driven to the nearest township, reported what had happened and asked for townships around to be alerted to see if anyone was missing.

If she had done that the hiker would have heard about it, surely, or his friends would have done so.

But she hadn't. Why not? It didn't go with her supposed concern over the pills at all.

. . .

Kay said slowly, "If you went to a chemist you could get drugs. Couldn't you?"

"And give you a chance of making trouble? I'm not that much of a fool. Bind you and gag you and cover you with rugs and you'd still do something. I'd have to leave you in the station wagon while I went into the place, and you'd do something like banging yourself against the sides of the wagon—anything to make passersby look inside. I still think he's shamming anyway. I expected him to come awake in sheer fright when I started in on you and you yelled, but he didn't, He's tough though, and he's quick-witted. He could still be shamming. If he is, he'll be sorry."

"What are you going to do?" Kay whispered it. She felt so tired it was difficult to even think about the situation any more. Her fingers and arms, where the woman had twisted and bruised unmercifully some time before in an effort to make Johnnie come awake, were throbbing with pain. The only consolation about it was that Johnnie, if he was shamming, had had the wits to remain still and silent.

The woman didn't answer her question. She walked away and began on preparations for the evening. There was already a flask of over-stewed tea prepared. Kay knew that in a little while she was going to be offered some, with a sleeping tablet in it, but she knew she was going to accept without arguing, too. She was too tired and exhausted to try and fight and she was hoping that a night of sleep, even forced sleep, might clear her wits for the following day.

She turned her gaze away from the flask. It reminded her of the hiker and her foolish attempt that had been so promptly outwitted.

She turned her attention to the water container and went back to slowly probing at her previous idea. If she could upset it there would be no water and the woman would have to go in search of some. That meant going on to the trails and tracks again. And tomorrow was Saturday, her mind reminded after some wearying effort. There might be week-end hikers about. Not many. The woman, Kay was certain, would never have come to an area where she expected to see hikers, and the one who had come on Thursday had been there alone—had said indeed the way across the valley had been too rugged for the rest of his friends, and that he himself had nearly given the hike away.

But someone she thought hopefully, might drive up the fire trails as the station wagon had done. So if the woman could be forced out of hiding again there was a chance, a very faint chance, of them meeting up with someone.

It was something to hold on to at least.

.　　.　　.

The woman, she thought a little while later, would never cease to surprise. She had taken the portable radio from the back of the wagon and set it on the ground. She said, round-eyed gaze on Kay, "This might help rouse Johnnie if he's really out; or might make him give himself away if he's not. Besides, it'll do no harm to be able to talk later on of things we listened to."

She should, Kay thought wearily, have become used to the sudden callous reminder of brutal planning, but she wasn't. The knowledge that the woman was thinking of what she would later tell of this trip, when Johnnie and his foster mother were disposed of, galled her unmercifully.

She said furiously, "But you're not going to get away with this, you know. You're not!"

The woman didn't even answer.

Kay sat helplessly silent. She was conscious of the music or the sound of voices from the little white and gold radio. Her head was actually nodding when she began to take in what was happening. Then she jerked awake.

She looked up and saw the woman was watching her.

"Asking us to ring Quidong," the woman spoke reflectively. "About a Sydney appointment. About Johnnie that will be. Why, I wonder?" After a little while she reached out and silenced the radio. Then she nodded slowly. She said to Kay, "It'll mean the day of our appointment is altered. That's what it is."

Kay forced herself to bring out the words. "Are you going to ring?" she whispered.

The woman laughed softly.

"Planning how you're going to yell to Stuart? Or that fool of a Webber? Or Jess? You won't have the chance, Kay. I'll see to that. Yes, I'll have to ring, or that fool of a husband of yours might take it into his head to get someone out looking for us. Just to make sure Johnnie isn't upset by missing his dad, for instance. Yes, I'll ring in the morning," she nodded slowly. "But don't think it's going to help you. *You* won't get a chance to get near the phone."

But how are you going to manage that, Kay wondered, and hope came slowly back.

．　．　．

Miss Webber, in a flowered housegown that gave her an unfortunate resemblance to billowing curtains, sat at the kitchen table at Quidong, drinking tea with Stuart. It was still piccaninny dawn, with not even a trace of pink or orange or blue in the pale pearl grey of the sky.

She said, "Well, it's funny in a way I suppose, but," she nodded comfortably, lifting her cup again, "there's sure to be an explanation."

He said with sudden anger, "Yes, there's always an explanation! Of every damn thing that ever happens! Yesterday there was Coombs explaining away . . . oh to the devil with it," he finished morosely. "You should have let that youngster go back. You should have let him ring this morning. Is there any way of getting in touch with him?"

Her eyes had a blank, puzzled look. She said, after a moment, "He gave me his name and the name of some hotel there. I think . . ." she gave a sudden nervous giggle, "that he maybe felt an apology was due to him or something. If you really . . . but I'm sure you're being silly."

He said flatly, "If Kay doesn't ring this morning I'll get in touch with him. Was he staying at this place? Moving on?"

"Staying for the weekend. So he said."

He nodded. "If Kay doesn't ring by . . . by ten . . . I'll get in touch with the youngster."

.   .   .

Kay woke with the familiar headache that the pills seemed to give her, only this time it was far worse because she hadn't been allowed to come slowly awake, but was ruthlessly shaken into consciousness.

Her arms were tied, but she knew that that must have been done just before she woke, otherwise the agony would have been unbearable, with the combination of yesterday's brutality and dagger-like pricklings from being pinioned.

She dragged herself into a sitting position and saw the woman was watching her. She saw, too, that the ground all round her was wet and that her movements had disturbed a grubby piece of tarpaulin that had been tossed over her in the night.

As though I was a dog, she thought angrily. A dog to be given a rag to cover it, but not to be called under shelter. A dog that might bite.

The thought was faintly amusing.

She looked at the sky and realised there would be no more rain for a while at least. It was going to be a sun-filled dawn, in a little while.

She sat wondering why the woman had jerked her awake like that, then she was given a mug of tea and a piece of bread. She fell on both, heedless of the woman's disgusted look. Then she was given a small bowl of water and told to wash herself as best she could. Then the high-crowned red straw hat was tossed to her and she was told to put it on as best she could.

"It'll cover your hair—it's a mess," the woman said flatly. "But

I'm not wasting time while you fiddle with it. Kneel down. Hurry up! I'm going to loosen your arms. You can wriggle them free, then put the stockings in the back of the wagon and get behind the wheel. Hurry up."

As she moved behind the kneeling girl she added curtly, "I want to get to a phone before anyone's around. We'll be at a phone box by the time the Caragnoo exchange is open. I'll speak to Stuart if he's around. If not, to Webber or Jess. You'll do as you're told. There, now get your arms free and get behind the wheel. Hurry up."

Kay moved sluggishly. Not from disobedience, but because her body felt an alien thing—as though it were no longer controlled by her mind at all.

She thought, as she slid behind the wheel, that a call box would be near a township surely. The woman wouldn't dare take the station wagon right into the town, so it would be a box somewhere on the outskirts of such a town.

If, Kay planned as she began the bumpy journey over tussocky ground to the trail again, she refused, when the call box came in sight, to stop as ordered, and simply drove on at high speed, the woman wouldn't dare shoot and they would finally land in the town itself. Wouldn't they? And then . . .

From behind the woman said, "We're not going into a town. Or near one."

Kay could hear the words being repeated over and over even when the cold flat voice had stopped speaking. "We're not going into a town . . . or near one," she repeated to herself over and over again.

Finally she managed to ask, "Where are we going then?"

"Garage. Remember it from my last trip this way. One man place. Like the one we pulled into the other night, and when we get there it'll·be like the Caragnoo exchange—just open. Put on a bit of speed. You're moving too slowly." As Kay reluctantly obeyed, the woman went on, "When we get there I'm leaving you and Johnnie in the wagon. He's covered up, except for his face. He'll look as though he's sleeping. You'll look as though you're sleepy too. You'll close your eyes and lean back, to fob off any conversation.

"I'll pull into the side of the place. Tell him I just want to use the phone for the moment. That'll be in the office. That'll have glass in the front—they all do. I'll be able to see you as I call Quidong. I'm not having you near the phone where you can yell blue murder and perhaps get help."

Kay said, sudden amusement in her voice, "So I just sit prettily in the car and never let out a peep."

"That's right. I'll have the ignition keys so you can't drive away. And if you try running away or if you try attracting the garage man's attention I'll shoot the pair of you. Get that?"

She gave a sudden jerk of laughter. "Frighten you? I mean it. I'll fake a hold-up for the garage chap. Won't matter about you. I wouldn't be having you drive now, only there isn't time to deal with you properly and I'm not rushing things and making a mistake."

As always, the callousness of planning, the calm assumption that nothing would prevent the plans being carried to their conclusion, made Kay furiously angry.

She said, "I suppose it's going to look quite natural for you to stroll into a garage office clutching a rifle? I can picture it!" She started to laugh, because it was suddenly utterly ridiculous that the woman hadn't thought of that obvious point for herself. "The man will think you're after the takings and intend holding him up!"

"Rifles aren't the only things that shoot."

"What do you mean by that?" Kay threw over her shoulder.

"Revolvers of course. Yes, I've got one, Kay. A relic of old Mings' Malayan days, actually. It was in the place when I turned up, anyway. I prefer a rifle because I'm used to shooting with that, but make me use the little chap and I'll use it. Get it?"

.   .   .

The garage was small, and a little shabby. It stood on a triangular piece of ground and on two arms it was bounded by bush and at the front by the road with bush clustering the other side of it. As Kay pulled slowly in to one side of the white building she could see, through the trees on the left, a small fibro cottage. It would belong to the garage man, she knew. She wondered how many

169

people were inside the cottage and how long it would take them to come running if a shot sounded.

But it mustn't sound, she realised despairingly. The woman was quite capable of shooting anyone who came. She had spoken of faking a hold-up. It would still look like that if the man's wife was found shot in the road, too. It would look as though she had come running to help him and been killed in turn.

And there might, she thought, closing her eyes at the horrible picture it conjured up, be children in the cottage. They might run out, too.

The woman said softly, "Take out the ignition key and hand it to me over your shoulder. Don't look round. Now I'm going to get out."

Kay heard the door open. The woman said in that same soft voice, "I'm going into the office now. I'll tell the man—he's coming now—I just want to use the phone and that you'll have a snooze till I come back. Lean back and close your eyes. That's it. Remember what I told you. The office is right in sight of this point. Try any tricks and I'll shoot. Both you and the man."

Her voice lifted. Her steps began to move away as she called, "Good morning. Could I use the phone? It'll be a long call I'm afraid."

"Yours as long as you like it, lady," was the cheerful response. "Would you like me to get the number?"

"Thanks, but I can manage. I'm used to country exchanges. Don't worry about the wagon—the rest of the party will have a cat-nap while I'm busy."

Kay could hear the voice retreating into the distance, sayng, "Yes, lovely day. Fine camping weather. Lovely area around here. Quiet, but that's best if you ask me . . . yes . . ."

Kay opened her eyes. The sun had come up and there was a cooling wind on her face. She wanted to call Johnnie's name, to ask if he knew what was happening, but didn't dare. She could see the ugly brown face looking directly at her. The woman would see her lips move, she knew, and if they kept on moving she would think Johnnie was awake. Johnnie would suffer for that later on.

But he was going to suffer anyway, she thought despairingly, looking round her slowly. She wondered if she dared risk calling to the man. He had his back turned to her doing something near the petrol pumps. Her gaze turned towards the barely seen cottage. She licked at dry, aching lips and knew she could do nothing at all.

The best she could hope for was someone coming along and pulling in at the garage, but at that hour of the morning, in that quiet place, it was unlikely. And if the woman saw a car coming she would probably hurry from the office and get the wagon moving before ever the other car pulled in.

But Kay sat there, praying one would come. Soon.

. . .

They both started to their feet when the phone rang, but Stuart was picking up the receiver when Miss Webber was still hurrying through the kitchen doorway.

He jerked at her, as she joined him, "an eastern call." They were both silent as the seconds ticked by.

Then Stuart said, almost unbelievingly, "Miss Mings?" Then he laughed. It was loud, hilarious, filled with relief. He felt a fool. A wildly exhilarated fool.

To her startled, "What's the joke?" he stammered, "I've been worried. Terribly worried."

"Why?" The voice came tinnily.

"It's a long story." He started to tell her, the words pouring out, but she broke in before he was able to explain the question that had come to him in the night and left him worrying till then.

She gave a jerk of laughter as she said, "I knew the pill was gone, all right. Found out that night. Webber's right, of course. I always count the horrible things. Nearly had a fit when Kay told me she'd taken one. Johnnie was whining about his head while I was heating some soup for him and Kay had seen my bottle, thought it was aspirin of some kind and took one. There was no harm done. Except to the youngster of course. We owe him an apology, but not knowing where he is . . ."

He said sharply, "Didn't you do anything to find out where he was—if he was safe—when Kay told you? He could have staggered around in a daze and . . ."

She said quickly, "Those pills don't leave you staggering—

you're asleep in a couple of minutes. Expect Webber's worried you by telling you the song and dance I put on when she tried to get one off me? Actually they're not dangerous—except to kids of course. But I wasn't having Webber start cadging them off me. Felt she could buy her own. I knew the youngster would have flopped flat and stayed till he woke up and they don't leave any after effects."

"And what would have happened," he asked dryly, "if he hadn't had all the soup—but just a small portion—enough to make him woolly-witted, for instance?"

There was silence. Then she said shortly, "Never thought of it. Foolish of me."

More than foolish, he thought angrily. It had been criminal carelessness, but there was no use in saying that. Probably, he thought, she was mentally kicking herself right then, poor old thing.

He asked quickly, "How is Kay? And Johnnie?"

"Fine," the tinny voice held a stronger note. "Enjoying themselves immensely. Told you Johnnie'd be set on camping after one taste, didn't I?"

"Yet he tried to run away?"

"The hiker tell you that? The little devil expected to have his pants warmed of course for throwing his dinner at Kay."

"Why did he?" he demanded, then snapped impatiently as the exchange cut in, "Yes of course I want the call to continue. Indefinitely. Miss Mings," he went on urgently, "why did Johnnie act like that?"

"Well . . ." there was doubt in the tinny voice, then it hurried on, "he tried shoplifting in a little store. Oh, don't start worrying, man! Over now. Boy got a talking to and got into a panic. After his dash into the bush he felt sorry for himself—banged his head you know and we all had things out. You'd think he was related to an angel at the moment." She gave a jerk of laughter, "that reminds me—we heard the call of course—what's wrong with the Sydney appointment?"

"Nothing. I put that in so Kay wouldn't panic and you wouldn't, thinking something was wrong here." He went on to tell her of Ellen Waters.

She said, after a long moment of silence. "I see. All right. We'll drive in some time tomorrow." As though realising that that might sound as though she was completely indifferent to her old friend's trouble she went on quickly, "We'd made plans for today. I don't want to drag Johnnie straight away now he's happy for the moment. We'll drive in first thing tomorrow."

He shrugged. If she wanted to put Johnnie ahead of a friend of a dozen years standing there was nothing he could do about it, he reflected, but he wondered how Kay would react. At that he said, "I want to talk to Kay, Miss Mings. And to Johnnie too—I've got quite a few things to say to him. Will you bring them to . . ."

"Never thought you wanted them. Thought it was me that'd do. Left them in the bush and drove on out myself."

Anger and disappointment swept over him, then died. It was useless blaming her, he knew. She couldn't guess at his desperate need to talk to Kay. She couldn't know that he wanted to say simply, "Kay, I love you," and if she did know she would probably laugh he reflected wryly. There wasn't much of romance in her. Just common sense. Then he amended, not too much common sense either—to cease worrying about Alex without wondering if he had reached safety.

He said, "Tell Kay to ring me. As soon as she can."

"Right you are. Anything more? Everything all right at Quidong?"

"Fine. Just fine," he murmured absently.

When he put the receiver down Miss Webber asked, "It's all right?"

"Yes. She says so."

She smiled and he realised guiltily that he had impressed his own fear and panic on to her. She reached into the pocket of her housecoat and pulled out a slip of paper. She said gaily, "So we won't need this after all, will we? It's that hotel phone number—where Alex is." She tore it into pieces and tossed them into the basket beside the phone table.

CHAPTER SIXTEEN

JOHNNIE was awake, Kay thought despairingly, and she couldn't talk to him properly. She couldn't untie him. She couldn't even get out of the car. To do so would mean her own death and the death of the garage man, and of anyone who came out of the cottage.

She sat tensely at the first soft, "Kay," but to the other, following, louder ones she said, trying not to move her lips, trying to keep her face out of the woman's sight, "Be quiet. She can see me. She mustn't know you're awake."

His rough small voice whispered, "O.K. don't you talk then, but I've been hoping and hoping she'd leave me untied, see'n go away for a bit and then I'd've sloped. She meant that, about shootin', didn't she?"

"Yes."

"There's a cottage over there. See?"

"Yes."

"If you honked and honked someone'd come out'n then there'd be someone else'n then . . ."

She tried to move her face out of the woman's sight. She whispered, lips barely moving, "There might be children. A woman. They might be . . ."

"Shot? Jeez!"

He didn't say anything more. There were a thousand things she wanted to say to him; a thousand questions to ask but she didn't dare.

Then she saw the woman coming out of the office. She thought of Stuart and felt sick. Whatever he had wanted he was satisfied now. The tiny lifeline he had held out to her was out of her reach, too.

She heard the woman say, "Thanks for the phone. We'll have the tank filled up."

The woman came forward. The ignition key was thrust out towards Kay. The woman said pleasantly, "Pull up to the pumps,

174

Kay." She went on, as the girl fumbled the key into place, "That was Stuart I spoke to."

Kay couldn't answer. She edged the station wagon slowly beside the pumps. The woman walked beside it, close beside it, her hand in the pocket of her slacks. She said then, standing beside it while the garage man walked to the other side, pump hose in hand, "Poor old Waters is dying. Ellen's flown to Sydney and Stuart wants us to follow in and stay with her till it's over. Told him we'll go in tomorrow."

Tomorrow, Kay thought. One day and one night more for the woman to get what she wanted out of Johnnie and cope with both of them. Tomorrow she would tell the world Johnnie and his foster mother were lost in the rugged bush. Only they wouldn't be lost in that particular area at all—they'd be buried somewhere miles and miles away from where they were supposed to be lost.

Kay let the rest of what the woman was saying flow over her, but she paid no attention. Then she jerked out of abstraction as the garage man said, "Did you know your plate's nearly gone, lady? Hanging by one screw."

He had moved round to the back and was squatting down, while the woman gave an annoyed exclamation and moved slowly so that she could see both the back of the station wagon and Kay.

She said shortly, "Must be all the bumping on the trails. Jerked it loose I suppose, but . . ."

"You've got two plates," he said sharply, "Different number, too—what the . . ."

Kay saw knowledge leap like a flame into the brown, owl-like gaze. She turned slowly. She could see Johnnie's wide, horrified gaze fixed on the woman through the station wagon window.

And the garage man was standing up. He was holding the two plates. He was staring from the woman to Kay herself. Kay held his gaze. Her head was turned away from the woman. Kay continued to hold his gaze as she mouthed silently, desperately, then she let her gaze slide away.

The woman was saying, "So *that's* where it was. Johnnie, you're the limit. The little wretch pinched the plates off my second car just before we left and he wouldn't tell me where he'd put them." She laughed. She went on chuckling, "Do you know that's the one place I never thought of looking! He's a clever little devil, but there's a limit . . . would you screw the proper plate back? I'll stick the other in the glove compartment. I suppose the other's under the front plate. I'll fix it up later. Did you ever hear of a kid getting up to that before?"

She went on talking, quickly, easily, bluffly, as the man silently fixed the one plate into position; as she slid into the back seat beside Johnnie; as the man stood aside, turning to put the screwdriver into the small box near the pumps; then she said softly; "Start moving, Kay."

She began to speak to the man again as the station wagon started to move. She went on speaking, calling back a bright good-bye, as the station wagon swung out onto the road and picked up speed.

Then abruptly she was silent. As abruptly she gave a great jerk of laughter and was silent again.

She said, "So that's that."

That's that, Kay thought wearily, in echo.

Johnnie said, his voice wavering, "I tried to get 'em off. I pinched y'little screwdriver out of your sewing machine to fix 'em, Kay'n I still had it when we took off, see, and then I came round by that creek and I tried gettin' them off, only I flopped. I guess . . . I guess I just loosened that one . . ." his voice trailed off.

"So you're awake are you?" the woman said. "Where did you get that trick of rolling your eyes up when someone pressed your lids open? Oh don't tell me—out of some blood-and-thunder. Knew you were shamming though."

She was silent again.

Then she said shortly, "Continue along this road. Take the second turning on the right. I'll direct you from there."

No, you won't, Kay told herself viciously. The tank was full she remembered. The station wagon could take miles in its stride now and it was going to. They weren't going to turn off anywhere. They were going to continue until they came to a town and they were going to tear into it like a bat from hell. When the time came when she should obey orders and turn off she was going to press her foot down and let the station wagon eat up the road. The woman would never dare shoot if they were going at high speed. They'd go on and on and sooner or later they'd meet other cars. They'd be reported sooner or later. The police might come. And a township had to loom up somewhere.

When the woman said, "That's the turning, there," Kay eased the speed down till she was sure the woman was off guard, then she pressed down her bare foot. The station wagon gave a shuddering lurch, then jumped forward, the tyres screeching as they tore into the road.

Kay heard the woman calling, felt something pressing against the back of her neck, but she paid no attention.

And then she knew it was no good. She had no strength left to keep her foot down, her sweating hands grasping the wheel or to control the speeding station wagon. She tried desperately to will herself into action, but her tired and weakened body wouldn't respond. She could feel her foot and her hands sliding away.

After a minute the station wagon rocked to a halt.

The woman said, "That was a fool trick. Now reverse. Go back to the turning. Turn off. Do as you're told."

· · ·

Miss Webber called, "It's *another* call from the east. It's . . ."

Stuart snatched at the receiver. He yelled, "Kay!" then realised he was a fool again. It couldn't be Kay. It wasn't ten minutes since Miss Mings had hung up, with Kay far away in the bush somewhere.

A man's voice asked, "You just had a phone call? The exchange here says the woman asked for your number?"

"Woman . . . Miss Mings?"

"Don't know her name . . ." the voice went on, crisply, questioningly, then answered questions in turn.

Miss Webber had been standing curiously in the doorway. As he went on speaking, she inched forward. When he put down the receiver she asked in alarm, "What is it?"

"I . . . don't know. Johnnie *did* find those plates. He screwed them under the ordinary plates on the station wagon. He wouldn't have done that for some fool trick."

"But . . . "

"And Kay and Johnnie were with her and she lied. She said they weren't. That I couldn't speak to them. And Kay mouthed

'Help. Help.' over and over again at the man." He shook off her hand. "A garage mechanic that was. The station wagon pulled in there while Miss Mings rang. And the mechanic found the double plates. And Kay mouthed at him. He thought she was crazy. But Miss Mings was in a flap. She tried to fob him off with Johnnie having played a trick on her by hiding the plates of her other car. That's another lie. She hasn't another car. You said yourself Miss Mings never did things for people without expecting some sort of gain. And I laughed. Because I couldn't see what sort of gain she could get out of Johnnie. But why didn't she tell me she was going away? She's always given me a week's notice of her going before, but I never heard a word of this trip till the Saturday. And I thought it odd, even then, because the cattle were ready to trek out. She's usually around for that."

He was upturning the waste basket, scrabbling through the bits of paper. He looked up at her to jerk, "She wasn't at the show on Friday afternoon. She said she was expecting a phone call—about the cattle actually—and she went back to Quidong. She said."

She said flatly, "You've gone mad. Are you trying to make out Miss Mings is some sort of monster or something or that . . ."

"She lied to me. She said Kay and Johnnie were in the bush and I couldn't speak to them. And they were there with her."

"But that doesn't mean," she started to laugh, doubling up in amusement, "Oh you great silly, she's terribly mean! She'd have to pay for the phone call even if you reversed the charges. She wouldn't want Kay and Johnnie talking on and on while the cost mounted."

He said flatly, "She was frightened. She started to babble to the mechanic. She was so upset she left in a hurry and she never paid for the petrol. She never paid for the phone call either."

She went on laughing. She said, "I'm sure she was so embarrassed she could have died. Johnnie being found out that way and . . . she just wanted to get away. She'll be back soon, more embarrassed than ever."

"Will she? Why did she tell the mechanic that lie about the plates being from her other car? She hasn't got another car and you know it."

She pointed out reasonably, "She had to say something. She

couldn't go into explanations of Johnnie's wild story about that woman in red. Don't be silly. The man would have thought he had a group of lunatics in the place. She said the most sensible thing and honestly . . ."

"Why did Kay mouth at him like that?" he demanded furiously. "Why did she mouth 'Help!' over and over again."

She sat down, pressing her hands down on her plump knees. She said with composure, "She did *not* say 'Help'. She said . . . and I don't blame her, 'Hell!' She was probably saying it over and over under her breath as a relief for her feelings over all the embarrassment and worry and I, for one, don't blame her."

She gazed at him triumphantly, and added, "There's always a reasonable explanation for things. I've told you that before."

He gazed at her blankly. He asked, "Where did those second number plates come from? Why hasn't someone reported a loss by this?"

"They have. I'm sure of it. It was someone who came to the show, you understand, who drove away—probably hundreds of miles —some man probably who came just to look over the cattle— someone, anyway, who drove away and probably stayed at several places on the way home, and he doesn't know where the number plates disappeared."

She looked at him severely, "And really, Stuart, Miss Mings is a highly respected woman. She owns Quidong and . . ."

"That's right," he said evenly, "everything has an explanation, as you say, and I'm horribly afraid the police are going to agree with you and dither and fumble . . . and it's no good. I've got to find Kay. The police might keep a look-out for the station wagon on the roads, but they won't search the mountains. Not until I can produce a lot of things that *can't* be explained away with a little clever thinking."

He looked down at the little jigsaw of torn paper on the floor. "I'm ringing Alex and asking him to try and find her. Ellen Waters," his voice was abstracted, "was flown east. I'm going to ask the same people to fly me as close to the mountains as possible. If I'm a fool, I can take the laughter. What I can't take is the idea that Kay was with Miss Mings, and Miss Mings lied about it, and Kay never asked for a word with me. I was there, the other end of the line, but she didn't want to speak to me, or she couldn't. I'm going to find out which it is—both need an explanation."

•   •   •

The connection was better than it had been when Miss Mings had called, and whoever was speaking was shouting into the bargain. The words came with a roar, and when they weren't answered they were repeated, with an anxious "You hear me?"

"I hear you," Stuart said, hearing a flat note of despair in his own voice. "Alex has gone. You're sure? He's really gone?"

•   •   •

"Knew you couldn't keep that up for long," the woman said evenly. "Haven't the strength, have you? Marvellous how you can kid yourself, in that state, that you can kick the world in the face, then start doing it and find you've merely given it a tap. But no more tricks from now on. Or Johnnie'll suffer. I don't need him any more."

"Y'bloody old bellyache," Johnnie said tersely.

Kay's lips twitched, and then she felt a mild surprise that she could still experience humour. She ought to be crying, she thought wearily. Or pleading. Doing anything anyway, other than meekly, and wearily driving on as ordered. But the woman, she knew, had things all her own way.

Her thoughts slid away to Johnnie. She remembered how she and Stuart had dubbed him a coward because he was scared of bullocks and horses and the cattle dogs. It flicked her on the raw now to remember that judgement. How many nine-year-olds, she wondered, or how many adults, would have shown the coolness and fortitude he'd put up in the past few days? He'd kept silent and still under shakings and pinchings; under having pins stuck in him; under lack of food; under bumpings and bangings in their journeyings; under threats to himself and to her. She felt tears pricking under her lids and bit down hard on her lower lip to stop them going any further. She churned her dulled wits into slow action once more and tried to plan out what to do.

There was so little time left, she realised, and she had already tried so many things and got nowhere. The only thing she could think of was to drive to wherever the woman ordered and then make one desperate effort, when she was told to get out, to overpower the woman some way. She remembered how, before, the woman had always pinioned her arms immediately she had stopped the wagon. So this time, she planned, she would stop and instantly slide forward and away from the seat, grab the door handle and throw herself out. The woman would have to put the rifle aside for the moment, ready to grab her victim's arms. It would take her a couple of seconds at least to grab the rifle again, and more to aim and fire. If Johnnie could bang his feet up at the critical time . . . but he wouldn't know, of course, what she intended. He might be startled into stillness . . .

The woman suddenly snapped, "Stop!"

Kay automatically jammed on the brakes. The station wagon skidded to a halt and the rifle touched the back of her neck.

The woman said, "Sit still. I've just remembered—I was in such a dither with shock I drove off and never paid for the petrol or the trunk call."

To Johnnie's exultant, "He'll tell the cops!" she said flatly, "Shut up."

Then she said, "He'll think it a simple mistake. He won't do anything unless I don't go back and fix things with him. That means we've got to go back." She fell silent then said shortly, "No, don't start up yet. I want to think."

After a couple more minutes she added, "Start up. Reverse. Go back to the place where we turned off. Turn left. Go back towards the garage. If there are any other cars about we'll pull up well out of sight till they've gone so don't start planning trouble. Go on—get moving."

So even the faint hope that the police might be set in search of them was denied them, Kay thought wearily, as she turned the station wagon and started back. She wondered what would happen if there was another car there, if she drove in ignoring the woman's command to stop, and yelled for help?

Then she knew she couldn't do it. Unless she could see who was in the other car she couldn't do it. She couldn't risk having children injured. And if the woman faked a hold-up at the garage she might calmly do away with whoever was in the car—no matter if it was two or three people. It would be accounted for by the police thinking the car had pulled in while the hold-up was going on and the gunman had simply shot down innocent bystanders so he would have time to get well away.

But when they came in sight of the garage again it looked deserted. The woman said exultantly, "Good. Drive in. Stop where you did before. Johnnie, lie back and close your eyes. You're asleep. Understand? Try anything and I'll shoot you. I'll shoot Kay. I'll shoot the man in the garage. Get me? There'll be no help forthcoming out of any tricks. Only the death of that man, and Kay and yourself."

She added, as Kay eased up ready to pull in at the side of the white building, "And no trouble from you either, Kay. Watch your step."

Kay's gaze searched the deserted road. If only a car would come, she thought, she could yell to the driver—tell him to get the police—and if he understood and was quick-witted he might get away and help would come. But more probably, she thought helplessly, he would stop the car and gape at her in astonishment. People simply didn't believe they could walk into trouble and tragedy. The driver would stop and gape and probably lean out to ask, "Whatever's the matter?"

The woman had got out of the car again and had demanded the ignition key. Kay handed it to her without looking at her. Her gaze was on the garage man coming out of the glass-fronted office. She wondered what he had made of her silent mouthing. Apparently nothing because he looked quite normal. He didn't look excited or curious or angry or anything but blank-faced.

The woman said heartily, going to meet him, "I'm hardly game to meet your eye! I was so flustered I drove off without thinking any more about payment, but I soon remembered and here I am to apologise and pay up."

He nodded. "I thought you'd be back."

His gaze moved away from her, towards Kay. He said, still watching Kay, "But just in case, I got the exchange to give me the name you phoned and I rang. You're Miss Mings. Of Caragnoo. Out in the south-west."

Kay stared at him. He'd rung Quidong! That was all she could think of for a moment. He'd rung Quidong. What had he said? Had he told Stuart about her mouthing? About the plates? About the . . .

The woman said, "So I owe you for two phone calls. Yes, I'm Hilary Mings. Never thought you'd have the idea of doing that—is it a case of once bitten, twice wary? Been stung before, I mean?" Her laughter jerked out.

He shrugged his narrow shoulders, rubbing over his long bony chin with one hand. His gaze was still on Kay. "It happens. You get someone in who wants to call somewhere. Then another comes. While you're fixing that the first chap's finished his call and driven off. This chap I spoke to—Heath—he was upset. Said you'd lied to him. He wanted to speak to his wife and you said he couldn't because she wasn't around, and I told him there was a girl with you."

Kay drew a long breath. She looked at the woman and saw the brown skin was reddening, either with shock or temper.

Then the woman gave a jerk of laughter. She said, "Hear that, Kay? Now look at the pickle you've got me into with Heath. Told you you ought to speak to him and clear things up." She turned back to the man, shrugging, "Just a domestic rift. A word here, a word there . . . you married?"

"Uh huh."

His gaze was still on Kay. He asked flatly, "The boy had a spat with this Heath, too? He said he'd wanted to speak to the boy and you said . . ."

"Oh good lord!" The woman sounded exasperated, "I'd had to be a tell-tale—had to admit the boy's been playing up and Heath sounded in a temper. Couldn't see any sense in waking the boy to collect a good telling-off, and then have him turn sulky. Do you mean to say you've been worrying," she asked in what sounded like astonishment.

"Heath was worried. And I told him *she'd*," he nodded towards Kay, "been mouthing 'help' at me. I told him . . ."

"What! Kay, what in the name of . . ."

Kay looked into the reddened, enraged face. The woman wasn't looking at the man any more. She was coming towards the station wagon. Her furious expression could be seen by Kay and Johnnie alone, and her voice held only startled surprise when she said, "Were you talking to yourself again? I know whispering to yourself 'Help me, help me' when Johnnie's annoyed you, calms you down a bit, but you should have realised this time that . . ." She swung round on the man again, but she still had her face half turned towards the station wagon, so she could watch it, as she said, "I'm sorry all this's happened—our holiday's been a mess from start to finish. First the boy tried shoplifting . . ."

Kay listened to the bluff, earnest voice telling of Johnnie's misdeeds, giving the name of the store and the town, and the name of the garage where they had stopped for petrol; where Kay had cried out in reproach to Johnnie and where the garage man had stared in avid surprise.

So now, she thought despairingly, this man can ring the other garage and he'll learn what she's saying is true. He'll believe that I was praying "help me" in an effort to control my temper.

But Stuart . . . she thought in wild hope. What was Stuart thinking?

Then the woman said, "Heavens above, I'd better ring Quidong again I expect, before Heath has a litter of kittens." Her big teeth showed in a grin at the man. "Can I use the phone again? Then I'll settle up with you. Would you get the number for me—I found that girl on your exchange a bit difficult to hear before . . ."

The man led the way into the office. He came out again in a few minutes and began polishing the glass over the office front. Then after a minute he stopped that and came towards the station wagon.

Kay licked at her lips. Her gaze flickered from him to the woman in the office. She saw the woman's right hand was in the pocket of her slacks. If the man would only come right to the station wagon, Kay prayed, and block the woman's view of her face she might be able to warn him, then she realised in panic that if that happened the woman might simply shoot him.

But if she did that wouldn't Stuart later on put two and two together, she wondered, and then realised that Stuart probably didn't know the name of the garage or where it was. Even if he did, by the time the papers reported it he would have something else to worry about—he'd be rushing east to try and help find her and Johnnie. By the time that was over the brief sensation about the garage hold-up would be over, too.

The man stopped a little way from the wagon. He asked, "All right?"

She nodded, trying to smile.

The woman called, "Kay!" then added, "Stuart wants to talk to you."

Kay opened the door. She went hurrying across to the office, then wondered, looking back, if the man would wonder about her bare feet. But he wouldn't, she remembered despairingly, read anything much into the fact. A lot of people preferred to kick off their shoes—he'd think she'd done that for a minute while not driving and then forgotten them when she was called.

When she entered the office the woman said softly, "Reassure him." She hesitated, her owl-like gaze going over the younger woman. She can see the light in my eyes, Kay thought. She knows I'm going to warn Stuart. She had debated in that hurrying passage, what she would do and had decided. It was a possible chance of saving Johnnie, against the possible death of the garage man, she had decided. If she told Stuart—warned him—screamed to him —help might come in time. It wouldn't even be much use for the woman to shoot the man. If he didn't try stopping them getting away he might be all right.

Then the woman said, "Look," and jerked her head towards the corner of the office.

Kay's gaze swung round. She stared. There was a playpen there. There was a baby. About twelve months old, she thought. It smiled at her in wide friendliness, trying to pull itself upright, going on grinning as she stared.

The woman said softly, "One trick and I'll shoot the kid. I'll have nothing to lose remember."

Kay closed her eyes. Johnnie's life against the baby's, she thought despairingly. She clutched the receiver and managed, "Stuart?"

His voice sounded shatteringly loud. He demanded, "Are you all right?" When she said "Yes," he demanded, "Why didn't you ask to speak to me before?"

"I . . . I didn't know it was you," she answered. The woman

had pushed a piece of paper in front of her. The words were scratched there for her to see. She simply repeated them. "I thought it would be Miss Webber, or Jess. I thought you'd be gone to work."

Her gaze went to the corner of the office again. The baby was trying to chatter at her. She heard Stuart ask, "What's that?"

She said slowly, "A baby. He's trying to talk to me."

He didn't comment on that. He demanded instead, "Where's Johnnie?"

She looked at the paper where new writing was appearing. She said, "Out in the station wagon. He's asleep, I think. Do you want him?"

"No. If you say it's all right."

"Everything's all right."

"You're going to Sydney tomorrow?"

"Yes."

"You're going back to your bush camp now?"

"Yes."

"Where is it?"

She looked down at the paper "In some valley. It's lovely down there."

"And you're all right?"

"Of course. Why not?"

"I was worried."

"We're quite all right."

"Kay . . . I love you."

She stood silent, surprised and faintly uneasy at the note of desperation in his voice.

She said, after a long moment, "I love you," then repeated it and let the receiver slide from her clasp.

She heard the woman speaking. Then the phone was replaced. The woman drew a long breath. She said, "It was a damn good thing we came back. I'd like to give you something to remember about that mouthing of yours." Her voice was cold and flat and unemotional which made the words seem worse than ever. "And that fool had told Heath about the double plates."

At Kay's quick lifting of her head, she added impatiently, "Don't get ideas. You never told Heath that Johnnie had babbled of number plates, did you? No, I thought not. He was only puzzled as to why I'd said they were off my other car. I explained that away easily. I told him I was so shocked and flabbergasted all I could think of was getting away before some more of Johnnie's misbehaviour was revealed, too. I told him I intended having things out with Johnnie and as soon as I knew where the plates came from I'd see they were returned."

She frowned, "I'll have to think up something before I go back. But he'll have other things to think of by then. Get moving. And no tricks. I've fobbed this fool off, thank heavens. He looked at Johnnie once but moved smartly away again. I was half afraid he'd try sticky-bearing. Hurry up and get back to the wagon."

Her voice eased into normalcy as she called, "All set. I can't apologise enough for all this fussing. And how much do I owe you now? I've got the cost of my two calls for you, and there's the one you made and the petrol . . . if you'll tot it up?"

Kay slid behind the wheel again. She said softly, knowing the two in the office couldn't hear, "I couldn't do anything, Johnnie. There was a baby in the office. She . . . she threatened to kill him if I said anything to Stuart to warn him."

"Bloody old bellyache," he said staunchly.

"Dear Johnnie . . ." she said thickly. She knew she was close to breaking down. It was a relief when the woman came back, still talking.

Another minute and they were moving again. The woman gave a long sigh. She said flatly, "I've aged ten years. Take the turning we took before. And put on a bit of speed, but don't try that fool antic you got up to before." Then she added, "What did you say to Johnnie while I was in the office? I could see you were speaking."

"I told him about the baby."

She gave a jerk of laughter. "A bit of luck. The fool's wife had gone to her mother's because mum had a pain somewhere and he was baby-sitting for the morning. There's the turning ahead. Take it. No tricks, mind."

. . .

In the driving mirror Kay could see the cloud of dust spreading out behind them. She had started the journey with hope—hope that they would meet another car and she could somehow attract attention—but it had slowly died away. They were retracing their journey out she knew. Soon they would be back where they had started that morning. Where they would go from there she hadn't the faintest idea, except that it would be somehow deserted. And that it was going to be the end of the journey for herself and Johnnie she knew quite definitely. The only thing she could think of was her former plan to defeat the woman when they finally pulled up—to throw herself forwards and out. That the woman would remain in the car and reach for the gun was definite. But Johnnie might delay her just sufficiently for Kay to scramble into the scrub. Then the woman would have to jump out and follow. She didn't try dwelling on the cat and mouse game that would ensue. She forced aside the remembrance that she was weak and the woman was strong, desperate, determined and armed.

She kept going back over the journey from Quidong, asking herself uselessly what would have happened if she had done this or something else; if she had plotted that or defiantly done something quite different. Worst of all was the remembrance of the picnic lunch, of Johnnie's attempted flight, of herself being the one to drag him back.

She was thinking of that when she saw them. For a moment she stared ahead in dazed uncomprehension. She saw a little man with knobbly knees and huge boots and a fierce sprout of black beard, and a girl in tartan slacks and a knitted cap with a pompom on it. She saw fat bare legs in brief pink shorts and a broad shouldered figure in what was obviously cast-off soldier's jungle-greens. She could see another man in a scout-master's uniform and behind him two wide-eyed scouts, and a short, squat man with a babyishly-round face.

She started to pull up as something jabbed the back of her neck. The woman's voice ordered, "Drive on. Straight through them. They'll jump aside, you'll see, thinking us just a mob of fools who think we own the trail. Go on ..."

Then the bearded man cupped his hands round his mouth. His voice whipped forward to press on Kay's consciousness with her own name.

"Kay Heath!" the voice demanded.

She said, "They know me. They're looking for *me*!" She kept repeating it, ignoring the pressure on her neck, the urgent commands to drive on. "You can't ignore them. You can't do anything. You can't shoot them all. You can't . . ."

It was the realisation of that that cleared her wits. Her hand reached out, grabbed the ignition key and hurled it, straight into the surrounding bush. She could see the glint of it arching and falling, as the woman screamed.

Kay turned. She said, "You can't shoot them. Not all of them. You can't," and then, just as she had planned, she fell forward, gripped the door handle and tumbled out into the door, her voice screaming into the sunlight, "Help me!"

.   .   .

Johnnie whispered, "Jeez, do you think the old bellyache'll get away?"

His mouth, he realised in dismay, was filling up and his eyes, too, but he wasn't, he told himself determinedly, going to blub in front of all those faces. And anyway it was all right. A miracle had happened and Felt Hat—he couldn't think of her any more as Miss Mings—had gone dashing into the bush and he was lying in the wagon with his head on Kay's lap and she'd been crying all over him.

He said faintly, "Jeez, you're soppy."

He saw her smile faintly. She said, "Dear Johnnie . . ."

He felt his eyes starting to fill up again. He said hurriedly, "I was awake for ages. She stuck a pin in me. And I heard you yell, but . . ." his anxious gaze searched her pale face, "I couldn't do nothin', could I?"

"No," she said, "Nothing."

"But Jeez," he whispered, remembering, "When I heard you yell I nearly died!"

.   .   .

Kay looked into the young, anxious face without really seeing it. She knew, because her dulled mind was telling her so, that he

189

had saved her. He had told her his name was Alex Jamieson. He was explaining shyly:

"You see, when I hung up after I'd talked with that woman I got worried all over again. I thought it was jolly odd neither of you'd tried to do anything about me and I said it was probably because the old woman *hadn't* counted up her pills as expected and you still didn't know anything was wrong. I got a real scare on," he grinned at her, "so I hiked back to the creek, but you were gone. It left me worrying what if you took several of the pills to help your face-ache, and then dropped. The old lady might just think it was exhaustion and leave you. I thought of ringing that Quidong place some time this morning and asking if you'd rung and been warned and then I got another scare on, and thought—if you hadn't it might be too late to help you if we started off late. So I rounded up a mob and we started out at dawn."

She took all that in, after some effort, with the rest of his explanation. Then she said stupidly, "You mean, you came—you stopped me—just to tell me the sleeping tablets were dangerous?"

"That's right," he agreed.

Kay started to laugh. She went on laughing and laughing and couldn't stop.

. . .

A long time later, in the little cottage hospital where she and Johnnie had been taken they told her Stuart was coming up the steps. She went running, in spite of her bruised feet and her tired body, out into the corridor and on to the sheltering veranda.

He said simply, "Kay," and his arms closed round her.

Then she started to babble. He said, when she was silent again. "I didn't dare say a word to you and that woman for fear of scaring her and making her do something to you straight away. I'd told the garage man if you came back not to scare you either, or to try talking to you or Johnnie, unless he had someone there who could help him—who could stop you leaving. He hadn't, so I had to depend on Alex. The hotel had told me he'd left to go and find you. It was all I had to hold on to."

She started to babble again and to laugh as she remembered Alex's serious face and his talk of sleeping pills. Stuart kissed her mouth into silence. He said, "You're all right. You're both all right. Hold on to that."

She nodded, her body pressed against his. "I'm all right," she echoed. "We're both all right." Then she lifted her face. She said, with an echo in her voice of a cocky, rough-edged voice she would never forget, "but, Jeez, we nearly died!"